just like ziggy

Other Books by Julie Oleszek

THE FIFTH FLOOR

just like ziggy

a novel

by julie oleszek

mockingbird publishing
batavia, il

Published by Mockingbird Publishing, LLC
This is a work of fiction. All of the characters, organizations, and events portrayed in this novel are either products of the author's imagination or are used fictitiously.

Printed in the United States of America.

Cover design by Elizabeth Watters

Oleszek, Julie
Just Like Ziggy: a novel/Julie Oleszek. – First Edition.

ISBN 978-0-9862705-3-6 (pbk)
ISBN 978-0-9862705-4-3 (eBook)

First Printing, 2016
Mockingbird Publishing, LLC
JulieOleszek.com

For Mom and Dad

one

In complete darkness, I sat motionless upon the golden couch in our living room.

"What are you doing, Anna?" my mother's voice sounded frightened.

I placed my index finger over my lips, "Shhh, come with me." I rose from the couch and pulled at my mother's hand, leading her to the big window that looked out onto our backyard. "Don't let her see you," I told my mother, shielding her from the window with the drapes. "She's out there, waiting."

"Waiting for what?" my mother whispered. I detected panic in her shaky voice.

"For me to come home. She's waited so long. Look."

We peeked from behind the curtain, taking care not to be seen. Liz was swinging, smiling and singing.

"Listen," I whispered.

The room went still. So did our breathing.

"Anna, Anna, where are you? Anna, Anna, I've come for you. Anna, Anna, it's time to come home. Anna, Anna,

I'm afraid to be alone."

Her singing was beautiful, like angels fluttering their wings in unison.

"No, Anna!" my mother screamed. "It's not your time. You must not follow Liz!"

"But Mom, I must go. She's waiting," I giggled, climbing onto the window's sill, ready to jump.

"Anna! No!"

My eyes burst open like dams holding back oceans of water. I stood on my mattress, with one foot on the bed's footboard, and gasped for air. A sliver of light from the hall illuminated a small portion of my bedroom. I hurriedly lay down before anyone found me this way.

two

"Have you been taking your medicine?" Dr. Ellison asked.

Dr. Ellison is my psychiatrist. She is about 5'7" and has a glowing complexion and shiny chestnut hair that bounces just above her shoulders.

"Yes," I said.

Actually, I hadn't taken medication since I left the fifth floor three days ago, but exposing my cover-up would only concern Dr. Ellison. So I figured I was doing her a favor by keeping this little fib to myself. Besides, she had the power to persuade my mother to send me back to the fifth floor. That was an option I was determined to avoid unless I was dead.

Dr. Ellison looked at me seriously, probably studying my eyes and listening for changes in my breathing.

"How have you been feeling?" she asked after a long pause. It took effort to steady my nerves, feeling vulnerable in Dr. Ellison's office and wondering if she sensed my lie.

Three months ago, I sat in this chair staring out the

same large window across from me. The scenery remained the same, with bloated clouds illuminating the blue sky with their brilliant white. However, the full-bloomed trees of today differed from the bare branches of that cold day in early March when I first arrived at this office. Then, frost had settled in the corners of the window. Today, heat waves could be seen dancing through the thick, humid air, both typical of Chicago's weather.

This small office was where it began, or quite possibly, where it had ended depending on who's recalling the past events. In February, at the age of seventeen, I had stopped eating. I hadn't been trying to lose weight or anything. It was because I'd given up on living. When days of starvation grew into weeks, my mother made an appointment for me to see a psychiatrist. I was too weak to care. Within an hour of meeting Dr. Ellison, it was obvious that my plan to call it quits was totally at odds with Dr. Ellison's plan to keep me alive. She simply would not allow me to die on her watch.

Twenty days without a single bite of food had left my body weak and unable to convince Dr. Ellison that she was wrong, that I should be left alone in my misery. If Dr. Ellison knew I'd killed my sister, Liz, she would have let me die. I deserved it.

For nine years, my family had lived with that tragic memory. I am the ninth child in a family of ten brothers and sisters. My younger sister Bridgett was three when it happened. Tim had just turned twelve. Kyle was fourteen and Marie fifteen. Meg was seventeen. Gabe was eighteen. Jim was twenty, stationed in England and Frances—twenty-one, married and living in Maine. I was seven.

Dr. Ellison immediately made my mother drive me to a locked psych unit on the fifth floor of Advocate Hospital. The worst part about it was that Dr. Ellison sat next to me in the back seat of my mother's car. Maybe she realized I could convince my mother to drive straight home instead. Since then, I've come to call the psych ward simply the fifth floor.

"Anna. Are you eating?" Dr. Ellison asked now. Her tone heightened, trying to get my attention.

"Yes," I replied snidely.

"We'll get you on the scale on the way out."

"Why? I'm eating. And it's not like my mom's going to sit by and watch me starve again," I said with contempt.

I lied. My mom would allow it. Not that she would want it this way. It's just that our family's deep-rooted independence would keep her from pressing the issue. Dr. Ellison gave my mother two prescriptions before leaving the fifth floor, to fill before I arrived home. For the last three days, I had taken one pill from each bottle and flushed them down the commode.

On the morning of my release, we sat in a large conference room while Dr. Ellison drilled my parents on what to expect and what the next months would involve. It was embarrassing to have my doctor and parents talking about my life. Anna will be accountable for this. She'll be required to do that, Dr. Ellison reiterated, looking at the three of us around the table. I wanted to drop dead from humiliation.

Many times during the earlier weeks of my stay, Dr. Ellison's approach had frustrated me tremendously, but I finally figured out that it was because she cared. It wasn't that my parents didn't care, well, speaking for my mother, she does. It's just in a different kind of way. She'd rather use some kind of figurative language like "stay as fit as a fiddle," instead of "take your meds." Medicine, doctor visits, or *I'm sick* were ugly words in our family. They stood for weakness or lazing on the couch wanting sympathy, which never got any attention from anyone but our mother.

Anyone who stayed home from school became an easy target for teasing. "She's faking!" I heard a sibling mock more than once as I lay in bed teary-eyed from a throbbing earache. Sometimes it seems like the only time anyone paid attention to me was to tease. I don't like to remember those days when the teasing was relentless, but it stuck in my head. Unfortunately, Dr. Ellison brought up things that reminded me.

My mom seemed to be listening to Dr. Ellison during the meeting, consistently nodding. My father's focus never left Dr. Ellison, though I suspect he was thinking of things he needed to be doing, like paying bills. When Dr. Ellison restated the importance of family communication, my father answered, "This seems to be all the rage today. I can count on one hand the number of times my father and I talked before I left for college, but we understood each other."

"Anna," Dr. Ellison said, interrupting my thoughts yet again. "It is necessary that you take your medicine. It will help you manage daily events and minimize nightmares," she added in a louder tone like she thought it would make a difference.

If medicine couldn't cure something physical, like a brain tumor, it definitely wasn't going to cure something mental, like nightmares. "Mm-hm."

"You'll be here three times a week for a weigh-in and therapy. You are not to go below ninety-seven pounds."

"Yeah, I know. You've mentioned this like a hundred times," I said harsher then I intended. "I'm just saying that I can take care of it myself. I don't need to be bothered about food or weight."

"After a month or two," Dr. Ellison replied. "I will reevaluate and decide if you need this kind of close monitoring."

Maybe Dr. Ellison wanted good things for me, but that didn't imply she could run my life. It was driving me nuts. She needed to stay out of my business, but she wouldn't, and for some ridiculous reason my mother agreed with everything she said. I would refuse, but because Dr. Ellison wouldn't hesitate to take me to the fifth floor again, I couldn't.

Staff on the fifth floor thrived on patients sharing emotions and open communication, which was the complete opposite of the way I was raised. I had done for myself for as long as I can remember. Having a big family will do that. It was sink or swim. Some called it tough love. I called it tough.

Why the blood tests? I seriously wanted to ask,

suspecting it was to monitor my iron and meds. I couldn't say I blamed Dr. Ellison. I fainted several times on the fifth floor, once knocking my head against the bathroom countertop on the way down to the floor.

"What's it been like at home?"

"Fine."

"Have nightmares returned?"

"No."

"How about Liz? Have you been able to talk to anyone about her?" Dr. Ellison asked.

She knew this was a touchy subject. I didn't talk about my dead sister. Neither did my siblings. Most of my friends didn't know about her, a secret I thought worth keeping. Dr. Ellison disagreed. "Avoiding Liz's name will only continue to hurt Anna and the others," Dr. Ellison informed my parents during my stay on the fifth floor. I suppose my parents listened respectfully, but nothing really changed at home.

Three months ago I was sure of my murderous acts. Then I had intense therapy with Dr. Ellison, a nurse named Carol and Chad (a mental health technician). They were all in charge of my life for the last three months. After I let go of my horrible memories, my care team was able to convince me that I had nothing to do with Liz's death. She died of a brain tumor. Unfortunately her brain tumor just happened to be growing secretly at the same time I messed up an acrobatic trick we were performing on our backyard swing set. Liz fell like a dead weight, her head racing toward the dirt. Soon afterward, she died. I was seven years old. Liz was ten. She was my closest sister. The one I played with every day, adoring her and looking up to her. Then one day, shortly after falling, she didn't exist. Just like that.

"Anna, about Liz's death? Have you been able to talk to your parents or your siblings?"

"No, I haven't."

I wanted to. I was curious about Liz and all the things my siblings might know about her that I didn't, but sappy emotions and deep conversations didn't exist at home. We avoided talking about crap like emotional support and dead people.

"You are unfocused today. This worries me," Dr. Ellison said.

"I'm fine," I said, nervous she might ask for a blood test this very moment, exposing my fib about taking meds.

Growing up in a large family, I learned that saying nothing was better than saying something. I kept problems to myself to avoid being teased by my older siblings. My mom listened if I had a complaint, but rarely intervened in sibling rivalry. At times she offered advice, but deciphering her figurative language was so difficult, I gave up asking for help.

Every cloud has a silver lining, she told me when I was five to explain away my missing Meg and Marie. When Frances got married, they moved into her vacant bedroom. For the first time in my life, I shared a bedroom with only two sisters, Liz and Bridgett, instead of four. The following afternoon I lay on the grass in our backyard looking for those clouds with silver linings. I hadn't found a single one.

Being older, I'd been able to unravel most of Mom's expressions, but even today there are a few that puzzle me.

My dad, well, he wasn't interested in such trivial things. I wouldn't tell him anyway. He was the working kind of dad, not the fun-with-his-children kind of dad. As long as he had his beer, TV newscast and stamp collection, he was content.

"Well, then let's discuss it here," Dr. Ellison continued.

"Why can't we just say it's over with? Liz is gone. I get it. I'm not going to freak out about it."

"Anna, I am not asking you to dwell on Liz, but three months of therapy is not going to heal nine years of grief. The anniversary of her death will be here soon. I want you to enjoy great memories of Liz."

"This is beyond stupid!" Exasperated puffs of air escaped my lungs. I wanted to hold it in, but I couldn't because I needed Dr. Ellison to understand that I didn't want to remember when Liz and I were kids. Dr. Ellison stayed quiet, giving me time to finish, but I had to fight off a wave of dizziness without her knowing.

"Can we just say 1974 was a bad year?"

"What would you suggest we talk about then?" Dr. Ellison calmly asked.

"I don't even see why I need to be here, but if you're going to insist then maybe you can explain why you want to force pills down my throat? Why I'm weighed like a sack of potatoes? Why I have to answer all these questions?"

Tears began to form in my eyes. I stopped and concentrated. It only took a second before I was able to hold back tears. I lowered my eyes to my hands. If I looked at Dr. Ellison I would probably burst out crying.

"Anna," she said. "You cannot leave the hospital and expect to continue like nothing happened. To let you go home without any follow-up appointments would be setting you up for failure. I won't let that happen."

I wanted to scream at Dr. Ellison that I wouldn't be returning to her office, but her intentions had been clear from the first time we met. She was not the threatening type. If I didn't show up for an appointment, she'd probably send the police to drag me to her office or worse—back to the fifth floor. I looked at the clock — 3:52 p.m. I sat for the next eight minutes without a word. Dr. Ellison followed when I stood up to leave.

"Let's get you weighed," she said, with a genuine smile. "I know this isn't easy, Anna, but let's agree to make the best of it."

The scale was at the end of the long hallway. I was sure if my mother looked through the reception window, she could see me, which would embarrass me even more. I stepped hard onto the scale. Dr. Ellison slid the upper weight to fifty. Then she moved the weight below to forty. She gave it short thrusts, inching it up to forty-four, forty-six. The weight teetered back and forth until it reached ninety-six pounds.

"Let's say by Friday you are up to ninety-seven." She smiled. "Agreed?"

I had expected a lecture. I nodded, genuinely grateful.

I walked out to the reception area, sliding past my

mom. “I’ll be outside.”

Dr. Ellison would give my mother a quick recap. I couldn’t stand the thought of my life being discussed.

three

I had been too sick for schoolwork while on the fifth floor, and by the time I left the hospital, schools had been closed nearly two weeks for summer break. I couldn't start my senior year in August until I officially completed my junior year. So I had to go through a summer tutoring program. My high school (East Catholic, EC for short) didn't provide social services like private tutors for misfits like me, so some teacher from the local public high school, Downers Grove South, would be tutoring me.

The only benefit to summer school was being distracted from things I was desperately trying to forget. I was scheduled with Dr. Ellison on Mondays, Wednesdays and Fridays for the next one hundred years. Mondays through Fridays would be spent with the tutor, Mrs. or Mr. Whoever, for the rest of summer.

I walked over to my dresser, unscrewed the two medicine containers and took out one pill each. I tucked them into my sock and headed for the bathroom to flush them down with my morning pee. *How will I manage blood tests?* I thought. *And weight?* For now, weight was the bigger problem. I looked fat at ninety-six pounds. Ninety would be perfect, but there was no way Dr. Ellison would allow one ounce under ninety-seven come Friday.

I turned on the shower to mask any movement in the bathroom before stripping off my pajamas and socks and kicking them into one corner. One look at my ugly body and I grabbed for a towel. I wrapped it around my chest so that it hung loosely past my lower half, covering my middle. "Much better," I whispered.

My shoulder-length hair was frizzy in some areas and straight in others, a typical heap of a mess from going to bed with a wet head. My eyes blended with my nougat-brown hair color and my skin looked more sallow than ever, a sure giveaway of being locked up. A few acne spots dotted my chin and forehead. I investigated to see what I could do about getting rid of them. *Don't touch your face*, my mother would say. *You don't want scars*.

There was not a single line on my face, not a single chicken pox mark or freckle. I had never noticed this *granted beauty* until a few weeks ago. That was Jonny Love's expression for understanding the beauty in everyday living. Jonny Love was a quirky but kindhearted friend from the fifth floor. I never fully understood why Jonny was committed to Advocate's fifth floor, mainly because I hadn't asked him. I was too wrapped up in my own egotistical ways.

I looked into the mirror again. My belly protruded,

bulging the towel. There wasn't an exercise or diet that had ever come close to flattening my stomach.

"Unfortunately Anna, you've got my stomach." My mother said when I complained after months of sit-ups and miles of running. "I'm shaped like a barrel," she continued, making me feel worse. When she noticed her explanation wasn't helping, she tried to make it sound better. "You're short," she reminded me, like I might have forgotten. "I always had an urge to stretch you."

"Nice out, Mom! Thanks. You've been a great help!" I left the house, slamming the door behind me. I would have kept my tears inside, but the night sky and blustery wind allowed bawling without being seen or heard.

I SLID INTO the shower, wet my hair and lathered the shampoo into bubbles. I thought back to the time when washing my hair was an exhausting chore. I hadn't wanted to live, let alone try to make my hair presentable or to smell clean. I cared about nothing.

"Anna, what are you doing in there? Cooking a turkey?" Bridg yelled from outside the door.

"Yep," I said.

"I need to get in before your tutor gets here."

I hated the thought of Mom and Bridg being home while the tutor was here. Mrs. Whatever-Her-Name's presence was a sign that I was absent from school, when all my friends and Bridg were in class, like the rest of the world. I was locked up on the fifth floor learning firsthand about charts and procedures and pounds and ounces instead of geometry, like every other seventeen-year-old.

"Be out in a sec," I called after turning off the water. I lowered my head, letting my hair hang loosely in front of my face, wrapped a towel around it and flipped it up and over my head so it hung like a nun's habit down my back. I dried myself quickly, dropped the towel, and reached for my clothes. I wanted to get out of Bridg's way because later it might be me begging to use the bathroom. Steam poured out when I opened the door. Bridg waved it away, pretending to choke as she slunk past and closed the door. I envied the way Bridg would look when she came out of the bathroom. Her dark brown hair would be styled so that loose curls feathered away from her face and her bangs curled under just above her arched eyebrows. A light coat of black mascara, which Mom barely tolerated at Bridgett's age, would highlight her greenish-gray eyes.

I came from the kitchen at the sound of the doorbell. The tutor followed my mother up the stairs and into the living room, carrying a multi-colored patchwork shoulder bag with one large, bright red apple hand-sewn on the side. It screamed, *Look at me I'm a teacher!* The tutor was tall but pudgy around her middle, unlike my sister Marie, who was tall and thin.

"Anna, this is Mrs. Frank," my mother said.

"Hello Anna. I'm glad to finally meet you. How are you?"

"Fine. Thanks."

"Fine as well." Mrs. Frank stumbled, realizing I hadn't asked how she was in return.

"Oops, I jumped ahead of myself. Well, I'm good if you were wondering, but maybe you weren't. In that case, I'm glad to be here."

Mrs. Frank was obviously nervous.

"Can I get you a cup of tea or coffee?" my mom asked.

Yeah, right. That's going to help her nerves.

"I'm sorry. I'm a bit nervous. You'd think after seventeen years of teaching third-grade students I'd have conversations like this memorized. Well, quite honestly this is my first tutoring job."

"Water instead?" my mother asked.

"Yes, please." Mrs. Frank took a much-needed breath. "Anna, I have spoken with your teachers and we've determined where to continue your studies. Six weeks isn't much time, but you'll be able to catch up if you're willing to apply yourself."

Just when I thought I couldn't be embarrassed anymore, Mrs. Frank proved me wrong. She talked to me like I was back in the third grade. In the bathroom the blow dryer was on full blast. I would only have a few minutes before Bridg turned it off. I had to get Mrs. Frank away from the bathroom before Bridg overheard any of this elementary school chatter.

"So basically the whole summer," I said, looking at Mom and then back at Mrs. Frank, my arms crossed to illustrate my irritation.

Mrs. Frank's tone changed from sweet to casual. "We will see."

We sat at the dining room table, in adjacent chairs,

and Mrs. Frank pulled out my all-too-familiar textbooks and notebooks. It was all here, everything I had left in my locker. I hadn't cared about a single subject months ago and I didn't give a crap today, either.

"Unless you have a preference, I have a schedule that I think will be helpful."

I just spent the last three months living by a daily schedule, requesting a signature and charting my every move. Group. Signature. One-on-one therapy. Signature. When I peed, it was charted. Breakfast. Lunch. Dinner. Charted. Charted. Charted. Sneeze. Charted.

"I don't care. You can choose," I said.

"Well, it's essential that we touch on each subject every day. Starting tomorrow, I'll arrive by eight. We'll work until one with a couple ten-minute breaks in between, that allows fifty minutes for each subject."

"Now," Mrs. Frank continued, pulling out her notepad and thumbing through three or four pages. "According to Mr. O'Connor, numbers are your strong suit so I thought we could either begin or end our day with geometry."

I perked up, confused and intrigued. *He thinks I'm good with numbers?*

Mrs. Frank looked at me for an answer. "First is fine," I said.

"Great, let's begin with geometry." She wrote the word, slowly sounding it out. "Geeee-ahhhmmm-iii-treeee."

I snuck a peek at her spelling to make sure it was correct.

"Then, we'll move on to health, evolution, English, and social studies. How does that sound?"

"Fine." I said again.

"Today will be a brief review—to remind you where you left off."

I pulled the geometry textbook from the pile and fished around for my yellow notebook. Opening it reminded me that I had barely gotten into second semester before all hell broke loose. Page after page was covered with chicken scratches rather than my typical neat and precise handwriting. I had a habit of writing everything down to strengthen my chances of acing tests, but one glance at my geometry notes showed me I had given up believing this helped. I couldn't remember exactly when I had made the decision to simply accept a D+ average.

Doodling covered the margins, and more bizarre, I hadn't scrawled hearts or I love so-and-so, like most of my friends, especially Janet. Every boy she dated, she chicken-scratched her would-be married name. Janet Ashley Peterson. Janet A. Ewing. Janet Ashley Perntolozzi. She'd been writing Anthony Perntolozzi's last name since the beginning of junior year, using all sorts of creative script. Bold letters. Shadowed letters. Cursive with extra special loops and curves. I wondered if she'd moved on from Anthony, because Janet was so pretty that she had her pick of boys.

My scribbling was a long string of cursive lower case b's and y's covering the margins from the bottom up on the left and from the top down on the right. I didn't remember ever doing this, but it was my handwriting and without a doubt my doodling.

By the time we moved on to English, I was exhausted. It was only 11:30 and I swore the clock was moving backwards. When I reached for the English notebook on the opposite side of the table, a rush of dizziness made me grab at the table. I tried to steady myself as I fought to stay standing. Quickly, I pretended to have simply lost my balance. I grabbed the notebook and sat down. I looked down praying that Mrs. Frank hadn't noticed, and then the dizziness was gone.

I opened my purple notebook. Again, just like my geometry, health, and evolution notebooks, strings of cursive b's and y's were written in the margins, leaving almost no white space. *If I was subconsciously writing bye to the world, I had misspelled it. Just another example of how bright I am,* I thought sarcastically.

Ten pages of my English notebook were crammed with sentence diagrams. *Who cares where the subject belongs on the diagram line? Or whether a word is a preposition, participle, article or any other part of speech?*

Back in junior high, my English teacher Mr. Gommet had nearly blown his blood vessels from his temples when I couldn't come up with a sentence's verb. The following summer, after reading Teen magazine from cover to cover, I went back through the articles looking up words, identifying the parts of speech in an old worn dictionary I had garbage-picked for a Mother's Day gift. I couldn't risk the embarrassment again, so I studied. Then something weird happened. Words began to intrigue me.

"Really?" I said in disgust to Mrs. Frank. "Diagrams are a waste of time." I sat back in my chair with my arms crossed ready to argue about the importance of direct and indirect objects.

"Well, you're in luck because Mrs. Allen advised me that this semester you are to put words together, not pull them apart."

"In what way?"

"Writing."

"What kind of writing?" I asked, trying to keep my excitement contained.

"Narrative, persuasive and expository writing. Two weeks for each," Mrs. Frank said smiling, like she somehow knew I liked to write.

four

By Thursday afternoon my head pounded from a headache that was steadily growing worse. I found an almost empty bottle of Tylenol in the medicine cabinet. I looked for the expiration date thinking about the crazy sicko who had laced Tylenol capsules with cyanide last year. The bottle was labeled 1983. I shook two of the five remaining pills into my hand and popped them in my mouth, hoping I wouldn't be poisoned. "Crap!" I sarcastically mumbled. "Three months stuck on the fifth floor and then I die . . . from tainted Tylenol." *What luck.*

Thursday night I lay in bed staring at the ceiling and worrying. Oreo, our black and white beagle, was curled beside me with her nose tucked under her tail. Yesterday, I managed to stay at ninety-six pounds, but I hadn't eaten much of anything since. Unless I stuffed myself tomorrow, I would never make the ninety-seven pound mark.

I fumbled around in my nightstand for the journal Chad gave me on the fifth floor. He hoped that I would write about my nightmares, but there was absolutely no chance I'd agree to something so ridiculous. The moment I woke from each one I was already pushing it away, trying to forget.

I turned to my first entry and read it.

Dear Liz,

I miss you so much.

Frayed fragments of paper reminded me that I had ripped an earlier entry from the journal's binding. I tried to remember what I had written, but didn't have a clue. The second entry was a letter to Liz. I had written about how I imagined Heaven and how much she was loved. *Love.* Reading or even thinking the word sounded completely foreign. I searched for a pen and turned to the third page.

Thursday, June 21, 1984

Dear Liz,

Being alone is horrible. Sometimes I can feel your presence like you're watching over me, and other times you seem to be disappearing from my thoughts. December will be ten years since Dad carried you away to the hospital. You never returned, but why should I waste my time telling you this? You know what happened. I think you do, anyway. It's crappy, you know—being left behind. Many times, I wish I had died with you. I know it's not my fault, but that doesn't make me feel any better.

I reread the entry before closing my journal. I lay awake thinking of too many things. The moment sleep came, terrifying nightmares often shook me awake. I sifted through my mind, fighting exhaustion. *Tomorrow. Mrs. Frank. Homework. Dr. Ellison.* "Weight," I mumbled. I couldn't stand the thought of it. Dr. Ellison's power over what should be in my control was driving me crazy.

I took a deep breath. My mind was racing. *Tomorrow. What should I do about my weight?* was the last thought I remembered before falling asleep.

"Anna, Anna."

I sat straight up in bed. I was called again from somewhere in our house.

"Anna, Anna."

I tiptoed down the hall, careful not to wake my parents or Bridg. The light from the stove overhang was lit, sending a dim glow through the kitchen doorway, but the rest of the house was pitch black.

"In here."

I rounded the corner into the kitchen. Liz had one hand on the screen door that led to the small porch with steps down to our backyard. In the other hand she had two Baggies. One filled with pickles and the other a mayonnaise sandwich.

"C'mon. Let's go."

"Where?" I asked.

"To the swing set. We can have our lunch on the glider."

"But it's night," I said, frozen and staring at Liz from the kitchen entryway.

"I'm going. C'mon, Anna," Liz said, pleading with me.

"No, I can't!" I yelled.

"You're going to miss me," she giggled, opening the screened door wide enough to exit.

"No, don't go!" I screamed.

I suddenly awoke. My pajamas were soaked. I quickly felt my underwear to make sure I hadn't wet myself.

"Anna, Anna," she said, standing over me. I screamed into the pitch dark. When my eyes adjusted to the darkness, my mother was standing at my bedside.

"Are you okay?" she asked.

I panted. Uncertain of so many things I fell back onto my pillow. My mother sat on the edge of my bed, just like she always did after I'd awakened from a nightmare. Part of me wanted her there and the other part wanted to be left alone.

five

"*I* hope you tell Dr. Ellison about your nightmares," Mom said as we drove north on Finley Road to Dr. Ellison's office in Lombard.

"Mom, please, I hate talking about this stuff. Besides, she doesn't need to know."

"She does, Anna. She can help you."

"I'm fine," I said, exasperated.

I drowned out the next twenty minutes with music. My stomach gurgled from stuffing myself with a large glass of milk and a bologna sandwich smothered in mustard mashed between two pieces of toast.

Mom parked in the lot before turning toward me. "Do you want me to tell her for you?" she asked over the music, reaching to turn it down.

"You're kidding, right? She doesn't need to know, Mom. I told you it's no big deal."

I could see the anguish on my mother's face. She disagreed, but she was reluctant to go against my wishes.

"Don't say anything," I said insensitively, immediately changing my tone to be more sympathetic, realizing I had no right to undercut my mom's worry, "Please, Mom, don't say anything just yet. Wait until I'm ready. She knows I have nightmares. If the time is right, and she asks, then I'll tell her," I fibbed.

We entered the medical building, took the elevator up three floors, and stepped into the open atrium. My mother headed to Dr. Ellison's office. I headed to the bathroom. I checked the first three stalls for feet. No one. In the end stall, I carefully took the two large index cards from my underwear to make a few adjustments since they were uncomfortable on our drive over. The twenty washers I took from Kyle's science table early this morning remained securely taped on one side of each card. I pulled up my jeans, which I swore had increased my body heat by ten degrees on such a hot day. I quietly jumped around in the bathroom stall, making sure nothing fell to the floor through either pant leg.

"NINETY-SEVEN POUNDS. That's progress," Dr. Ellison said, charting my weight.

I followed Dr. Ellison into her office and sat in the leather chair. Sitting on washers was more painful than I thought it would be. *Fifty minutes.* I concentrated on being still instead of wriggling, trying to prevent the metal washers from imprinting my tender skin.

Dr. Ellison crossed her arms, probably pondering why I was squirming in my chair. I hope she thought it was because I was nervous in her office and not because of the crap load of metal cutting through my skin. She pulled an old-fashioned oval mirror with a plastic handle from her desk drawer. It looked like a replica of the sterling silver mirror my mom had sitting on her dresser, which she had received from her mother as a wedding gift.

Dr. Ellison handed it to me. "I want you to look in the mirror for one minute."

A minute! I cursed. Twenty washers pressed hard against my skin made every minute pass like an hour.

"Why?" I said, furrowing my eyebrows, wanting to argue.

"It's a good exercise. Look at yourself and tell me what you see."

Seriously, my friends and family would laugh at the stupidity of this absurd exercise. Dr. Ellison's closed door hid me from any onlooker wandering from another office. This was a no-win situation for me. I'd held out on Dr. Ellison before, avoiding eye contact or giving her the silent treatment, but whatever course of action I took only turned out to be a great opportunity for her to catch up on paperwork as the seconds ticked by like hours for me. I was stuck until I tried it.

I had to get my mind off my butt. The washers were buried so deep in my skin I'd need a chisel to remove them. Dr. Ellison set the timer. *One-one thousand, two-one thousands, three . . .* I counted. Fifteen seconds seemed like minutes. One washer dug into my right side and caused my blood pressure to rise. Both sets of my cheeks, face and butt, were on fire. I felt faint and my head pounded, probably from overheating in those jeans, and I was pretty sure I was about to die if I didn't get some water.

The timer beeped. I placed the mirror in my lap. "I don't feel good," I said hastily. "I need a drink."

Dr. Ellison left and returned with a cup of water. I drank it down, gulping between huge breaths. If she didn't let me leave soon, she'd see me die right here. It was obvious the washers were a huge mistake, but dying right there was okay with me at the moment. I looked at the clock. *Twenty-two minutes more to suffer.*

"More please?" I almost begged, giving away my urgency.

"Why don't we stop for the day?" Dr. Ellison said after I gulped down another foam cup of water.

When I was on the fifth floor, Dr. Ellison threatened to place a feeding tube down my throat before I finally convinced her I would eat. Today, I was getting an unbelievable reprieve. If not for my reddened face and the raging thirst that had gotten me out of here early, Dr. Ellison might have figured out that I had cheated on my weigh-in.

In the bathroom, I fumbled with my jeans button even before I was completely hidden behind the stall's door. When I yanked the cards from my underwear, the washers peeled from my skin like Band-Aids ripped from unshaven legs. I sat on the commode giving myself a second to regain my balance, adjust my body heat and breathe.

"Anna, are you in there?" my mother called.

"I'll be out in a sec."

I waited until I heard the bathroom door bump against its frame. Exiting the stall, I threw everything in the trash and walked from the bathroom, my heart beating in sync with my pounding head.

six

Nardil and Lithium. *To improve your overall mental health. You'll feel happier and worry less,* Dr. Ellison explained like a commercial when I asked about the pills. *Happier? Worry less? Yeah right.* I read the instructions on the bottles. Nardil. Take twice a day. Lithium. Take with food two times a day. "Shoot!" I whispered to myself. "I should have flushed four pills a day, not two." *I'm so stupid.*

I counted the number of days I'd been home. Nine. I took nine pills from each container and put them in my shorts pocket, but then rethought my plan. After the washers in my underwear didn't work as smoothly as I'd hoped, I was more aware of how easy it is to mess up lies. *Had Mom been counting to see what I'd taken?* I wondered. Though I was 99% sure she had not touched these bottles since placing them on my dresser nine days ago, I couldn't take any chances. I put the pills back in the bottles, deciding it was best to start flushing two pills of each medication starting today. I opened my bedroom door and headed to the bathroom.

Bridg's bedroom door was closed, as always. We hadn't talked much since I'd been home. I didn't have anything to say to her and I figured she felt the same way. In the hallway I remembered Liz and I sprinting from the living room before gliding over the waxed floor, competing to get farther with each slide. After Liz's death, it was Bridg and me who soared over the floor. The hallway seemed so wide and long back then.

This morning there was not a sound. I figured our parents were at church without Bridg and me. We stopped going last year after Mom finally gave up trying to make us. Like our older sisters, Bridg and I argued too often about why we couldn't wear shorts or short skirts to Mass. "It's disgraceful, girls—to show off your bodies in that way, especially in church." Meg, Marie and Frances rebelled by wearing string bikinis to the pool. My mother wanted them to wear one-piece suits with high necks and full coverage on the bottom.

I sat on the bathroom countertop with my knees folded up to my chin. I had yet to flush the pills down the commode because I didn't want to disturb the quiet. Having no one to talk with felt odd. The past three months had been more talk than I could handle and now the silence overwhelmed me. Most fifth floor patients spoke of memories and family, like this was their normal. But it was difficult for me to explain the reasons I was furious that Liz's death had ruined every opportunity of a normal childhood.

THE LARGE MIRROR showed who I really was. My eyes

swelled before one bloated tear rolled down my cheek. I looked at my distorted, anguished face gazing back at me. *I'm ugly. I'm fat and stupid and useless.* I closed my eyes tightly, squeezed out a river of tears and tucked my head into my folded knees. I wanted to believe I was good. I wanted to believe Bridg and I could be close. I wanted to believe someone would ask about my hospital stay without being mortified or refer to it as a horrible place because they didn't know any better. I wanted to believe my family and friends would understand, but none of it seemed possible. I lifted my head and looked into the mirror again. *I wanted to die.*

Long before entering the hospital's fifth floor I had let Bridg down. We had separated long before I moved into Marie's room after she married a year ago. That was just the final blow.

I had tried too hard to change Bridg so that she could take Liz's place. Too late, I realized this was an impossibility, just as impossible as it had been for me to take on Liz's responsibilities as an older sister. Yet I tried to make both happen after she died. I taught Bridg to do the walk-a-bird walk, Liz's silly drunken sailor walk, crisscrossing her legs and stumbling around, but it wasn't the same. I tried to take care of Bridg like Liz took care of me, but I failed at this so often that Bridg came to rely on her friends for comfort. She disappeared most weekends to a friend's house and was often gone after school. Everything had been snatched away from me, but everything had been taken away from Bridg too. Each of us was fighting for survival, alone.

Bridg would not be up for some time. My parents wouldn't be home any time soon. I stretched my legs across the countertop. I closed my eyes and concentrated. *It's not that you can't, it's that you won't*. Chad had used these words over and over, suggesting I could make things better if I was willing to work at it. By the time I left the fifth floor, he had me convinced. I felt ready to conquer the world. Being home a few days had drastically changed that thinking.

Medication. What bullshit! It didn't help Liz any. I hopped from the countertop and threw the melted pills from my orange-stained hands into the commode and flushed them down. I looked into the mirror again, figuring I better be prepared for the stupid mirror activity tomorrow. "What do I see?" An ugly face and a fat body—that's what. *It wasn't that I couldn't, it was that I was going to*. I grabbed hold of my cheeks, pinching them hard. "First thing I need to do is take off this extra weight," I mumbled.

Then as if some demon called my name, I quietly opened the bathroom door and tiptoed across the hall and into the kitchen. I raided the fridge and the cupboards for bits of leftover dinners or other foods that could go missing unnoticed. Before the fifth floor I hadn't cared if I starved to death or given a crap about food. Now I couldn't think of anything but food. *It was so unfair*. Bridg and Marie had no idea how lucky they were to be tall and skinny. I quickly and quietly walked down the hall to my room with a handful of walnuts and a half package of saltine crackers.

My parents were at church. Kyle was away at school. Tim was on summer break from college but he was away on some canoe trip and wouldn't be home for days. I hadn't seen him since Christmas of last year. Marie and her husband were living in their new apartment in Wheaton. Meg was raising her family in Fort Worth. Frances now lived in Plainfield. Gabe recently moved to Darien. Jim lived near Carbondale taking college classes. And Liz was dead. We were without a doubt one big happy family. I ached, wanting it to be true, but realized how ridiculous it all sounded. I entered my bedroom and closed the door behind me, tears slipping from my chin.

seven

My father left for work on Monday morning at 4:33. I had been awake for hours, listening for any welcoming sound, but other than my father's travel bag thumping against my parents' bedroom door on his way out, the house was still.

On the fifth floor, I often lay awake waiting for Brian, the night shift MHT, to stroll into the bedroom every hour making sure there were no escapes on his watch. His presence was reassuring, a fact I carefully hid. Showing that would have been like telling the world I was defenseless. My mother's words echoed through my thoughts. *Never say or write anything you don't want the whole world to know. Never. Never. Never.* I didn't care much to listen until I was in first grade and finally understood. Out at recess, I told Charlie Parks I was his girlfriend. He told our teacher, Mrs. Caroline. I had heard my older siblings talk this way and thought it was no big deal. Mrs. Caroline disagreed.

My heart ached. I wanted to act different, but I had no idea how. Other families hugged like it was normal, so why didn't we? Before the fifth floor, I never considered what it would be like to be embraced, but after seeing friends and family smile and laugh with tight hello squeezes, I thought about it often.

My mother left for morning Mass at seven o'clock. When her car buzzed down the street, I emerged from under the thin sheet, sweaty after spending the night sweltering in the remnants of yesterday's ninety-degree heat.

Showering rinsed the salty layer from my skin but barely cooled my body. I was sticky and damp again by the time I pulled on my shirt and shorts. My dad refused to get central air conditioning. Why should he? He was rarely home during the workweek. He spent many days in chilled hotels and restaurants. There was no need for him to think of us drowned in sweat. Even Mrs. Frank, I had noticed last week, had gone from a T-shirt and pants to a tank and shorts. Her pudginess provided enough heat to dampen her shirt in various places as the morning progressed.

Mrs. Frank rang the doorbell and popped her head in. "Hello," she called out.

"Jeez," I mumbled. I seriously needed to tell her not to ring the bell or bounce right in like she owned the place. I'd rather Bridg sleep instead of having the pleasure of witnessing her dumb sister being tutored. I hurriedly popped two pills from the prescription bottles into my mouth, gagging on the chalkiness and the thought of being forced to do this. I quietly walked past Bridg's bedroom door and down the hallway to meet Mrs. Frank.

"Anna," she said, delighted like a grandparent visiting their grandchild after years and noting they'd grown like a weed. "How are you this morning?"

"Fine," I said, quietly indicating my sleeping sister.

"Did you have an enjoyable weekend?" she whispered as we pulled our chairs up to the table.

"Yeah," I lied.

"What did you do?"

"Nothing special."

"My weekend was pleasant. My husband and I went to Brookfield Zoo. Have you been there lately? They're always adding new exhibits."

It could have been that I'd only had three hours of sleep or maybe it was because I couldn't stand the thought of animals in captivity. For whichever reason, I began to cry. *Not now. What the heck has happened to me?* I used to be able to hold back tears with ease. Now I couldn't stop them from coming if my life depended on it. Crying was for weaklings and for kids who needed their hands held. And here I was, with tears welling up in the corners of my eyes. I turned my head trying to think of anything but Ziggy, the elephant Brookfield selfishly claimed as theirs, but it was impossible. Out of control, the memory raced forward like a speeding bullet.

CROWDS OF PEOPLE gawked at something called Ziggy. People let me wriggle through because I was only five years old. When I finally reached the railing the most beautiful animal I'd ever seen mesmerized me. A man standing next to me threw a peanut into the pen and Ziggy turned around, gently touching it with his trunk before lifting it to his mouth. When I saw Ziggy's eyes, I knew something wasn't right.

"What's wrong, Ziggy?" I whispered.

He looked right at me with his tiny eyes.

"He hears me, Sissy."

"No, he doesn't," Liz said. "He's too far away."

"Are you okay, Ziggy?" I said louder, and waved just in case he didn't hear me.

He turned away. His back faced the crowds of people. He swayed back and forth. He lifted his right foot off the bed of straw. This was when I noticed the chain wrapped tightly around Ziggy's ankle.

"Look, Sissy!" I panicked. "Why is Ziggy hooked to the wall?

"I don't know."

I wriggled through the crowd back to my parents.

"Why is Ziggy hooked?" I shrieked, looking at Mom.

"Chained, not hooked." Dad said. "Because he probably hurt someone."

More concerned with Ziggy than how my father might react, I looked up at him. For once I was unafraid to speak, though my voice wavered. My insides raged as if it were I tied down with chains. "I'd hurt someone too if I was chained to a wall," I sneered.

"You better not," my father scowled, condemning me with his stern look. He strolled away, his hands in his pockets jingling loose change.

I sent thoughts toward Ziggy hoping he could read my mind. *I'm sorry I can't help you.*

MRS. FRANK LAID down her notepad and pen, and reached for my hand, but I pulled away. "What's wrong?" She asked, her voice heavy with concern.

I wanted to tell her, just like I wanted to cut the chain binding Ziggy's ankle.

"Did I say something to upset you?"

I couldn't hang on a second longer. I pushed my chair away from the table and ran to the bathroom. The mirror reflected streams of tears running down my cheeks. I switched off the light, wanting blackness to engulf me like a hug. I turned the tap on full blast trying to force the faucet's lever past its limits to mask the sound of my crying. *How could anyone be so cruel, to shackle an elephant to a wall?* A flash brightened the small space and I turned thinking someone had opened the door.

"THIRTY YEARS THAT elephant was chained to the wall." My mother had said, standing at the bulletin board in front of Ziggy's pen reading the news article about the elephant's death three years later.

Liz, pet Ziggy and make it okay, I prayed, hoping Liz could hear me all the way from Heaven. "Mom, do you think he's in Heaven?" My voice quivered. Tears formed in the corners of my eyes.

"Animals don't go to Heaven, Anna."

"Then will he come back to life?"

"Anna," Mom said concerned, looking at me curiously. "What in the world are you talking about?"

"Like Lazarus. Jesus brought him back to life. Remember? He just popped up and walked from his tomb."

"Lazarus was a person, not an animal. There's a difference."

I GASPED FOR air on the bathroom floor, my chest convulsing. "I was eight, Mom. Eight!" I muttered with contempt. "I'm sorry Dizzy Lizzy." I shook my head at my mistake. "I mean Ziggy—I'm sorry Ziggy."

The garage door opened as my mother returned from church. Mrs. Frank stopped her at the top of the steps and the two spoke.

"Anna," Mom said, knocking. "Can I come in?"

"Not now. I'll be out in a second."

Except for the fact that my eyes were almost swollen shut and my skin was beet red, I was fine. I opened the door. "I'm fine. It's nothing."

"It's more than nothing, Anna. You've been in there for the last thirty minutes," Mrs. Frank said.

My mom waited. She didn't know what to do. Neither did I.

"Was it about the zoo?" Mrs. Frank added.

"It was," I reluctantly mumbled. One thing I discovered on the fifth floor was that it was better to say something than keep silent. That was totally the opposite of my experience for the first seventeen years of my life. Saying something appeased most people. Saying nothing kept them searching for answers. "An old memory just got to me." I continued. "Sorry, I didn't mean to get all weepy." I squeezed between Mrs. Frank and my mother and headed for the dining room table. "I'm fine now."

"She'll be okay," my mother said, so I figured Mrs. Frank must have eyed her in a certain way when my back was turned.

Mrs. Frank's look revealed her confusion. It was the same look Chad gave when my mom first visited the fifth floor and he noticed we didn't hug. *Get used to it, Teach, cuz this is the way our family is* I thought sarcastically.

eight

Opening the one small window in the dining room provided little comfort in the steaming heat. Mrs. Frank and I took extra breaks to fill our glasses with ice cubes and tap water. Today, I figured, my weight shouldn't be a problem with ten extra pounds of humidity in the frizzy curls on top of my head. My mind was on the scheduled blood test. Thinking about it had my blood boiling, which didn't help my already reddened face and hot cheeks. I had no idea if taking a regular dose of pills today would be enough to fool Dr. Ellison with the test results, but I hoped so.

"Ready for writing?" Mrs. Frank said, fanning her face with one of my notebooks.

"Mm-hm," I said, trying to imply that writing was no different from the other subjects, but honestly I looked forward to it.

"For the next two weeks we're going to be working on expository writing." Mrs. Frank smiled. "Do you know about expository writing?" she asked, her elementary tone returning.

I gave her a crooked smile and rolled my eyes, hoping she'd catch my drift that she had slipped back in to third grade mode.

"Well, of course you do," she quickly added.

Realizing that Mrs. Frank was trying, I immediately felt bad. Shoot. Anyone bold enough to be dragged into this house and tolerate this heat deserved to be thrown a bone. It was just that the one-on-one attention was smothering. She came every morning smiling and ready to battle the heat because she was either nuts or truly liked this tutoring thing. Maybe she needed to see my face brighten with discovery, like a little kid excited by a magic trick. That wasn't so weird, I guess. Maybe I wanted to learn as much as Mrs. Frank wanted to teach.

"So then tell me. What is an expository essay?" Mrs. Frank asked, smiling.

"It's an essay that explains something."

"Exactly. It also can be a piece of writing that describes something or informs the reader of the topic. How about we brainstorm a list of topics that interest you?"

I pulled my green notebook out, opened it to a clean page and stared at it. I could have probably thought of several ideas on my own in the middle of the night, but being asked like this, on the spot, while Mrs. Frank was at the kitchen sink guzzling a gallon of water made me gasp from anxiety.

Though I liked to write, I didn't want Mrs. Frank scrutinizing my feelings. I'd written many reports before, but consistently chose subjects without any emotional content. Quoting an encyclopedia was easy and safe. I wasn't upset when a teacher marked my paper in red ink when it was a subject I didn't care much about. I had thought about writing essays that meant something to me. But I had decided long ago the risk was too great. Seeing red marks strewn across words that revealed my true passion for writing and exposed my emotions was no different from slicing my wrists.

"Let me help you," Mrs. Frank said, returning from the kitchen and eyeing the white page. "Two heads are better than one. Something I said today, about Brookfield Zoo, upset you. You should write about it. When a writer uses emotions to write, the reader senses the importance of the subject."

I listened quietly, thinking again of Ziggy. "But an expository shouldn't have emotion in it. It's more factual."

"An expository *essay*. Not necessarily," Mrs. Frank said, bubbling from inside, happy to explain. "All writing needs to connect with your reader. For example, if you wrote an expository essay—let's say about the benefits of zoos—with no emotion, the reader will walk away unmoved, forgetting what he or she just read."

Mrs. Frank paused, letting what she had just said sink into my brain like I was an elementary student needing time to digest. I nodded, urging her forward.

"But emotion without opinion is different. Emotion, dispersed throughout the piece, grabs the reader's attention. Opinion has the opposite effect."

I wanted to ask a ton of questions. *How did this work?*

How could a writer fill an expository essay with emotion, without the reader knowing? What kinds of words worked best with this kind of writing? Instead, I nodded again, pressing for more.

"A memory of the Brookfield Zoo sparked an emotion today. This spark will electrify your writing. Leave out your beliefs, feelings and reaction to the subject, but let the reader know you are writing about a subject in which you are well versed. This, as well as unwavering focus on the main idea, is thought-provoking."

I had never heard it explained this way. I was amazed Mrs. Frank knew so much about it since she was a third grade teacher. I wrote *zoo* on the first line in my notebook. Mrs. Frank was obviously pleased I'd considered it.

"Okay, that's one idea. How about someone you admire or a sport you know a lot about?"

"Yeah, I guess."

"How about I give you five minutes to write a list of ideas?" Mrs. Frank said, picking up the notebook and fanning her face. Again, she got up to fill her glass with water. Her shorts were stuck to her butt and legs and a line of sweat was left behind on the wood chair. She pulled at her shorts to straighten them as she headed for the kitchen. I stared at the one idea on the white page. When Mrs. Frank returned, she saw that I listed another idea. *The Importance of Air Conditioning.*

"Boy, isn't that the truth." Mrs. Frank laughed, slumping back into the chair. "Write this down," she said, sitting forward and pointing to a blank line in my notebook,

"How to kill your teacher."

I looked at Mrs. Frank in shock. She looked at me surprised, realizing she's let down her guard. "Oh dear, did I just say that?"

"Yep," I confirmed.

In the next second, we were both laughing. If my brothers Gabe and Kyle were here, they would comment, "Imagine the headline. Teacher drowns in a puddle of her own sweat."

I pictured the front page and began a new round of laughter. I knew exactly what I'd write. *How to write a proper obituary.* Thinking about it had me chuckling to myself. Who would ever think to write an essay on the proper way to write a death notice? From Mrs. Frank's reaction to the heat, I knew she would appreciate the humor behind it.

"I have an idea," Mrs. Frank said. "Why don't we stop for the day? It's supposed to reach ninety-one degrees today. All this week will be just as hot."

Chicago weather was hard to predict. June could be as cold as March or as hot as August. This June was sweltering.

"Any chance we could meet at the Downers Grove Library for the rest of the summer?" She asked.

There wasn't much chance I'd be seen by classmates since EC, my high school, was ten miles away in Lombard. Besides, it would be awesome to be anywhere but home while being tutored. Woodridge, the next town over, would be even better. There was only one kid on the EC bus that was dropped in Woodridge. The chance of seeing someone there was less than seeing someone in my town. And the Woodridge Library was even closer.

"Where do you live?"

"Darien," she said, "but . . ." she hesitated stretching her thoughts into words, ". . . we can't meet at my house because the kids would be too distracting," she said hesitantly, not understanding where my question was leading.

"Not your house. I thought we could meet in Woodridge instead. It's closer for both of us."

As much as I hated to admit it, I needed my mom's approval because of the car and needing a ride. Before Mrs. Frank could ask to talk with my mother, I quickly stood. "I'll go talk to my mom." There was one thing I didn't need and that was my teacher and my mother planning my life. Dr. Ellison was bad enough. I pushed my chair away from the table. My shorts were glued to my legs and butt. It was only now I realized how freakin' hot it was in this house. It angered me thinking we didn't have air conditioning.

Mom arrived home from Mass every morning and headed to her bedroom to stay out of our way while Mrs. Frank was here. I think it was because she knew how I felt about being tutored.

"Mom," I said, knocking and then opening my parents' bedroom door. Mom was propped up against the headboard eating mini-sized Snickers bars and reading the mail. There were four wrappers and a paper towel smeared with melted chocolate next to her. I assumed this was from wiping her chocolatey fingers since she frowned upon licking fingers, chocolatey or not.

"Can I use the car so Mrs. Frank and I can work at the Woodridge Library?"

"What time?"

"Eight," I said frustrated, knowing the problem lay in Mom getting to morning Mass.

"Let me talk to Mrs. Frank," she said, pushing herself up from the bed.

"Mom, please . . ." I said quietly, giving her a desperate look. ". . . let me work it out."

"See if nine-thirty works," she suggested.

I closed the bedroom door quietly not wanting to wake Bridg across the hall and tiptoed back to the dining room where Mrs. Frank had downed her water and was back to fanning herself.

"Will nine-thirty work?"

Mrs. Frank switched her eyes away from me and up toward the ceiling contemplating how this could be managed. The sweltering heat, for once, was on my side. *Thank you, Dad.*

"I'll tell you what, I'll check first with your school counselor, but I'm thinking we could meet from ten to two each day, since writing is mostly done on your own time. We could switch our ten-minute breaks to five-minute breaks. How does this sound?"

"Good," I said.

"I'm going to advise you to eat a hearty breakfast because we'll be working more aggressively. Think you can handle it?" Mrs. Frank smiled. I returned the smile knowing

I owed her big. *She's not so bad, for a teacher.*

nine

My mother hadn't asked that I drive myself to Dr. Ellison's yet and I was glad. When or if she did, I'd go alone, but honestly, as much as I hated being driven around like a child, I liked that she went with me—in the car and waiting outside Dr. Ellison's office. It felt strange to think this way—the idea that not everything had to be done without help. But still my old ideas kept me from wanting my mother to know that I needed her.

We were cooled from the sweltering heat when we entered the small medical building with Dr. Ellison's office. After we stepped from the elevator onto the third floor, I headed to the bathroom and my mother headed to Dr. Ellison's waiting room. It was difficult to escape looking into the long glass mirror that took up one entire bathroom wall. My complexion had tanned quickly since being released from the fifth floor. It helped hide my flushed cheeks.

Dr. Ellison was speaking with my mother as I entered the waiting room from the lobby. "Perfect," she said. "We were just discussing today's blood work. The lab is on the second floor. I have you scheduled on Mondays. Before or after we meet is up to you."

I eyed Dr. Ellison, then my mom, and then the appointment lady, Allison, sitting behind the sliding glass window. "Whatever," I huffed, heading toward the open door from the waiting room to the small hallway where the offices were located.

"Good morning, Anna," Allison said, showing a white smile. "It's good to see you."

"Hi," I replied, continuing to Dr. Ellison's office. I figure she was nice enough since she'd taken the time to learn the correct pronunciation of our last name, may-hart, without the tiniest slip, like most people make.

I dropped into the puffy leather chair in Dr. Ellison's office facing the big glass window.

How things had changed in three months. Before I first entered the hospital's fifth floor I had been seeing flashes of my dead sister and having disturbing memories. Now, I felt . . . well . . . confused. I had learned to live with hallucinations, but after months of daily therapy sessions, when I returned home my life went from predictable to unpredictable.

Dr. Ellison closed her office door and sat in the leather chair across from me, against the window.

She was seated before I confronted her with an angry scowl. "This blood thing is ridiculous, you know! Why do you need it anyway?"

"To test your iron level," she said calmly, ignoring my raised voice. "I don't want you passing out or feeling the least bit faint. The lab is in room 201. How was your weekend?" she asked.

"Fine."

"Have you seen friends since you've been home?"

"No."

"Why not?"

"I don't know. I guess I don't want to see anyone right now."

"The sooner you see your friends the sooner you'll have some normalcy again. It'll feel good to go out with them."

"Yeah, I guess."

"What are you afraid of?"

I gave Dr. Ellison a sharp look. "I'm not afraid of anything. I just don't want to go out."

"Anna, I realize it bothers you to have been in the hospital, but it's essential that you reunite with your friends."

Dr. Ellison waited for me to remark on what she'd said, but I held out.

"It's normal if they ask questions about what happened. They're curious, just as you'd be in their place," she continued.

"That's not true," I said sharply. "I wouldn't ask. I might want to know, but I wouldn't ask."

"Why wouldn't you?"

"Because it wouldn't be any of my business." I curled my knees up to my chin, placing my feet on the edge of the chair. This time Dr. Ellison quieted, waiting for me to continue. “Anyway, what would I tell them?”

“How do you respond at home when your siblings or parents ask questions?”

“There’s nothing to say.” I was confused by her assumption that I would go home and sing praises about being locked on a psych floor.

“So when they have a question, you say nothing?” Dr. Ellison asked.

“They don’t ask. It’s only Bridgett at home anyway and I’m pretty sure she doesn’t want anything to do with me.”

“Why do you think that?

My vision became blurred from tears. I wanted Dr. Ellison to know so she could help fix the problem, but I didn’t know what the problem was. Well, not exactly anyway.

“I can just tell. She doesn’t talk to me. I’m pretty sure she hates me because I was in the hospital.”

“Have you asked her?”

I expelled a big breath. “And say what? Hey, Bridg, what’s up with you hating my guts? Oh yeah, and then how do I respond if she says something like, hate your guts? Nah! I hate all of you.” I smirked, covering my hurt at knowing those awful words were probably true.

“I’ve met Bridgett. She doesn’t seem at all like a girl who would say that. And I’m sure you wouldn’t ask her in that way.” Dr. Ellison said.

“It’s just that we don’t ask things like ‘What’s wrong?’ or ‘What did I do to upset you?’ in our family. It would be awkward. It’s different from the hospital, Dr. Ellison. You seriously need to spend two hours in my house if you don't believe me."

"There is no shame in needing help or talking about things we struggle with, Anna. You need to understand this."

"I get it. I just don't need to talk about it."

"If you understood or didn't need to talk about it, then you'd ask Bridgett how you can make things better. Or you'd be going out with friends and beginning to have fun, but instead you are sitting at home doing nothing."

"I'm busy at home. I have school and homework."

Dr. Ellison paused. "How about role-play? I'll play the part of Bridgett or a friend if you prefer. Janet? She's a friend, right?"

"How do you know about Janet?" I asked, letting my curiosity get the best of me.

"She told Dottie that she was your best friend when she came to visit you at the hospital."

Janet had come to the fifth floor for a visit, but I had refused to see her. I had told Dottie, the receptionist who sits in the waiting area between the locked and unlocked wards, to send her away. I imagine Janet felt so hurt. Soon after her visit, she sent a get-well card that I read a few times, but I never cared enough to write her back. She probably hated me, and I wouldn't blame her if she did. I'd feel the same way. I regret that I treated her badly.

Janet and I had been best friends since the first day of high school. We sat at the same lab table in biology and connected immediately. She loves to talk and I was willing to listen. Janet is smart and I'm not. She's pretty and I'm a plain Jane, as my mother would call a girl like me. Janet has boyfriend after boyfriend and I only have Janet. She is popular and I go unseen and unknown, yet we became best friends.

Janet tells me about her boyfriends and social life. She loves expanding on every conversation. She especially revels in airing her dirty laundry about the things she does with boys. I listened carefully my freshman year, learning as much as I could without letting on that most of what she said was the first time I'd heard such things. Shoot! If not for sex ed in fifth grade, the book *Are You There God, It's Me Margaret* soon after, and Janet's loose ways, I'd be living in the dark ages. It doesn't matter that I have three older sisters. I had only been clued in that babies don't come from kissing by listening to the older neighborhood kids.

Sophomore year was different. Janet and I no longer had classes together, but we remained best friends. I was placed into the classes teachers referred to as basic with easier curriculums, but the students knew the classes were for idiots. Mr. Elliott, the sophomore counselor, remarked, "I think it best we place you in basic studies so your academics have a chance to mature." *What a jerk!*

My chest tightened. My throat swelled. My thoughts wavered. Labored breath came from deep in my throat.

Breathe. Anna, breathe. I learned self-talk from Carol, my nurse on the fifth floor, and it was my only solution in dodging Dr. Ellison's questions. I tried desperately to gasp for air without her knowing.

Dr. Ellison rose from her chair and before I was completely aware of her intentions she was at my side wrapping a cuff around my arm.

No freakin' way was I dealing with this medical crap. I forcefully pulled at the cuff and then slid it down over my hand when I couldn't get it unwrapped from my arm.

"I don't need you worrying about me! Weighing me or syphoning my blood either! Or forcing me to take medicine! This is so ridiculous!" I shouted through clenched teeth to avoid being heard through the walls. "I'll tell you why I don't go out with friends," I continued. "Because I spend all my time here with you."

Dr. Ellison leaned slightly against her desk, holding the cuff in one hand and her stethoscope in the other. She listened to me vent and took mental notes. *Well, two could play this game.* My tone was filled with anger, but now I'd added stubbornness. Lifting my eyebrows and quieting my breath, I went in for more. "I'm not role-playing. I'm not five! I'm not ten! I'm seventeen!"

I had absolutely no more to say. My eyes remained on hers for seconds too long. I was pathetically uncomfortable. My wave of dizziness made Dr. Ellison's body appear to sway. I shifted my eyes to my hands. Dr. Ellison changed her position, but not for the better. She pulled her desk chair closer to my side. She placed the cuff and stethoscope in her lap. *She'd better be kidding.*

"Anna, your health is important to me—your emotional health as much as your physical health. This is not going to change. You're here instead of in the hospital because you've already worked through so much, but it's not over. Suppressed memories take time to resurface. We've talked about this.

"It can be difficult to understand the aftermath of traumatic events. Gaining strength from an emotional tragedy is no different from a person who's been seriously injured in a car accident. The mind and body both need time to heal. You need to allow yourself this time, and unless you change this destructive perception of yourself, things will not get better. Once you understand why it's so difficult for you to see your potential, then changing your thinking is a real possibility."

Dr. Ellison's voice was kind, but firm. I continued staring at my lap, but listened intently.

"When I mentioned Bridgett and Janet, something inside was triggered. To help you, I need to understand what you're thinking. It's important that you continue to progress from your hospital stay."

I nodded slightly to let Dr. Ellison know that she'd been heard, but my eyes remained focused on my hands. That was my only hope to avoid crying like a child.

"You have many more choices than you did for the last three months. It's true that I am requiring you to be here, and I'll continue to monitor your health, but listening to suggestions and helping yourself is your choice. It takes courage and strength to change for the better. I can help you through all of it, but I cannot force you to accept my help. Like you said, you are seventeen. In less than a year you will officially be an adult. You need to work toward future goals, with the help of others who care about you and love you. This is normal. Everybody needs feedback. Survival depends on it."

Quiet filled the room. More than a minute passed. Dr. Ellison took the cuff from her lap and I lifted my arm toward her. I accepted the hiss of the air being released from the cuff. My lungs too released trapped air. *Survival depended on it.*

MY MOTHER LOOKED up from her book when I entered the waiting room. "I'll see you at the car," I said walking past her.

She'd pay the bill, giving me some leeway to cross the atrium to the stairway exit. On the landing between floors three and two, I plopped myself on a stair and leaned back against the cool concrete wall. Growing up I had wished to hear the things Dr. Ellison expressed in one session. *You're smart. You're pretty.* I would have settled for *you're kind,* but hugs and kisses and encouraging comments were simply overlooked. *Was I loved by anyone?* Liz loved me, or at least she cared enough to play with me.

Had I been so innocent to think that relentless teasing was love? I understood Dr. Ellison's point of view, about changing. Being who I am had taken me to the fifth floor and gotten me where I was today.

ten

I strolled to the reception desk in room 201 acting relaxed.

"Hi," I nervously smiled. "I'm here for a blood test."

"Do you have paperwork?" A girl who looked to be my age said showing a friendly smile.

I handed her the form Dr. Ellison had given me.

"Sign right here," the girl said, handing a clipboard over the small desk. "It will be just a moment."

"Anna Mmmeee-dart," a man in a white doctor's jacket said, butchering my last name.

"May-Hart. The d is silent," I corrected.

He smiled. "I wasn't even close.

"That's okay. Most people don't pronounce it right."

"Is it Irish?"

He reminded me of Isaac, one of the MHTs on the fifth floor—easygoing and good-humored. I nodded. "Mm-hm, Yeah."

"How are you today?" he said, as we walked down a short hallway.

"Fine."

"I'm Guy." *Who names their kid Guy?* "We'll be together twice a month." He smiled, looking up from the paperwork.

"It's just a quick finger prick."

"Oh, I thought it was going to be a blood test."

"I suppose it is a blood test, but Dr. Ellison is only testing your iron so a finger prick will give us what we need."

My stomach knotted tighter. "Nothing else, like the medications I take?" I asked, my chest swelling.

"The order says iron only."

Guy squeezed my finger after piercing it, and the blood rushed to the surface. He soaked it up through a little tube. "Nothing to it," he said, handing me a cotton ball. "Here, keep this pressed."

My mother stood leaning up against the car. I was not sure if it was because of the sun's position, but her silhouette looked old and worn out. My parents have at least ten to fifteen years on most of my friends' parents, but never had I considered them old. Today, Mom looked seriously aged. Her eyes were closed and her head was tilted toward the sun as if she was trying to catch every ray to tan her skin. I noticed wrinkles, so much more than before. The way she leaned against the car with slumped shoulders showed she was tired. She had gained a few pounds in the last months since she'd taken up eating chocolate and popcorn loaded with salt and butter. These bad habits overtook her healthy habits of a good diet and exercise when I was hauled off to the fifth floor.

Every morning when I was growing up, my mother lay on the living room rug doing scissor exercises, crossing her slightly lifted legs back and forth, across one another. Then she did bends and toe touches. Bridg and I joined her, trying to hold out longer with our backs flat on the floor and our legs slightly lifted and holding our breath. I looked at her stomach. From where I was standing, I could see through her lightweight shirt that her toned stomach had turned to pudginess.

"Hey Mom."

My mother jumped. What seemed old a moment ago had been lost to a straightening posture.

"Ready?" she asked. "Do you want to drive?"

On the way home, my mother looked as if she was sleeping or praying. My heart was heavy. I never intended to hurt her. *Ten kids. One dead. Seven gone. One a disaster. And Bridg, only thirteen—the one who needed her most.*

IT WAS PAST nine in the evening. My mom and Bridg were playing *Payday,* Bridg's favorite board game, in Bridg's room and before that, they played *Go to the Head of the Class*. Mom asked if I wanted to play when I passed by on my way to my room, but I turned her down.

I pulled *To Kill a Mockingbird* from the bottom drawer of my nightstand and stared at its faded green cloth cover. It reminded me of Ben, my trusted friend from the fifth floor. One evening he had given me this book. I slid my hand over the coarse burlap-like cover. I wanted to trust others like Ben so easily could do. But trust who? "People like fat Mrs. Meyerson?" I mumbled angrily.

"You flunked English, Anna," I mimicked, hatefully. What was she thinking? Rubbing salt in my wounds would produce an A? "Hey Mrs. Meyerson!" I sneered, drowning the words into my pillow. "Just thought I'd bring your enormous size to your attention. In case you are unaware—you're fat."

I lay my head sideways onto my pillow. People like the nurses and MHTs on the fifth floor were willing to help because it was their job, but what about others? It was different now that I was home.

eleven

Thunder rumbled in the distance as I headed out the door for my first tutoring session at the library. *Turn left on Dunham. Turn right on Janes Avenue? Or is it left?* I recited, hoping the route would come back.

"There's an umbrella on the back seat if you need one," my mother called out her bedroom window as I backed from the garage.

I gave a quick wave to let her know I'd heard her and to say thanks for the car. She let me drive today, which means she was pretty much trapped in the house, and unless a parent of one of Bridgett's friends picked her up, so was my sister. By the time I'd made it to the first stoplight a mile from our home, lightning flashed in the distance. The darkening sky indicated a big thunderstorm was on its way. I looked in back to make sure the umbrella was where my mom said it was when the first large droplets of rain fell on the windshield. When I pulled into the parking lot, the crack of lightning and boom of thunder caused me to scream and shield my head. “Crap!” I shouted, looking around quickly to see if anyone saw my reaction. Another flash completely brightened the sky. The wind pushed the rain sideways.

“I FOUND ONE for you, Sissy,” I said enthusiastically, handing over the book I had pulled from the shelf.

“Tales of the Fourth Grade Nothing by Judy Blume,” Liz read. “But I’m going into fifth grade.” She turned it over to read the back cover. “Okay, I’ll get it. It sounds funny,” she giggled. She added it to her pile of books “What do you have so far?

“How to Eat Fred Worms,” I said showing Liz the cover.

“Fried.” Liz flipped through the pages and then read the back cover, “Neat,” she said. I felt proud reading books like my big sister.

“There’s Lowly!” Bridgett said in her baby three-year-old voice. She sat on Mom’s lap with a Richard Scary book open.

“Mom,” I whispered showing her my first selection.

“Will you help me with some of the words?”

“Sure,” she said, and then glanced out the library window. “Hurry up, girls. It’s about to storm.”

Bridgett, Liz and I piled into Mom’s stifling blue station wagon with our books as lightning lit the sky followed by a thunderous crack. My sisters and I screamed.

“Lizzy, for Heaven’s sake. Why are you wearing that purple dress?” Mom scolded.

Sissy’s white skin and blond hair shone with beads of sweat from wearing the wooly purple dress on such a warm day.

"Because it's my favorite dress." Liz said, smiling.

"Well I guess it's neither here nor there," Mom said, buckling Bridg into her lap belt. Liz and I sat next to her. Seatbelts weren't needed when you're seven and ten.

"If I get hot, I can take it off in the car," Sissy giggled. Her blue eyes twinkled.

"Hang on girls," Mom called from the driver's seat as we traveled down the gravel drive to our house, bumping and jostling around in back.

The door slammed. Liz and I ran up the stairs.

"Dad," I smiled so hard it hurt. "Look what I found for Sissy," I said, showing him *Tales of the Fourth Grade Nothing*.

"It's Lizzy. Not Sissy."

"SHIT!" I SCREAMED with another loud crack of thunder. I slammed my palms against the steering wheel in absolute anger. "Sissy! Sissy! Sissy!" I yelled in defiance of so many things.

I reached for the umbrella in the back. Not that it would keep me at all dry in this downpour. I sprinted into the cooled building. My Keds were soaked.

"Sorry I'm late," I said to Mrs. Frank. "Be back in a second." I headed to the bathroom to dry myself, but it didn't do much good.

"Any better?" Mrs. Frank said. She seemed to be happier than I had ever noticed. I guessed the absence of sweat rolling down her neck and back was the reason. Unfortunately, I was wet and freezing.

BY THE END of our Thursday session, Mrs. Frank asked about my expository writing assignment and if I had any questions. Since I worked on writing at home she only saw the end product, which I figured bothered her. She wanted to be involved in every subject, but I guessed air conditioning over jungle-like humidity trumped her need for involvement.

When I arrived home, I headed to my bedroom. Oreo followed me in before I locked the door and flung myself onto my bed. It was unmade, a habit I began after realizing how stubborn I had become in perfecting tight sheets and a perfectly smooth bedspread over the ten years after Liz's death. Just months ago, such imperfection would have been unthinkable.

I should be working on homework and finishing the obituary, but I just couldn't motivate myself. Yesterday's visit to Dr. Ellison proved she wasn't testing anything but my iron level. It was low and she was concerned. I weighed in at ninety-eight pounds. I couldn't seem to get it just right and it was driving me nuts. The fact I hadn't added coins to my pockets or worn sneakers and jeans instead of sandals and shorts made it worse. Had I used all my schemes, I probably would have weighed a hundred pounds or more. My weight increase was due to my lack of control. Even more bothersome was everyone's denial about it, holding their breath hoping I would continue this weight gain.

When I first stopped eating, I noticed Mom's worried looks. Even Gabe commented on how skinny I was when he visited after work. Marie had taken me to McDonalds hoping I would order my usual. Nobody's ideas had worked. I refused to listen. I had been losing weight because I didn't want to live. But as long as everyone thought it was about the food, there was no need to explain. Acting like I was simply on a diet was much easier than explaining the complicated truth: that I didn't want to live.

Now it was worse because I was so confused about everything. I didn't know what I wanted. Sometimes, I wanted to run away. Just disappear. Have the world leave me alone. At other times I wanted to be helped, relieved from this confusion. On the fifth floor it was easier thinking about how other families acted compared to mine. Sometimes I wished for a family who openly gave each other bear hugs and genuine smiles, but then I couldn't be part of what I already had.

So what if we didn't hug each other? Frances, Jim and Gabe showered Bridgett and me with Christmas gifts when we were small. Meg played my favorite 45s on her record player. Marie didn't want me hanging around her when I was a kid, but it's different now that we're older. Even if it were only Bridgett and I, without any other siblings, I still wouldn't trade what I have to gain hugs from another family.

But what is so wrong with wishing for both?

Gabe hadn't referred to me as Big Rat since I was a child. I remember hating that nickname once I realized it wasn't appealing. Today, I craved the attention a nickname like Big Rat brought. Back then I was somebody. Today I'm nobody.

twelve

"Where's Anna?" I heard Timmy ask my mother, who was in the kitchen making dinner. Pots and pans had been clanging together for the last fifteen minutes.

Tim returned home from his college canoe trip a few days ago. He was working full time at the Hobson pool as the manager and lifeguard like Meg had years ago. Most days, I didn't see him until dinnertime when he had a two-hour break before heading back for the evening swim hours.

I figured Tim would be knocking at my bedroom door in the next minute so I quietly pushed myself up from my bed, careful to keep the bedspring from squeaking, and tiptoed to the door. Holding the small push button lock with my thumb, so the popping of the button lock couldn't be heard, I quietly and quickly turned the handle to unlock the door. I nervously tiptoed back to my bed and sat propped up against the wall, feeling dizzy from the quick movements. I grabbed a book, opened it to the middle and checked to make sure it was not upside-down. A moment later, there was a knock on my door.

"Can I come in? Timmy asked.

"Sure."

"Are you interested in a job?" my brother asked, standing halfway in the doorway, like he was ready to turn and get back to more important things.

Tim was five years older than I was. He wore a pair of cutoff jeans. A towel hung around his neck like it did every day when he arrived home from his job. The sun had already darkened his winter-white skin into a dark golden tan and bleached his blonde hair almost white.

I had not been looking for a job, but making money was always a plus. "Where?"

"Seventy-fifth Street Pool. They need a pass checker from five to nine. Three fifty an hour—that's fifteen cents more than minimum wage. Want it?"

"I guess it sounds okay."

"Great, I'll tell Sue. She's the manager there."

I tiptoed to my bedroom door and locked it again, stopping short when I heard another knock.

"What?" Came from Bridg's room.

Her bedroom door opened. "How's it going?" Timmy asked.

"Fine." Bridg responded.

I listened carefully. It's not that I was eavesdropping, it's just that I'd always done this in order to learn from others. It's how I connected to the world without humiliation. On the fifth floor I had to learn that it was okay to ask questions but outside, it was different. Outside, I was pegged as quiet instead of dumb. Being quiet is not a weakness. Stupid is.

"Hey, what's up?" Timmy asked Bridg. From the close distance of his quiet voice, I assumed he stood with one foot in the hallway and one foot in her bedroom just like he had a moment ago when talking with me. I presumed Bridg was on her bed, probably reading.

"Nothing. Why?" Bridg asked.

"You've been so quiet since Anna's been home. I'm just making sure everything's okay."

"I'm fine," Bridg said, her voice much lower, with a lingering ache of loneliness.

"She'll get better soon." Timmy said.

At first, I wanted to scream. *I just spent the last three months returning from hell. I couldn't be any better if I tried.* But I was so taken aback by Tim's concern for Bridg that all I could do was quietly listen. *A family member reaching out to help another on an emotional level and using words like 'I'm making sure you're okay'?*

"It's not that," Bridg said. "Anna's not even the same person."

"I know. She needs to get through this."

"Something like that, I guess." Bridg said, seemingly unmoved. "Sometimes I wonder if Anna is putting Mom and me through this on purpose."

And now Bridgett responded like she wanted Tim to stay and listen?

"She'll get over it soon," Timmy said.

The door began to squeak closed and I tiptoed back to my bed, praying the creaky floor beneath my toes went unheard.

"Tim," Bridg said. I stopped short. "Thanks."

I flung back onto my bed and buried my face in my pillow and cried. Bridg was not only lonely, but she has a messed-up sister.

I reached for *To Kill A Mockingbird* from my nightstand. I automatically opened to page ninety-eight and read my favorite passage where Miss Maudie explained why it was a sin to kill a mockingbird. Bridg was another example of a mockingbird. She hadn't hurt so much as a fly, just as a mockingbird didn't invade people's gardens, and yet I chased her away with my screaming nightmares and hostility. It didn't take a rocket scientist to know why she spent so much time with friends. Who wouldn't want to get away from me? I wondered if she'd like me any better if I were gone permanently.

thirteen

I believed my obituary was a perfect essay to write. Maybe it would serve its purpose. I turned on my stomach, propped up on my forearms and stared at the blank page in my notebook. Oreo snored, curled up next to my waist. I leaned to one side and scratched the top of her head between her ears. "You'd miss me pup, wouldn't you?" She eyed me with one eye, wagging her tail, oblivious about death. It was strange, but I would stay alive to protect Oreo more than anyone else. Oreo wriggled an inch closer, sighed, and closed her eyes.

> *Obituaries are a dead person's final good-bye to the world, but there is a major flaw in these concluding, read-all-about-it reviews. Dead people don't write obituaries, their families do, which suggests, unfortunately, that what should be the final written words of the deceased ultimately becomes the words of family members.*

For example, how often have you read these familiar words? "Survived by her husband Buck and their two children Dasher and Dancer." Then it continues to list an assemblage of other people. Who cares? What about the poor old stiff? Shouldn't Jane Doe reap the benefits of her last hurrah? You can change this by writing your obituary before you die. Obituaries should include inspirations, wishes and future plans.

To begin, inspirations are important to the reader of the obituary. This tells the reader who you were as a human being. Your inspirations can be true or not. The idea is to get the reader hooked. Pull them into your life so that later, they will visit your gravesite with flowers and decorated Christmas wreaths.

For example, you might consider writing something similar to this. "Anna Maidhart, age 17, aspired to rescue animals from being locked in cages, chained to walls, and gawked at by humans.

Then, consider where you'd like to be buried. Go for your dreams here. Hey, if you've hooked your obituary reader, they'll be happy to grant your wishes. You want to be buried in Paris, why not? Maybe the savannah, where antelope and buffalo roam, is more your style, or next to your favorite pizza joint. Jane Doe might think a field with frolicking deer and blanketed with daisies to be more suitable. The point is this. Don't be caught dead in a place of your worst nightmares.

"Anna, the animal lover she was, has always dreamed of being buried down by the creek where she played, catching toads and minnows when she was a small child."

Lastly, future plans consist of your dreams coming true. Anything you have ever imagined can be included here. Who cares if it sounds like the impossible? You'll be dead, so there will be no need to worry about accomplishing your ultimate goals. Don't hold back. Go for your biggest and best future. It should look something like this.

"Though we are saddened to lose Anna at such a young age, it is important to mention that she would have made a difference. She had many future goals."

Anna planned to become an author of timeless best-selling novels and significant works that would change people for the better. Her future would have consisted of traveling to places like the redwoods, Himalayas, and the moon. These places, she had imagined, would have inspired her writing.

As you can see, it's not difficult to write your own obituary. Be prepared like the Boy

> *Scouts of America. You can be confident your friends and family will personally understand you in death, even if they didn't have a clue about you in life.*

WHAT A LOAD of crap! An accurate obituary would make for a very short piece of expository writing. *Anna was a hopeless teenager without a future.*

fourteen

On Wednesday, I met with Sue, the pool manager, at four-thirty, a half hour early so she could show me around. Sue actually looked like she belonged in water. Her feet pointed outward and she walked like a duck. Her body was perfectly streamlined for swimming and her hair was chlorine-bleached yellow and flattened to her head like she just came from underneath the sea.

"So you're a going to be a senior."

"Yes," I nod.

"What school?"

"EC."

"Oh, East Catholic? My niece goes there, Emily Hanson. Do you know her?

Just great. "No. What year is she?"

"She'll be a sophomore."

"Sorry, I don't know her."

"So here's the pool house. You can swim anytime for free during hours when you're off schedule. You can change in here or leave a towel and extra suit in the lockers if you want."

"Okay, thanks."

Here's the first aid station. If you notice someone entering the pool with a cut or scrape, send them here first and we'll take care of it."

"Okay." I said, as we continued to walk to each small building.

"These are the showers and bathrooms for our swimmers," Sue said, pointing to the two passageways into the locker rooms, one for men and one for women.

We walked to the baby pool. "No one over six is allowed in the baby pool and children must be accompanied by an adult. If someone asks, tell them we adhere to these rules. We don't want to be paying out the wazoo any more than we already are for insurance."

"I will."

We walked toward the large pool. It struck me before we stopped near the pool's edge. Shimmering sunrays spilled over the water's surface like flashlight beams reflecting off crinkled tinfoil.

I CLUNG TO the sidewall of the five-foot deep pool, my feet paddling to keep me afloat.

"Pluck up your courage, Anna." Mom called from the middle of the pool, in water up to her chest, holding Bridgett on her unseen hip.

"Let go, Anna. Let go," Liz called excitedly, trying to convince me that it was possible to let go of the sidewall without drowning.

I looked up at the lifeguard chair right above me. "Meg," I choked, sputtering water with every cough. "Watch me swim to Mom."

"I'm working, Anna. I can't," Meg said, scanning the pool for drowning kids.

"C'mon, Anna!" Liz hollered, "Let go!"

I took a huge breath and pushed off the cement wall toward the center of the pool. Dulled splashes from kids torpedoing into the water came from every direction, but nearby I heard Liz's muffled plea urging me forward. "C'mon Anna!"

"See, I knew you could do it!" Liz said, splashing wildly when I reached our mother.

"Lizzy stop splashing about like a fish out of water." Mom said, blocking the water from splashing into Bridg's eyes.

I wiped water from my eyes.

"ARE YOU OKAY?" Sue asked.

Yeah, why?"

"For a minute there it looked like you were crying. Anyway, that's it. Remember passes must be sewn onto suits, not pinned. If anyone gives you trouble I'll take care of it." Sue repeated, like I was unable to handle a simple situation.

By Friday, I was hoping for a problem to keep the job interesting. There was something to say for the expression, *Thank God it's Friday.* It had been a long week, and like the poster Marie bought for me, with a kitten hanging by one paw and a caption, *Hang in there!* I was just about to quit.

I handed my expository essay to Mrs. Frank when we were seated and ready to begin.

"Great, I can't wait to read it." Mrs. Frank said, placing it in a file folder and neatly into her apple decorated teacher bag.

I wished she wouldn't bring that thing to the library. It embarrassed the heck out of me and it didn't do much for her either. Though, I guess with kids at home, she wasn't worried about impressing anyone. Her chin length hair was neatly curled under and her makeup had been applied lightly, but her clumped mascara appeared to have been reapplied over yesterday's. I suppose it was unfair for me to nitpick because except for the apple bag, Mrs. Frank was put together. She seemed to care about her appearance. Her clothes were always ironed and accompanied by delicate jewelry.

"How old are your kids?" I asked.

If Mrs. Frank was surprised, like most teachers are when I bothered with a question, she didn't show it at all. I kept my mouth shut in junior high, and that hadn't changed in high school. I had a simple rule. Questions were only acceptable when survival depended on it. Most people liked to talk, especially when it was about them, which I saw as a welcome escape from my life. But it hadn't worked with either Dr. Ellison or the staff on the fifth floor.

"Thirteen in September. I have twins—a boy and a girl."

Although I wasn't really that interested in her kids, it

felt good to ask Mrs. Frank a simple question without overthinking what or how to ask. I wished I'd asked about geometry instead. I spent an hour trying to learn the translation rule and scale factor dilation and finding equations for circles by looking at endpoints of line segments. Angles and lines were easy to understand, but this circle crap was confusing. Mrs. Frank would probably smile eagerly if I asked, but a question like this was risky because maybe this information was something I should have already known.

"LET'S GET YOU on the scale first thing today." Dr. Ellison said as she opened the waiting room door from the hallway that led to her office. I moved quickly trying to avoid stares from other patients.

"God, why did you announce it in front of everyone?" I said angrily in a quiet voice when Dr. Ellison closed the door behind me.

"I apologize. It won't happen again." She pushed the top weight to fifty, the second weight to forty-six before nudging it with small jabs until it balanced at forty-eight.

I stepped off the scale wanting to scream, or at least kick the crap out of it, but instead I silently waited for this entire nightmare to just go away.

"Anna, let's go." Dr. Ellison said clearly, letting me know she was not interested in my defiant approach to something as simple as a balance teetering on a scale.

"Why does it bother you to have others know you're being weighed?" Dr. Ellison said once we were seated.

"Would you like it?"

"It wouldn't bother me. People are weighed all the time. A regular doctor's visit begins with a weigh-in. This is no different."

"It is different."

"In what way?"

"How many people do you know who get weighed three times a week? And I can't refuse because if I did you'd probably drag me back to the hospital." I quickly studied Dr. Ellison's eyes to see if that was true. "I hate that you think you have this much power over me."

I didn't need a mirror to see that my cheeks were burning with anger. My blood was boiling and pressure was building, causing my chest to ache as my heart pounded. I tried desperately to let air escape evenly so not to give Dr. Ellison any satisfaction that she has won this battle.

"It's not power. It's what I require of you, as your doctor, to keep you physically healthy so we have time for emotional issues. It won't be forever. The longer you maintain an appropriate weight like ninety-eight pounds, the less often you will need to be weighed. "

"It's no different than being chained to this chair. If I had any courage at all I would get up and leave, but I'm pretty much gutless, or a weakling."

"I disagree," Dr. Ellison said. "I think it requires courage to come here three times a week."

"So you're saying if I didn't come, you wouldn't hunt me down?"

"I hope I don't have to make that choice."

I sneered. "I come for my mom anyway, not you."

"Why your mother?"

"You have to ask? She's already had one daughter drop dead. Two would throw her over the edge, don't you think?"

"Why would there be two?"

"Oh my God, I meant nothing. I'm just saying she's praying day in and day out. If you haven't noticed the prayer books she reads while I'm trapped in here. She's probably begging God to save me or something . . . and before you ask . . . there is nothing to save me from, except for being here . . . all the time.

"Do you think of harming yourself, Anna?"

"No," I said with disgust.

"Do you think of killing yourself?"

"God! Why are you asking me these stupid questions?"

"Do you?"

"No, I don't!"

WHEN WE ARRIVED home I went straight for my journal.

June 22, 1984

Actually, Dr. Ellison, I do think about it. I think Liz and Ziggy are better off dead. Does that mean I want to die? I want to ask you this sometimes. But then what? I get sent back to Advocate's fifth floor? Sometimes, I feel cheated because I didn't even get a chance to be a kid before my sister died. I wanted to ask you today if this is normal, because I want to be normal like everyone else. Sometimes, I want your help. Other times, I don't. It's all so confusing, Dr. Ellison.

I closed my journal. Whoever said silence is golden was full of it.

fifteen

My mom agreed when I asked her if I could drive myself to work. She usually drove because she needed the car to haul Bridgett around, but tonight Bridg was at Jill's house for a slumber party. Though Mom could have probably used the car to get things done, I honestly felt she looked forward to hopping into bed without worrying about picking me up at nine o'clock.

I took my journal because after the initial crowd of kids at five, it slowed down, making my job behind the counter quite boring. On the way out, I grabbed one of Bridg's many books in case I decided to read. I looked at the cover. *Where the Red Fern Grows*. The cover showed a boy and two dogs. It was obviously one of Bridg's favorites since the pages were worn and many were dog-eared. Bridg loved to read as much as I avoided it. After Liz died, I stopped reading. Bridgett hadn't cared one way or another. The library had remained her magical place. For me, it had become a dungeon.

"Might be good," I said aloud to the empty room.

Sometimes I envied Bridgett's love for books and her belief that reading was fun. Maybe for the smart kids but after second grade, I was demoted from the cardinals to the black birds, the dumb kids group. Since then, unless the definition of fun is an overwhelming feeling of defeat, I found torture to be a better description.

I ARRIVED AT the pool ten minutes early. I hadn't eaten since breakfast and I was starving. I was not going to eat. If I gained weight instead of lost weight, no one would bother me, but even worse, no one would bother with me. Just a few more pounds and I would go back to being totally invisible at home, at school—everywhere.

I checked in about fifteen people, mostly grade-school kids, some with passes and some paying customers. Friday night was usually slow and tonight was no exception. Families found other things to do like seeing the latest movie or entertaining in their backyards with burgers and beer. Grilled juicy burgers from somewhere across the street had me drooling. White smoke rose above the rooftops, blowing this way. If it wasn't for the intense gurgling in my stomach, I could have ignored the temptation to leave my post, but I was starving. I headed for the snack bar, asked for a bag of potato chips and anxiously took them back to my station.

One chip. That was all I needed. One chip. I swallowed it so quickly there was no time to savor the taste. The urge to cram every last chip down my throat was relentless. *Just one more.* I plucked a large chip from the bag. *One more chip couldn't be that bad.* My tongue burned for the salt. *Why is this so hard?* I wanted to scream without being heard. I tossed the chip back into the bag and pressed the package together, crumbling all the chips to dust. Then I threw the bag into the garbage can. I grabbed the red fern book and opened it to the first chapter. I read the first sentence, and then reread it three times more. The greasy potato-chip smell rising from the trash can underneath the counter was too much. I threw the book aside, ripped the package from the garbage, turned the bag upside down and shook its contents into the garbage can, followed by the bag. *No chance of eating them now.*

The sky darkened by six-thirty. I prayed it wouldn't storm so I could work the full shift. I needed to climb into bed and fall asleep before I had time to open the fridge and search for food. The pool was always closed at the first sign of lightning. Arriving home early would be a deal-breaker for the day's will power.

Fifteen minutes later the first flash lit the sky followed by a rumble of thunder from a distance. Seconds later, excitement burst from the pool deck as the lifeguards' whistles screamed. Their Friday night plans had just changed for the better. Mine just got worse. Unhappy swimmers filtered out the same doors they had happily barged in through an hour ago.

WHEN I STOPPED at the crossroads of 75th Street and Woodridge Drive, I turned left heading for Route 53 instead of straight through to continue toward home. Ten minutes later, I passed a McDonald's and the first whiff of greasy french fries and sizzling beef made me salivate like Pavlov's dog. I was exhausted just battling the unbearable temptation.

Instead, I pulled into a nearby Jewel grocery store. I wandered through the aisles trying to appear nonchalant as I searched for diet pills.

"Where can I find the Ex-Lax?" a gray-haired lady loudly asked the pharmacist. My ears perked as I listened intently—where to find the Ex-Lax. *Wrestlers*, I think. *Why hadn't I remembered this before now?* Bobby Peterson, Janet's ex-boyfriend had sneakily taken Ex-Lax tablets to reduce his weight before a match. I walked closer, to hear better, and acted as if I was interested in purchasing vitamin tablets. I watched from the corner of my eye to see where the lady was directed.

I pretended to be looking for someone as I searched for something— anything— that I could afford as cover for the box of Ex-Lax. I picked up Pert shampoo and a cheap pair of socks. I walked casually up the aisle where the old woman had gotten her Ex-Lax. Casually, I swept one box off the shelf as I passed by and quickly tucked them under the socks.

"I can help you here if you're ready," came from behind the cosmetic counter.

I turned ready to say, "No thanks," but it was an older person, maybe around forty, standing at the cash register. She wasn't twenty and she wasn't a cute guy so I quickly changed my mind and placed my three items on the counter. My face reddened.

"That will be $8.11."

I handed over ten dollars, cupped my hand nervously for the change, and exited the store. In the car, I let out a long-drawn-out, well-deserved breath. I nervously backed out from my parking spot, like I'd stolen something, thinking that at any second a security guard would be tapping on my window with handcuffs. I drove out of the Jewel parking lot and headed toward McDonald's.

I tried to act completely relaxed at the counter. "Um, I'll take a Quarter Pounder with cheese and a vanilla shake, please." I said, eyeing my surroundings. If I saw someone I knew I'd need an easy out.

"Do you want fries with that?" the lady behind the counter asked.

"Sure, why not?"

"What size?"

Large, I thought. "Medium," I said. "Please."

"Anything else?"

"No thanks. Um, do you still have apple pies?" I asked, knowing darn well they did. "I'll have one of those too. My sister loves them."

As soon as I was handed the bag I headed for the car in the far corner of the lot. I pulled a couple fries from the bag and stuffed them into my mouth before I unlocked the car door. I slid the driver's seat back with one hand while I fumbled around inside the bag with the other, reaching for the Quarter Pounder box. I gulped down two bites. My chest burned as the food pushed down my throat. When the burger was gone I continued to gorge on the fries and the apple pie. My stomach cramped, but I sucked down the vanilla shake.

I'd already been gone way too long after the first sight of lightning. I should have been home forty-five minutes ago. I'd use the shampoo as proof that I went to Jewel grocery store if I needed to explain.

MY STOMACH GURGLED less than thirty minutes after taking the two Ex-lax. Five minutes later, I walked to the bathroom, but I needed to run. I closed the door behind me, quickly turned on the fan and ran the water before throwing myself onto the commode. I was embarrassed that the release felt rewarding, but the thought of losing hundreds of calories from just two pills was satisfying.

"Anna, are you okay?" Mom called from outside the bathroom.

It was one-thirty in the morning and I had been having diarrhea every half-hour. I had literally rubbed my skin raw and it burned painfully. The illusion that I could reverse the McDonald's binge simply by taking laxatives was exhilarating.

"I'm fine. I think I have the flu or something," I lied.

It finally stopped by three. After that I slept until noon.

sixteen

Sleeping late on Saturday did not help my exhaustion. I lay on my side with bent legs, my knees pressed together and my hands tucked under the pillow. The room was becoming steadily hotter as the minutes ticked by. "This is ridiculous," I mumbled under my breath, throwing off the sheet. I knocked on Bridg's bedroom door and opened it. She was lying on her bed, uncovered and sweltering, reading *Bop*, her favorite teen magazine.

"Hey, want to go buy a window air conditioner?"

Bridgett hopped off her bed. "Yep."

I rushed, taking a one-minute cool shower and leaving my hair untouched. Sweat quickly surfaced from my pores causing my clothes to stick as I dressed.

Bridg showered seconds after I left the bathroom.

"How are you feeling?" my mother asked.

"I'm much better," I said, sympathetic to her worried look.

Except for my imprisonment on a psych unit and Liz's

death, it was rare for someone in my family to get sick, even with a cold. But when one of us did, my mother's face showed her worry. It was the only time she showed emotion. Usually she was too busy with housework and errands to show her feelings.

"Can Bridg and I take the car to Sears to buy a window air conditioner? Seriously Mom, I cannot take this heat any longer."

My mother agreed, like I knew she would. I pulled myself up to the highest closet shelf using the clothes hamper as a step stool. I moved a bunch of junk to the side, groped for my rainy-day canister and dug out babysitting money from the last couple years. I was saving for a car, but right now avoiding a heat stroke was more important. There was no way in heck we were getting central air like most our neighbors had in the past years. My dad was holding out—for what, I had no idea.

BRIDGETT AND I spent over an hour sweating like pigs trying to get the window unit into my bedroom window. I bought cheap and I regretted it. I wasn't sure which it was, the loss of hydration, the laxatives or the hard labor, but I was having another dizzy spell. I leaned against the wall to rest when Bridg ran for a rubber hammer.

"I know where I'm sleeping tonight," Bridg said on her return.

Since Marie married last summer and I moved into her bedroom, I'd missed sharing a room with Bridgett. So when I heard her excitement I was thrilled.

I banged the sides of the air conditioner so it fit snug against the window ledge and window. "Crap!" I whispered as I missed and hit the window. Three cracks crept diagonally across one windowpane. Bridge ran for the scotch tape while I held the unit in place. Sweat dripped down my neck and back. Finally, the air conditioner was firmly in place and the blind lowered to hide the taped cracks. Bridg plugged the unit into the wall and cool air flowed from the vents as the unit hummed with power. We both stood in front of it cooling ourselves. I lifted my hair, turning around to let the coolness breathe on my neck.

There was a knock on my bedroom door before our dad popped his head in. "Who called Frances?" He asked, holding the phone bill.

"Me," I said offended, like he might have thought I was trying to rip him off. Though, I hadn't planned on mentioning it either. There was always a slight chance it could slip by.

"You owe me $12.07."

When he left the room, Bridg and I shook our heads, but said nothing about what had just happened. "Want to go to Micky D's?" Bridg asked.

Two nights of junk food would have fat leaching into my body, even with last night's purge. Besides, it worried me to eat in front of Bridgett. I wanted her to think that I had enough willpower to avoid foods like McDonald's and Burger King. But because Bridgett needed me for a ride I jumped at the opportunity. If she could drive, she'd probably be choosing to be with her friends instead, but I didn't care because right now it was just us. Anyway, one Ex-Lax instead of two should eliminate the McDonald's again.

"Mom!" Bridg yelled. "We're home!"

We headed to the humid but cooler basement with our bag of McDonald's. Mom joined us. My father was upstairs battling the heat alone. He'd rather swelter than spend time with us as a family. He said he didn't want dinner in a bag. He'd make a sardine and onion sandwich with mayo and savor it with a cold beer.

Downstairs we ate our fast food and watched a full episode of *Different Strokes*.

"I'll make popcorn. Get a floor bed ready," I said to Bridg, turning off the TV and heading upstairs into the stifling heat. Tonight had the feel of a slumber party when I was young and climbing into a sleeping bag in a crowded room of girls late into the night. Except it was only Bridg and me and it was only nine o'clock, but I didn't care. I was going to wrap myself in a blanket like it was a winter's night, and maybe write in my journal.

The popcorn began to pop when Bridg came around the corner from the hall into the kitchen. "Dad's in there!" she said completely disgusted.

"What?"

I followed Bridg down the hall. She swung open my bedroom door. We were blasted with cold air and the hollow echoes of our father's snores. My dad sleeps like the dead. He lay across my bed with his head at the foot near the cooling vents of the air conditioner. His dry, calloused feet with their long, yellowing toenails were nestled on my pillow

"Dad! Hey Dad!" I shouted louder and louder, but he didn't stir. "This is ridiculous!" I slammed the bedroom door, hoping it would wake him. Nothing.

"Mom," I said, opening my parents' bedroom door. "Dad is sleeping on my bed."

"For Pete's sake," she said climbing from her bed.

"Jimmy! Come to bed!" Mom called, shaking Dad's arm and then his leg. "Jimmy!"

"Alright," Dad mumbled. A few seconds later his snores resumed.

"You've got to be kidding," I sneered. "I'm so not paying part of the electric bill if he asks."

"Your father is a good man, Anna. Dad has never missed a day of work and he's a good provider."

"Well. Just forget it then," I huffed, embarrassed by Mom basically telling me off. She had the right, and I knew it. Most nights Dad would sleep, almost unconscious until three-thirty in the morning, and then rise from bed without an alarm, and get ready for work like he has every morning for as long as I could remember.

The smoke detector blared. Dad still snored without the slightest disturbance. I ran and grabbed a dishtowel from the kitchen and frantically fanned away the smoke from the burnt popcorn to stop the beeping.

"Don't throw it out. I'll eat it," Mom said rounding the corner into the kitchen. "It shouldn't go to waste."

As I passed the kitchen on my way downstairs,

loneliness settled around me when I saw my mother sitting by herself eating burnt popcorn.

seventeen

Sunday afternoon, Bridg and I headed to my room and stayed there watching TV in the cool of the air conditioning. We left only when it was absolutely necessary, one at a time, to use the bathroom or fetch dinner. The night before, I had tried to sleep on the living room couch before I moved to the sofa in the basement. The moist humidity of the basement was just as bad as the sweltering heat upstairs. Our slumber party cancelled, Bridg had stayed in her room and until Sunday morning, I didn't see or hear her. I was glad she hadn't died of heat stroke. On Sunday, we didn't dare leave my bed unguarded at any cost. Tonight we planned to sleep in luxurious cool even if it meant being stuck at home all day.

Bridg was reading yet another book, giving me the opportunity to pull *To Kill a Mockingbird* from my nightstand drawer. *How much I had learned from reading this book.* The author had used the diplomatic Atticus Finch and his impressionable children to teach readers about the world of injustice. Innocent Tom Robinson was killed because the small town where he lived couldn't see past his skin color. *Don't judge a book by its cover* would have been my mother's explanation.

I put *To Kill a Mockingbird* back in the drawer and reached for my English notebook on the floor next to my bed. I hadn't used Mrs. Frank's idea about zoos for my expository essay, but I had the perfect idea for my next writing assignment. I wrote the title, *Don't Judge a Book by Its Cover* on the top line and my thoughts flowed effortlessly onto the paper.

> *I was first introduced to Ziggy, an African elephant who was taken from the wild and chained to a wall at the Brookfield Zoo for over thirty years. His crime—capture. Are people so arrogant to think that animals, whether they are a four-ton elephant or a slithering worm, don't feel pain? Isn't it our duty to view the world with our hearts, not our eyes?*
>
> *Ziggy and I first became acquainted when I was five. Pushing through the legs of adults with other kids to see the large elephant was exciting. Making my way to the bottom of the railing I stared at the largest animal I had ever seen. A peanut was thrown into its pen, and the large trunk of this magnificent animal swung around, picked the peanut up with agility and took it into its mouth.*

When Ziggy turned for this quick moment to gather up the peanut, I saw something that changed me. His long eyelashes swept across his small eyes and though his eyes so tiny for such a big body, imbedded deep within them was sadness. His eyes could not hide his pain. My heart ached to save him, to free him. It was then that I fell in love with Ziggy and his chains became mine. Being five, I couldn't have understood the meaning of "Don't judge a book by its cover" but this would become my earliest recollection of this figurative language showing its ugly face.

Ziggy had given of himself against his will. Pulled from his home in the wild, he was forced to live in a cage, handled by elephants' worst enemy, humans. He was rumored to have killed a man, and because of this he was forced into thirty years of bondage. Had his keepers learned to look beyond Ziggy's cover, his size and power, they would have seen this animal's magnificent beauty and intelligence. Ziggy acted precisely, understanding his top priority—to survive. Isn't this an animal's main importance—to survive? Are we so bold to pretend we wouldn't act as Ziggy had if our own survival was threatened?

Like Ziggy, I suppose we all live in chains, suffer our own bondage, but unlike this magnificent animal, Americans are permitted to live an American dream upon American soil. The moment Ziggy floated into American waters, he deserved our same rights. All earthly inhabitants, people and animals alike, deserve justness not judgment. We need to take a stand. We need to look past physical appearances, and place our sights on the emotional effect that is created when inequality is permitted to flourish within our daily lives.

Imagine, will you—if you were Ziggy.

eighteen

By Monday morning I began to feel the daily routine at home was just like the routine on the fifth floor. Doctor visits and therapy sessions with meals spread out in between. At home it consisted of tutoring with Mrs. Frank, then to Dr. Ellison for an hour of therapy and then my job, by far the easiest part of my day. Later there was homework and studying.

Figuring out how to rid food from my stomach at just the right time so my bathroom visits went unnoticed was almost impossible. Sticking my finger down my throat was out of the question. I tried it and it didn't work. Except for horrendous gagging sounds, nothing happened; not a morsel of food found its way back up my throat.

The night before while Bridg slept in my room, I couldn't get to the Ex-Lax. I couldn't take a chance that Bridg would wake while I was pulling open my sock drawer. Today, I decided to swallow the pills no matter who was around. I quietly snuck one from the box and buried it deep in the pocket of my jeans shorts, taking care not to wake Bridg before heading to the library.

MRS. FRANK HAD me worried. She said little compared to her usual self. When we moved from one subject to the next there was barely any chitchat. Not that I minded, but I didn't like the uneasy vibes I felt coming for her. When I returned from a bathroom break, I could tell Mrs. Frank as on edge.

She turned directly toward me when I sat at our working table. "I need to talk to you."

"About what?" I asked nervously.

"Honestly, Anna, I am worried about you."

Immediately I thought the Ex-Lax had fallen from my pocket and Mrs. Frank had found it. My chest tightened. "Why?" I asked cautiously.

"Your expository essay is very upsetting."

I went dead silent, all sorts of red flags waving and bells sounding in my head. *Speak already!* I screamed within, trying to drain my flooded thoughts.

"I've never had a student choose to write an obituary. This piece," she said taking it from a manila folder and sliding it toward me, "has me concerned."

"Why?" I halfheartedly smiled, trying to act dumb.

"Why would you choose to write an obituary?" She asked empathically, softening her face.

"You don't need to be worried about some stupid assignment!"

"Anna. You wrote about your own death."

"No, I didn't. I wrote what my obituary should read if I die. *If,*" I repeated.

"You used your age." She pointed to where I wrote, *at age seventeen*.

"Well then, I guess I'm more creative than your other students," I said sarcastically, trying to steer the conversation in a different direction. When Mrs. Frank still looked concerned I approached the subject differently. "We talked about the heat last week and how it could kill us. Remember? It gave me the idea to write an obituary. It's not a big deal."

"I see it differently." Mrs. Frank argued.

I pushed my chair away from the table. The more we spoke about this the more uncomfortable I became. "So. I could have used age eighty. I didn't think about it, I guess."

"Anna," Mrs. Frank said, "I telephoned Dr. Ellison concerning this assignment."

"That was pathetically stupid," I choked. "Why would you do that?" My stomach knotted and my throat narrowed, making it difficult to hide my labored breath. Three months ago, in a situation like this, I would have walked away without a word, gotten in the car and driven home or walked, no matter how far.

If you want to be treated like the young adult that you are then you'll have to play the part, Chad had said. He had been disappointed at my attempt to skew medical evidence. Even though the evidence belonged to me, so whatever. Anyway, I was intrigued with his choice of words . . . *play the part.* Basically, quit being a spoiled brat and grow up. But he hadn't said it that way, like my siblings would have. I stayed seated next to Mrs. Frank trying to concentrate, but it was nearly impossible. Blood pumped hard through every vein in my body. If I could have spoken, I think I would've screamed. But it didn't matter much because I was speechless. *How could Mrs. Frank have done this to me?*

I left the library and considered driving anywhere except home. I could predict every word of Dr. Ellison's in reaction to Mrs. Frank's unnecessary phone call. If I were eighteen, this wouldn't be a problem. People like me had next to no rights. I once believed that deciding what to do and where to go was in my control, but I was wrong. It took less than an hour on the fifth floor to realize it was all an illusion. There were no rights at seventeen except for being allowed to breathe and sometimes even that was questionable.

Leaving the fifth floor meant I was ready to go home, didn't it? If I had not been ready to come home, Dr. Ellison would have seen to it that I was still behind locked doors. My stomach felt tortured. *Oh my God, she'd send me back to the fifth floor and Mom would agree.* My mother may not have control of my meds, but she would stop me if I decided to jump from a cliff or slit my wrists. *Would I jump?* I didn't think so. *No. No. I couldn't. Could I?* I pulled up in the driveway, turned off the engine and just sat, my fingers clutching the steering wheel of the Olds Cutlass. I couldn't stop the answer from rushing to the forefront of my brain, *Damn straight I could jump off a cliff.*

"Hey Mom," I called when I strolled through the front door, "Can I drive myself to Dr. Ellison's today?" I asked, acting completely innocent.

"How was tutoring?" she asked.

"Fine." I answered nervously wondering if she had heard from Dr. Ellison. "So, can I go alone?"

"Dr. Ellison wants me there today," Mom said.

The reaction I'd imagine a mother would have if her daughter's psychiatrist called about a personal obituary was different from my mother's completely unaffected manner. But heck, why should I be surprised?

"Are you joking?" I sneered. "I'm not going then. Dr. Ellison can't make me either!" *I hope I don't have to make that choice," she had said, which probably meant she'd have the cops retrieve me.*

"C'mon Mom! Let me go alone. I'll tell her you're sick or something. C'mon!" I begged. I was seventeen and begging. I attempted to act my age, but once my mouth opened it simply didn't happen.

nineteen

"This is comfy, the three of us ready to stare at walls." The snide remark passed over my lips before we were seated. I plopped down in the chair I'd claimed as mine since the first time I was there. "Enjoy the conversation and don't expect so much as a word from me!"

"Anna? What is making you so upset?" Dr. Ellison asked.

"This! That's what! I don't need my mother here, holding my hand."

My silent treatment lost energy by the second. My emotions went crazy. This feeling of wanting to silence myself, yet spewing anger felt a lot like my need to starve myself, but craving food.

"Do you know why I asked your mom to join us?"

"The stupid obituary Mrs. Frank blabbed about! I swear it was supposed to be funny because we had been talking about the heat and how we felt it could kill us on the spot. It was a joke! That's all! I swear!"

I looked at Dr. Ellison, while I tried to control my breath. I glanced quickly at my mother who was quietly following the conversation at one end of the leather couch. I felt sorry for my mom. I was obviously a constant disappointment, and still she liked me. *No! For some ridiculous reason, she loved me!* I was unable to understand how she could love an idiot, this two-year-old throwing-a-tantrum person that I had become.

"You need to calm down before we continue." Dr. Ellison said.

"Really? How wonderful!" I crossed my arms like I was shivering with cold. I tried to relax, by slumping forward in the chair. I wanted to straighten up, pretending to back up everything I'd just said, but honestly, I couldn't back any of it up. Since I'd been home, I'd lost all the confidence I had gained on the fifth floor. Maybe I wrote the obituary because I wished I were dead, or maybe I wrote it to be funny. I couldn't say for sure.

"So you wrote the obituary as a joke?"

Anxiety rose in my chest. "I'm not sure why I wrote it."

"Did you want me to find out about it?" Dr. Ellison asked.

"No." I said quickly, losing credibility.

Did I? Had I wanted Dr. Ellison to know how I felt? Was this whole obituary thing a subtle message?

"You're not very convincing." Dr. Ellison said.

"Is she taking her medicine?" Dr. Ellison asked my mother.

My mother looked at me, maybe hoping I could give

her the answer through telepathy.

"I don't know," my mom said.

"You do know I'm here, in this room, within earshot?" I mocked.

"Are you taking your medicine, Anna?" Dr. Ellison asked again.

"Yep." I said sarcastically.

Dr. Ellison uncrossed her legs and scooted herself a bit forward in her chair, turning toward my mom. "I think it's important for you to understand, this is not only Anna's problem. This is a family problem."

What? I looked over at Mom. Her expression barely changed with Dr. Ellison's words, though I noticed a slight shift in her eyes as if she thought it was true. *What the hell!* I wondered scornfully if Dr. Ellison could have done any better than my mom had, if one of her kids died.

"Yes," my mother agreed. "I haven't been a great mother, I'll admit."

"What? That's not true! I can't even believe you're saying it. She's a great mom," I said, narrowing my eyes toward Dr. Ellison, "What if your kid died?"

"Anna, really. Be careful what you wish for."

"I didn't wish for anything, Mom! God! Next time I won't defend you." My face reddened from embarrassment.

"I know you love your children. And Anna—you love your mother." Dr. Ellison said. "I'm referring to the lack of communication," she continued. "I need to know if you are taking your medication, but neither of you can answer my question with assurance or truth."

"My mom doesn't know because she trusts me."

"Are you taking your medicine?" my mother asked, throwing me off my game again.

Mom continued, "Dr. Ellison is right. There is a lack of communication. I don't check because I do trust you, but I also know better than to place such decisions on you," Mom said, her eyes full of regret. She turned toward Dr. Ellison. "I love my children. I've tried especially hard to show this to Anna and Bridgett after Lizzy died . . ."

I searched for near-impossible control as my eyes welled.

". . . it was too late for the others. I should have cried when Lizzy died, but I couldn't even let my kids see how heartbroken I was. I wanted to be strong for everyone. I never intended to do the wrong thing or hurt my children. I only did what I thought was best. I see now that my mistakes have been damaging to my family."

Silence filled the office.

"I'm so sorry, Anna. This has happened because of my stupidity. I cannot tell you how sorry I am."

"It's not your fault, Mom."

"I'm afraid it is. I just didn't know any better."

"We're not here to place blame," Dr. Ellison said.

I wondered if my mother wanted to hug me or rise from the couch and hold me in her arms. What if she did, but didn't know how? What if I showed her what I had seen on the fifth floor? What if I hugged her? "Mom," I said looking towards her, shifting my eyes to the floor and back.

"I . . ." I pushed myself away from the chair and went over and hugged my mother. She remained seated. We were in an awkward position for a hug. Mom's arms remained at her sides. Then I felt her awkwardly pat my back before I pulled away. My flushed cheeks grew even hotter in the seconds it took to get back to my chair.

The silence was slowly killing me.

"That was nice Anna," Mom said.

I swallowed a huge breath. "Okay."

"That was a big step. How did it make you feel?" Dr. Ellison said, her voice almost a whisper, like she too was on the verge of tears.

"Okay."

"It seemed difficult for you to return Anna's hug," Dr. Ellison said.

I began to ramble. "We don't hug. You know, it's not like you need to hug to know someone likes you and all. It's fine. It was kind of weird for me too. I know my mom likes me. We don't need to show it."

"Unfortunately, hugging is something I haven't shown my children often enough. I should have."

"We can't change the past, but we can change what happens now," Dr. Ellison said.

"That's right," my mom said. "Anna, you do know I love you, right?" Mom's face totally distorted as she lifted her shoulders in a lopsided shrug. As if this was some TV game show and she was completely unsure of her answer, but gave it her best shot anyway.

"God Mom! Yes! But you don't need to say it."

"What's so horrible about the word love?" Dr. Ellison asked.

"Please can we just stop talking about it?" I said, hurriedly.

"Anna, you need to take your medicine, and Mrs. Maedhart, you need to encourage Anna to do so."

"Encourage?" I said disgusted, lifting my eyebrows and puckering my lips around the sarcasm. "I don't need to be encouraged."

"You'll need to hand her the pills and watch her take them, making sure they're swallowed," Dr. Ellison said to my mother, ignoring my comment.

My blood bubbled. I held myself back from leaving. *My mother? Watching while I took pills?* I would think that after three months of working with me, Dr. Ellison would know my family better than this. We didn't do things like encourage each other or give pats on the back for taking medicine like good little boys and girls. It was each man for himself.

"No! Way!" I shouted.

"Anna, let's just try it," my mother said.

"You can't be serious," I said in disbelief. "Just because we got all . . . whatever, doesn't mean now you can run my life!"

My narrowed eyes slid from my mother to Dr. Ellison. "I'm not doing it! I *have* been taking my medicine," I lied, "But now, all bets are off! Don't bother writing prescriptions 'cuz I won't need them." Immediate relief flooded over me. I was done keeping the lie by pretending to pop pills.

"Anna, please. It will help you." My mother pleaded.

"Nope! Sorry Mom. You're not going to convince me no matter how hard you try. I'm not taking them!"

I sat back, sealing my arms to my sides and securing my hands tightly under my thighs to keep Dr. Ellison from noticing my shakiness. My mother, I was sure, was convinced I wouldn't be swallowing pills, but Dr. Ellison—she was thinking of what to do about it. I knew things were going to get worse, but this was the risk I took and now I had to live with it. I looked at the clock. Ten minutes remained. Silence erupted. I watched the second hand tick by, and from the corner of my eye, I saw Mom looking at me, sick with worry.

"There's a therapeutic school in Hinsdale. I would like Anna to attend. I will call tomorrow morning to see if they can take her," Dr. Ellison said glancing my way and then back at my mother.

"No!" I screamed. "I'm not going to some mental school!"

"Is it inpatient?" My mother asked.

"Mom!" I yelled. "Why are you asking? I'm not going. You cannot force me. I swear to God, I will run. Agkh," I grunted, slapping my hands down on my thighs hard, which caused an instant sting.

"Outpatient," Dr. Ellison said.

"I will run! You know I will! I did it before and I can do it again. Except you'll never find me!" I shouted at Dr. Ellison. "Do you hear me Mom? I will never be back!"

"Anna, we are trying to help you," Mom said.

"I don't want your help!"

Dr. Ellison only glanced my way momentarily before returning to this stupid conversation with my mom. "Anna will finish her summer courses there. She would be home by four o'clock each afternoon. I have two other patients there, and they are progressing nicely. I strongly recommend you get Anna enrolled."

"Mom. Please don't sign my life away."

Mom sighed, obviously tired. "Anna and Mrs. Frank have a rapport. I'd rather she didn't miss out on that entirely."

God! I was finally getting somewhere.

"Mrs. Maedhart. Honestly, this is very puzzling to me. I don't understand why you're unwilling to watch Anna take her medication and why you're considering part-time schooling instead of full-time. If it's a financial hardship . . ."

"It's not the money, Dr. Ellison. Please," Mom sighed then paused. "Nothing slipped past my mother. She was in control of every situation. Every decision, no matter how insignificant or critical, she made for me. I wanted something different for Anna —for all my children." Mom sighed again. "Enough already. It's six of one, half dozen of the other. Live in the present, right? All I'm pointing out is that my children have learned to be independent. Maybe I went overboard and caused more harm than good, but it's how I raised them."

"I suppose Anna could continue tutoring and simply attend group sessions at the therapeutic school. There are two-hour group therapy sessions on Tuesdays and Thursdays, but it is a mixture of teens and adults. I will continue to see Anna here on Mondays, Wednesdays and Fridays. Are you available to drive her to Hinsdale? Otherwise we can have her bussed."

"I'll drive her. Could Anna be given her medication by you or at the school?"

"God Mom! Stop with the medicine thing already."

"I cannot force you to take pills, Anna . . ." My mom's voice was raised ever so slightly, but enough to tell me she was done with this crap as much as I was. ". . . and I'm not willing to bring this between us."

"She'll be given her meds by me and the nurse at the facility."

"What about weekends? You plan on knocking on our front door?" I asked in contempt.

"Weekends will be up to your mother."

"Which means me. Wonderful." I grumbled sarcastically.

"One last thing. I'd like it if Bridgett came for one of our sessions."

"Why?" I asked.

"Because Bridgett is part of your family too."

"What makes you think she's going to sit in an office for an hour with me?" I said. I hoped Bridg would refuse because I'd rather keep family as far from my private life as possible.

I left without a word. No blood pressure, no weight and no finger prick. I got to the car . . . and no keys. Nothing but my mother's car, parked perfectly in its spot with the windows up and the doors locked. *Unbelievable!* A short time ago I was locked in on the fifth floor trying to get out and now I was locked out trying to get in. I suppose it didn't matter. Either in or out—both kept me trapped.

One thing was for sure. I hated the person I had become. The last month on the fifth floor, I was happy to be returning to my old self. The person people liked, a girl who took risks and danced to her sister's music. I wanted to be noticed again for my happy smile and the kindness that so many adults admired when I was younger. Like when my first grade teacher gave me the nickname Anna My Heart on the first day of school. I guess those days were gone forever.

This was the real me, I supposed. Mean, defiant, mad . . . and suicidal. It was the first time I thought of myself in that way. Always before I'd sugar-coat it by using a kinder term, like bummed or depressed, but crap, I was sick and tired of life being so difficult! I hated everything about it.

I couldn't stop thinking about what Mom had said as she drove home.

"Did your mom really make all your decisions?"

"Oh boy, did she ever. She was as sharp as a tack too—didn't miss a beat."

"What does all that mean, Mom? I mean, what was she like?"

"Astute. Well-liked by everyone. She was classy. Prim and proper, like most English women were," My mom pulled at her ironed but worn shirt. "Obviously, I take after my dad. I can be a slob."

"You are not, Mom." I light-heartedly smiled, matching my mom's reaction to her own comment.

"Well, maybe not, but Mother constantly wanted to open my head to see what was rolling around up there."

"Why?"

"My mother was very clever, and I wasn't. Never had it in me. But let me tell you, she got along with your father like they were two peas in a pod. Your dad and I would come home from a date, and I'd go up to bed. Your dad and my mother would have tea and talk for hours."

I couldn't ever remember a time when I heard my mother say anything even slightly negative about the grandma I never knew. My siblings didn't talk about her much, but when they did, it was of how much they adored her. My oldest sister Frances had spent every summer in Cazenovia, New York with our grandparents until she was sixteen. A few years ago, Frances claimed that summers with Grandma were the best times of her life.

twenty

It had been several years since our family had gotten together for the Fourth of July. All the siblings who lived in the area, who I didn't see often enough, would be there. Gabe would bring his family. Marie along with Frances and her family would come for Dad's grilled chicken. Mom would make her special holiday ring salad. It was much like potato salad with tiny ring noodles instead of potatoes. The noodles could only be found in upstate New York so Mom saved the salad for special occasions. I guess since I was home from the fifth floor it was an occasion worthy of ring salad. Just like it was when I returned home for my first weekend visit.

By noon, Marie — who was four months pregnant — and her husband arrived. They were followed by Gabe, my sister-in-law Gina and my nephews. Then came Frances and her family —my two nieces and baby nephew. Frances pulled her blonde bob back into a stubby ponytail before she helped Marie with the side dishes in the kitchen. My father arranged the charcoal in his Weber grill so it was distributed perfectly. Tim and my brothers-in-law sat on the top of the picnic table drinking beer as Dad spread the chicken over the hot coals. He watched the chicken closely, turning it every fifteen minutes or so while he drank with the guys.

Gina said to Dad, "Did you get the wallet I sent you for Father's Day?"

"I sure did." I saw my dad reach into his back pocket. I hoped Gina's feelings wouldn't be hurt. I listened closely and peeked from the corner of my eye while pretending to watch the kids play in the yard. "I exchanged it for this one," my dad grinned. "Thank you. I needed a wallet."

"Oh. Yes . . . I guess that one is nice . . .," Gina replied, casually.

Dad never minded hurt feelings, but I did.

I chased the kids in a game of backyard freeze tag until they were sweaty enough to convince their parents it was time for the sprinkler. Bridg was still in her room when I headed to the side of the house to hook up the hose. The spigot was below her open window. She was listening to Michael Jackson on her stereo and probably reading a book, too.

"Bridg," I yelled from below. "Bridg."

She came to the window. "Yeah?"

"Come out."

"What are you guys doing?"

"I'm getting the sprinkler ready for the kids. Everyone's here," I said, knowing she was aware of this, but hoping it would lure her outside anyway.

"Yeah, be there in a sec," she said.

I pulled the hose around to the backyard and set up the sprinkler. The kids began running through the frigid water shrieking.

Tim came from downstairs with water balloons. When the kids saw what he was up to, they jumped in circles shrieking louder. Bridg smiled in excitement and pulled her hair back in a rubber band to get ready for the game. Sometimes I forget Bridg is still young because of our nieces and nephews. I was ten when our first niece was born, but Bridge was only the youngest in the family for six years.

"I'm out," Gina said. "You guys are way too competitive for me."

We faced our partners standing three feet apart and tossed the water balloons gently, trying not to break them. Gabe was partnered with Tim while Bridg was my partner. Kids and couples were paired together.

"Go," Gina called.

Some nieces and nephews lasted past the first round only because their balloons had not popped the first time they hit the ground. After the third round only the adults were left.

Tim rubbed his hands together in preparation for the next catch. I scraped my palms up and down my thighs to wipe off the sweat.

"Don't miss, Bette," Dad yelled across the yard to Mom.

"Ditto on that, Anna," Bridg said.

"Bend your knees when going in for the catch," Frances yelled to her husband, showing him a proper knee bend for a successful catch. "And don't try to show off."

"I got this," he called back.

"Go," Gina called for the fifth time. The balloons were in the air. Gabe backed up for Tim's overthrow. "C'mon, Tim," he yelled as his hand went up, tipping the balloon, sending it bursting on the ground. "What were you thinking, man?" Gabe laughed. "I'm seven feet tall?"

"Man! We could have won," Tim said, punching the air in disappointment.

Dad sneered scornfully, "Ha! You don't deserve what you don't work for."

"Jimmy," Mom said to Dad. "Pride cometh before the fall."

Dejected, Tim walked back to the picnic bench and sat next to Gina. I felt sick that Dad had gotten to him, and sicker that I was actually glad it wasn't me being criticized this time. I wanted to yell, "good throw" or something that would make him feel better, but I knew I shouldn't. *Only give credit when credit is deserved.* There was absolutely nothing I could say to Tim to make the situation better because he overshot the throw. *But this is a stupid game so what did it matter?* I used to play for blood and guts too, but now—I took a deep breath before the next throw—*the only thing I knew for sure was that the fifth floor had really screwed with my thinking.*

Stakes were high when we moved to fifteen feet apart and even higher after seven rounds, at twenty feet apart.

Only Bridg and I remained in the game against Mom and Dad. Serious faces lined the sidelines. Dad's knees were bent just so, going in for the win.

Mom and Bridg sent the balloons sailing across the yard. Dad's balloon burst in his hands, soaking his face and shirt. Bridg's throw came right at me. I caught it to my chest, quickly closing my eyes in anticipation of water splattering all over, but it didn't. Bridg ran toward me with open palms for a double high five. I let the balloon drop and met her hands with mine. We celebrated only for a few seconds. Any longer and we'd be taunted as showoffs.

twenty-one

"God, I hate this," I said before slamming the car door and walking into the therapeutic school in Hinsdale. I took my sweet time walking up one flight of stairs to the ridiculous group therapy session.

"Welcome Anna. I'm Millie."

Millie was probably thirty. Her hair was bouncy like Dr. Ellison's, but it was jet black against her creamy skin. She led me into a kitchen area. There was a huge spread of food. Lunchmeat, bread and rolls, chips, pop and all sorts of side salads covered a large round table. Everyone was busy piling food on plates and talking.

"Get yourself a plate," Millie said, pointing to the counter with paper plates and napkins and plastic forks and cups. "And then we'll make our way into the conference room."

"No thanks. I'm not hungry." I said, casually eyeing the group. I didn't see anyone my age, like Dr. Ellison said there would be. There were two younger girls, but they looked like kids.

The conference room was large. Colorful pictures of nature scenes hung on the four walls.

"Sit anywhere you'd like," Millie said, pointing toward a collection of chairs and couches. I chose a chair so I wasn't forced to sit too close to someone.

"Hi, I'm Tom," a balding man said. He carried a plate filled with side salads and a sandwich crammed with lunch meat.

"Hi."

"And you are . . .?" he asked, taking a mouthful of coleslaw.

"Anna."

"Welcome." He chose a chair across from mine. Everyone trickled in to the room. Some introduced themselves, others didn't care, like me.

The room quieted once Millie got seated. "Everyone this is Anna, if you haven't met her yet."

The twin girls, who looked like they were twelve, spoke some kind of distorted language only they seemed to understand. While they talked, they twisted their hands in different directions, but it was odd the way it didn't make any sense, even to me. I learned about fifty words of sign language years ago and they stuck in my head. This twisted finger and hand thing they had going on was bizarre. As my mom would have said, *there was no rhyme or reason to it.*

"There's no formality here, Anna. If you want to speak, you can. And the same goes if you want to listen. That's fine too — well, for the first couple days," Millie lightheartedly laughed, "You won't get any better if you don't add to the conversation. We learn from each other and help each other. We'd love to get to know you better. It's important actually. Rich and I," she continued, pointing toward a man dressed in scrubs who broadened his smile and waved hello, "are the group's leaders, but we like it best when all of you do the talking," she said, making eye contact with others in the room.

"No lunch today?" Rich said to a girl in her twenties with stringy hair hanging in her face.

"Nah, not hungry."

"How about you start the conversation then while we eat and listen."

"Well, I feel like I've made some progress," the girl said. "A guy opened a can of pop the other day in the lunch room and I was barely startled."

Pop startled her?

By the end of the two hours I found out why when she brought it up again and then cried for the rest of the session. She had managed to escape after being raped, but was shot in the leg as she ran through a park screaming for help. The pop from opening a can of soda must remind her of the gunshot, I figured.

Then there was Paul, the older man with graying hair, who stopped walking in mid-step, on his way to the bathroom, and stood immobile. He rubbed his hands together frantically like he was trying to warm them after being frostbitten. Molly, the pregnant girl sitting to my left, had two seizures within the first hour. Every time Paul halted for his crazy ritual, Molly screamed at him to fucking stop, jolting me from my chair.

"How was it?" Mom asked when I threw myself into the passenger seat and slammed the car door shut.

"Two words. Pure torture!"

MY HOPES OF sharing my room with Bridg simply because it was cooler than the rest of the house had not panned out. Watching reruns like *MASH* became routine for us because Channel 32 was one of the few stations with decent reception on my nineteen-inch color TV. The seven other channels were filled with fuzzy squiggly lines and pixel dots. I looked forward to watching our shows with Oreo snuggled at my side and Bridg sitting on the bed near my feet. Every night I hoped that I'd stay awake past the second show. Bridg watched TV with me only as respite from her sweltering bedroom. I intently avoided sleep because I longed to spend more time with Bridg. When *The Jefferson's* or *Alice* ended, Bridg headed back to her bedroom to sleep alone in the stifling humidity. Even air conditioning couldn't keep her from leaving me.

The TV clicked off and my bedroom door creaked open and then closed as Bridg left. I woke for those few seconds, feeling empty and alone. I figured Bridg felt the same when I drifted off to sleep. For three months we were separated by ten miles, with Bridg at home and I on the fifth floor of Advocate Hospital Now we were separated by bedrooms less than ten steps apart, and yet the distance between us felt far greater.

I FILLED MY loneliness with food. Well, not exactly. I didn't eat the food. I prepared it. I made Tim's favorite submarine sandwiches with loads of deli meats and cheeses. I cooked spaghetti and meatballs, shepherd's pie or hotdogs and beans with pineapple chunks in the already scorching kitchen. There was plenty for Tim, Bridg and Mom with leftovers for Dad. And then I'd watch my family eat. I'd peer from around the freezer like I was looking for the ice cube trays or anything that would keep me from eating. I willed myself to starve as much as I willed my family to eat.

"Why aren't you eating?" Mom asked as she reached for a slice of Bridg's favorite homemade pizza.

"I'm not hungry. Besides I sampled way too much as I cooked," I said, like this would convince her that I had eaten more than enough.

"More for me, I guess," Tim said.

"Go for it," I said, closing the freezer door. "Looks like you have a choice between warm water and cold milk. Which will it be?"

My mother and Tim sat at the kitchen table eating the meal I'd prepared, but Bridg slid three pieces of pizza onto a plate, and scooped heaps of chocolate ice cream into a bowl to take to her room.

"Oinker," Tim said.

"C'mon guys," Mom complained, trying to stop this from going any further, on my account, I assumed. "Yep, and yet I'm skinnier than you," Bridg fought back.

"I was just kidding, Bridgett. Seriously."

Bridg headed toward her bedroom to be alone.

I HAD BECOME good at timing my Ex-Lax so nobody noticed my bathroom issues. Within a month of being home, my gut wasn't bothered even when I took three Ex-Lax. My skin no longer burned from constant bathroom visits. But losing weight after McDonald's binges and ice cream splurges was nearly impossible. Even taking four or five Ex-Lax pills at a time didn't help me lose weight. Instead I steadily gained about a half pound a week.

Quarter Pounders and french fries were taking their toll, but I couldn't stop eating. Mom sent me on errands for milk and bread or to the dry cleaners to pick up Dad's suits. Because I rarely ate in front of anyone, I gladly used these opportunities for quick drive-thru junk food stops. McDonald's had become my best friend and so had the pills that followed the food into my stomach.

twenty-two

"You must be so proud, finishing a week early," Mrs. Frank said.

"It's not like I had to take finals or anything."

"Still Anna, it's an accomplishment. You should be proud."

"Thanks," I said, shying away from the compliment.

We waved to each other as we pulled out of the parking lot. At the light, I turned left and Mrs. Frank turned right. I couldn't stop from thinking that in less than three weeks, I'd be attending East Catholic again. It scared me to death.

Janet stood in the driveway, waving me down when I pulled up.

"Hi," I said blushing. "What's going on?"

"That's what I'm wondering."

"Sorry Janet. It's just that . . . really, I don't have a reason for not calling. I should have."

"Don't should on yourself," she laughed, taking a drag

off her cigarette.

"That's pretty good. Did you think of that on your own?"

"Nah, it's a favorite of Anthony's. It's not working for me, is it?"

"No. Stick with shit." I laughed.

"You're coming back, right? To EC?"

"Yep. Should be a real blast."

"Thank God! I was worried you were bailing on me."

A WEEK LATER, Janet and I drove to EC together to pick up the books and class schedules for our senior year. Janet bought her beat-up Mustang for eight hundred dollars after working at Anderson's Book Shop in downtown Downers Grove for eighteen months.

"Hey, we have lunch period together." Janet said, excited about the daily chance to talk my ear off.

It turned out that after five weeks of summer tutoring with Mrs. Frank, my GPA was good enough to get placed back into average classes instead of the idiot classes. Janet's classes were all advanced so there was little likelihood of our schedules lining up and we both knew it.

When she dropped me at home, Janet reminded me that she'd pick me up by seven on Saturday night for the movies. It would be Janet, her boyfriend and me — the third wheel as usual.

"I'll be there," I said half smiling. I closed the Mustang by lifting the handle so the door held to the rusty frame. I walked up the driveway thinking of ways to get out of tagging along to the movies.

"How did it go?" my mother asked when I was up the stairs. "Did you see friends?"

This was an odd conversation. Mom typically didn't ask questions because details were not her strong suit. But I knew she was trying to change this about herself.

"Fine," I said.

"We're going camping," Bridg announced, coming down the hall.

"What? When?" I said, turning from Bridg to my mother.

"This weekend. We'll leave on Friday and stay until Monday."

"Why?" I said scowling, hinting that seniors don't camp with their parents. "Besides, I have work."

"I thought it would be nice for the four of us to get away before school started. Can someone work for you on Friday? We'll be back before you go to work on Monday."

"Where?" I asked.

"Wisconsin," Bridg said excited. "Devil's Lake."

Bridgett spent most weekends with friends. It was obvious this change in plans excited her. Maybe she wanted to be with us, to pretend we were a normal family. Camping was not something I enjoyed. I wasn't sure if Bridg really liked it either. We had gone with our parents a handful of times when we were younger, after Liz died, but it had been at least five years since the last time we camped.

"Well . . ." *A long weekend without Dr. Ellison. And no Saturday night movie.* ". . . I guess I can get someone to work for me."

Bridg quickly turned to leave the kitchen, like she was afraid plans might change in the next second if she didn't. "I'll pack right now," she said, heading to her room with a slight bounce.

twenty-three

Bridg and I competed to gather the largest pieces of firewood. When Bridg struggled but failed to drag a log heavier than herself back to our campsite, we had to change the rules. Each find must be carried back to camp, or it didn't count. After several trips to the campsite and back out into the woods we changed the rules again. Whoever had the most pieces of wood was the winner. At first I felt silly playing such a childish game, but as the competition grew more intense, I stopped worrying about my dignity and decided to have fun.

Even with four of us, assembling the old canvas eight-man tent was difficult. Dad reached to hoist the stabilizing center pole. His large beer belly hung over his slipping pants. Bridg and I eyed each other, horrified his pants would fall to his ankles at any second.

"For Pete's sake, Jim, pick up your pants. They're about to fall off you." Mom said.

Bridg and I looked away as my father struggled to get

the center pole into place with one hand and hold his pants with the other.

"Pull the ropes, girls."

The three of us pulled the ropes, stretching the canvas as Dad pounded the stakes into the ground.

"Well girls, looks like we have a place to call home," he said.

Mom inspected the musty tent inside and out. "It's on its last legs," she said when she found a large slit in the tent's screened front door where the zipper had separated from the canvas.

My father frowned. "This tent is good for another fifty years, Bette."

I agreed with Mom. Somehow the years of smoke, rainstorms and morning dew, from when my parents traveled to Maine every summer, had combined to create a rank mildew odor.

Dad built a fire as Mom poured baked beans into a pot. Bridg and I scouted around for long sticks, green enough to prevent them from burning before our hotdogs cooked. We had learned on earlier camping trips that a dry stick left us with half a stick in our hand and our hotdog sizzling in the fire, burning to a crisp.

We used our father's Swiss army knife, sliding it over the stick's outer skin, until we had tips shaven clean of bark with a well-defined point. I browned my hotdog. Bridg roasted hers so it barely looked cooked. My parents held theirs over the fire until each side was charred and bubbling.

"Are we having S'mores?" Bridg asked rummaging through the brown paper bag.

"You betcha," Dad said.

Bridg pulled open the bag of marshmallows as I opened the box of graham crackers and unwrapped the Hershey bars. We listened to the chatter of people a couple campsites down instead of talking.

I skewered two more marshmallows on my stick and held them above the dying flame. I avoided a second helping of chocolate and graham cracker. Bridg indulged in a double layer of Hershey's chocolate bar on her third S'more. I was envious. I wished I could eat like that and remain skinny, but I couldn't. Being short was a curse.

Millions of stars flickered overhead. I learned about the importance of nature from Jonny Love, a friend from the fifth floor. He would appreciate being here, sitting around the campfire listening to the crackle of wood burning and the hum of locusts in the trees.

By the next night, my abdomen cramped painfully because I hadn't packed the Ex-Lax. Earlier in the day, the effort of using the bathroom had taken too long so I gave up. At lunch I had eaten only leftover beans. It wasn't until after supper when Bridg built a fire, Mom washed dishes in a pan of boiling water, and Dad pumped fuel into the lantern, that I sneaked away from camp. The beans had finally done the trick.

On Sunday night, I got up to get extra napkins, sneakily licking my buttery fingers out of Mom's view, on the way to the picnic table. The four of us settled down around a blazing fire and finished the last of the Jiffy Pop popcorn. Camping trips in the past included bike riding with Bridg and hiking with our mom as our dad protected the goods and drank his beer back at the campsite. Tonight was different. Dad was aiming to be involved, which felt as awkward as when I hugged Mom at Dr. Ellison's.

I woke to three loud bangs, like two cars had just crashed. I bolted from my sleeping bag.

"It's me, Anna. Mom."

My eyes adjusted enough so I could make out the inside of the canvas tent and Mom's silhouette. Another loud clap stung my ears.

"Mom, what are you doing?" I whispered into the darkness.

"Trying to scare the raccoons away."

"Jimmy! Jimmy!" My mother yelled, struggling to wake my dad. I could hear him snoring outside the tent.

"What raccoons?" I asked.

"The ones on the table eating our peanut butter. Brazen—that's what they are. They must have opened the jar."

One raccoon scurried toward the tent. Mom grabbed the two frying pans and clashed them together again. No doubt the raccoons were after the candy bars and the open bag of Cheetos that Bridg had brought into the tent before bed.

"Jimmy!" My mother yelled. She sounded terrified, as if hordes of rabid raccoons, foaming at the mouth, were attacking us.

"I hope you're enjoying yourself, you filthy animals! So be it! Amen!" Mom shrieked as she clattered and banged the pans. The raccoons scampered away.

"Oh, for the love of Pete! Jimmy! Wake up!" Now Mom was flat-out exasperated.

I swiped the canvas flap to the side and peeked through the mesh. The moonlight gave a perfect view. My father was snoring with his fingers clutching a beer can and the left side of his face pressed flat against the picnic table. Two raccoons scrambled over the picnic table near my father's head. The cooler's lid lay in the dirt underneath the table. I began to laugh at the sight. Bridg stirred from sleep, asking what was happening. I could barely get it out without hysterically laughing and gasping for breath. Bridg began to laugh too, even though she had no idea what we were laughing at.

"For God's sake, Jimmy!" our mom yelled, clanging pans and scaring the raccoons away from the tent again.

"Get! Get!" We finally heard Dad shout. "Scram! Get out!"

Mom sat back on her heels, no doubt relieved that the raccoons were gone. I doubled over, gasping for control of my breathing. So did Bridg.

"What's going on in here?" Dad said, poking his head through the ripped screen.

"Honestly, Jimmy," Mom sighed. Then the puff of relief turned into a snicker that grew into a hearty laugh. The three of us couldn't answer Dad. We were too busy laughing and gasping for air.

BY MID-MORNING on Monday, we packed peanut butter and jelly sandwiches, ruffled potato chips, vanilla wafers and chilled cans of A&W root beer wrapped in tinfoil into a large picnic basket lined with yellow gingham. The morning was sunny and warm. Despite the humidity, a light breeze made it a comfortable August day for a picnic.

As we neared the pond a fragmented childhood memory sparked, like a match flaring before fading away. *The pond.* A few yards farther and again a gray image raced through my mind, lasting long enough to recognize this place from another time.

"How about here?" Mom said, interrupting the memory.

She and Bridg laid down a blanket as my father strolled toward the pond, his left hand jingling coins in his pants pocket. The breeze rippled the water just enough to push lily pads to the west bank where rotting tree trunks made good cover for minnows and for turtles. *Turtles. We'd been here before, Bridg and me.* I scanned the area searching for more. My attention narrowed on my father. He smoked a cigarette, standing near the water's edge. The sun's rays danced across each ripple of water, like music box ballerinas. And then it came, barreling toward me, changed from a dulled image to a vivid theater production.

"CATCH IT!" I hollered in excitement.

"Okay. Shhhh. Quiet." Our dad gathered the braided rope into long loops like he would a lasso, and then he swung the bucket far out into the pond.

"You must be quiet girls," Dad whispered. "C'mon little turtle. That's right. Climb back up on your log."

Bridg and I peered around our father so we could see.

"Pray for a turtle," I told Bridg. She put her hands together in prayer. I did too. *Please, please, please!*

The army-green canvas bucket rested on its side on the bottom of the shallow pond. The other half was above water, in full view. The rope dipped into the water with each little breezy ripple.

"That's right. Shhhh."

Slowly my dad pulled the bucket toward a small head poking up from under the water. He moved the bucket right behind the little turtle. Then with a swift jerk, he reeled the rope in, pulling hand over hand until the bucket reached the lake's edge near our feet. I jumped with excitement at the thought of my new pet, but again the bucket held only lily pads and pond water. Bridg and I sank with disappointment.

"It's not over girls. We'll get one yet." Dad emptied the bucket and threw it way out into the pond again.

"What are you going to name your turtle?" Bridg asked, trilling with excitement.

"I'm going to name it Liz," I whispered, staring at the baby turtle swimming towards our bucket.

Suddenly Dad jerked the bucket and started reeling it back in. "Anna," he said. His voice bubbled. "That's not a good idea." He dumped the water without looking inside for my turtle. "Let's call it a night, girls."

"OH MY GOD! Liz!" I heaved, buckling.

"Anna? Are you okay?" Mom shouted in a panic.

Bridg stared as Mom came toward me. I crouched on all fours desperately trying to stop gut -wrenching heaves. I sat back, cupping my mouth in case I vomited.

"We were here, Mom," I screeched. "When? When were we here?"

"The summer after . . ."

"Stop—don't—! I—I can't do this," I stumbled, putting my hands up, like I was pushing hard against a wall. "I can't do this."

My father finished his cigarette. I watched him head back to join us. Bridg grabbed the rest of her sandwich and a bag of chips and walked to the pond to be alone.

twenty-four

On the first day of school I woke early, pulled out the bathroom scale hidden under my bed, and stepped on it. At ninety-six pounds, I would allow myself to eat today even though I didn't have Ex-Lax to help me. I quit cold turkey yesterday to limit my bathroom visits during the school day. Taking eight Ex-Lax a day made me nervous anyway.

"Party year!" Janet beamed as I opened the car door and slid into the front seat. I smiled just to make her happy.

Climbing the five steps to EC's entrance, I almost crumpled in fear. It reminded me of the first day of my freshman year, when I walked through these doors panic-stricken. Most kids had tans from summer travel to expensive vacation spots. To my schoolmates from Ginger Creek and other upscale suburbs, turning sixteen meant a brand-new Lexus topped with a blossoming red bow.

"Hey Anthony," Janet yelled. She waved her hand excitedly at a cluster of our friends in the cafeteria. "C'mon Anna."

She was socializing the moment we were within earshot. Janet fit right in despite her milky skin that never tanned and pale blond coloring. She had blue eyes that sparkled like glass. Her creamy foundation looked painted on, its beige-to-white border surrounding her face. If not for her blue eye shadow and thick black mascara, she could easily blend into the scenery like a ghost. Janet's tall, muscular Italian boyfriend Anthony discussed the upcoming football game with his friend Murph Izak. Everyone else compared schedules. I acted interested, but except for Janet, my friends seemed unfamiliar, like a Fantasy Island episode where people float in and out through two different worlds.

"Hey, anyone need a ride?" Therese, who was always flashing her Lord & Taylor credit card, asked. "In my new 300ZX." She held up her car keys. Her underarm jiggled with the jingle of her keys. I guess the diet she always claimed to be on hadn't started working for her.

"Whaaaaaat?" Anthony said.

"New from Daddio. Who says divorce is a bad thing?" Therese gloated.

"Whatever, Anthony," Janet said, smacking him on arm. "What? My Mustang's not good enough for you?"

Murph Izak was slightly shorter than Anthony, though much cuter, a detail I kept from Janet. He was paying no attention to Therese, so I assumed he was not a superficial guy. That made him even more attractive. He chatted with Michelle and Patty about their classes. I wished I could sneak into their conversation, but they didn't even try to include me. It actually seemed like they were ignoring me on purpose. I backed away. They could go to hell for all I cared.

"Have you seen Mr. Surrick yet?" Samantha asked Janet.

I stood right next to Janet, but Sam didn't even attempt to make eye contact with me. It could be because she was about eight inches taller than I was—that's what I wanted to believe, anyway.

"No. Why?" Janet replied.

"Oh my God. He is gorgeous. I think he's been working out."

"Better looking than last year?" I asked awkwardly, trying to squeeze into the conversation.

"Totally better looking," she said, eyeing me for a second before turning the conversation back to Janet.

"Who's better looking?" Anthony chimed, giving Janet a questioning look.

"Mr. Surrick," Janet laughed.

"Why are all the girls all over him? He's an old dude."

"I wouldn't call twenty-three old. More like distinguished," Samantha said. "Plus you have Janet. I have no one . . . at the moment."

"No need to worry, babe. Not yet anyway." Janet teased.

Janet's flirtatious charm was exactly what I lacked. It drew guys like spilled honey draws ants. I had loads of street smarts, where Janet had next to none. Girls like Janet and Samantha, who thought guys loved them instead of just wanting sex from them, ended up crying in the bathroom. I'd listened to Janet's sob stories too many times to count. All the teachers liked Janet because she was good at every subject from science to art, current affairs to history, foreign language to world cultures.

The first bell rang and groups slowly separated, like they had five years instead of five minutes to get to class. My anxiety hurried me along. I hadn't uttered more than a quick hi and no one cared to notice me. No one bothered to ask about my summer or even worse, what it was like to be locked up with crazies. I didn't think it was a coincidence.

I sat down in Mrs. Simmons' algebra class wondering about Mr. O'Connor's comment that I was good with numbers. Was it true or had Mrs. Frank made it up? I looked around. Nerds and brainiacs were up front. Jocks, cheerleaders and other popular kids sat in the back row. I didn't want to belong to any group. My friends used to be so important to me, but now, I didn't care. What I wanted was out.

Mr. Simmons skimmed through the syllabus. "My final words are this," he said before the bell rang. "Don't let time go by without asking for help. You are the only one to blame if you should receive a poor grade."

Samantha and I had history with Mr. Surrick before lunch.

"He's so adorable," Samantha sighed, hugging her books close to her chest like she was wishing Mr. Surrick were nestled in her arms instead of her books.

"Yeah," I answered honestly, wondering why she

ignored me earlier in front of the others. Sam and I weren't best friends but we'd always gotten along.

We walked into class and Sam sat smack dab in front of Mr. Surrick's desk.

"How was your summer, Samantha?" he asked.

"Fantastic," she said, showing her white teeth while swinging her brunette hair over her shoulder, away from her face. She was determined to flaunt her boobs and charm. I was actually envious. I wanted what she had, including attention from the cutest teacher in school.

By lunch, I was in the last bathroom stall doubled over with cramps.

"Anna looked different than I expected." I heard Michelle say.

My insides jumped to attention. I cut my breathing in half hoping to remain undetected in the stall.

"What do you mean?" Patty asked.

"Samantha said that Therese said she got down to like seventy pounds or somethin' like that, but she actually looked like she did before."

"Why do you they think they put her in a psycho ward?"

Patty whispered like there might be someone nearby.

"I don't know, but I was uncomfortable around her today." Michelle said.

"I know. I felt bad. I wanted to ask her what happened, but Anna is like so quiet I didn't know if I should." Patty agreed.

"I don't know if I could return to school after being in

a crazy house." Michelle said. "Anyway what do you think of Murph? I think he's totally into me."

Peeping through the slit next to the stall door, I saw Michelle pulling her hair up into a stubby ponytail, leaving wisps of bangs all around and puckering her lips with freshly applied pink lipstick. Patty was cleaning her retainer.

twenty-five

By mid-October, I was seeing Dr. Ellison twice a week, on Mondays and Wednesdays. I no longer had to get blood tests to check my iron levels. Dr. Ellison tapered me off meds before I headed back to school because she figured I couldn't be trusted to take them without supervision. I felt guilty that she couldn't trust me. I wished she understood my grudge against meds.

My weight held steady at ninety-nine pounds. Weighing in was still a once-a-week routine that Dr. Ellison would not give up, no matter how much I complained. I had no choice but to eat.

JANET PICKED ME up for the first home game against St. Francis.

"You've totally got to pay attention to Murph tonight because," Janet said in excitement, "he totally wants to ask you out," she sang.

I turned toward Janet, pressing my back against the

Mustang's passenger door. "Are you kidding me?"

"Anthony called right before I left to get you. He said Murph's been trying to get your attention for months."

"For months? No he hasn't. He likes Michelle." I smirked.

"What? No way. He can't stand her," Janet said. "How about this weekend? A movie? Anthony and me. You and Murph. C'mon Anna. It will be *awesome*," Janet said, adding dramatic inflection like this might persuade me.

"I don't know Janet. I . . ."

"Don't even think about saying no." Janet interjected. "You know you like him. He's cute. What's the problem?"

Somehow Janet's persuasion paid off. "All right."

Now that I knew Michelle was history, thoughts of Murph filled my mind. I loved the way he combed his reddish blond hair. He wore it a bit longer on top so he had to sweep it aside every so often. His skin was a soft white. His freckles sparkled like his silver smile. Even his reason for refusing to eat anything for lunch, like pizza or sandwiches, was cute. He was afraid food would catch in his braces. He settled for strawberry-banana yogurt and Coke every day, chewing the ice when the pop was gone. He always lifted the cup to his mouth touching it to the bridge of his nose, tapping the bottom so he got every last little piece of ice. When he lowered the cup a small droplet of Coke remained on the bridge of his nose.

"WHY ARE YOU nervous? You've known Murph since sophomore year. Pretend we're seeing a movie as friends."

Janet said on the way to the theatre Saturday night.

"Right. We both know it's a date. You've dated a ton of guys so it's easy for you to say."

"What about Bill?" Janet laughed.

"We weren't on a date," I laughed. "And besides it was your fault."

"My fault? How do you figure?" Janet smiled, knowing absolutely it was her fault.

Bill joined us at the football game because he was a friend of one of Janet's previous boyfriends. Bill bought a pretzel at the concessions and offered it to me when he sat down next to me on the bleachers. Halfway through the pretzel, Bill claimed I owed him a kiss as payment.

"You wanna bet?" I said, disgusted. I pushed him away, accidentally smearing mustard on his new East Catholic Hawks jersey.

When we arrived, Murph and Anthony were standing at the theater entrance, waving as we pulled around the corner. Anthony pointed to his car and Janet squeezed into a parking spot next to his.

"When we meet up, don't kiss Anthony." I said to Janet. She was into showing off her handsome boyfriend every possible chance. She apparently didn't realize how embarrassing it was for me.

"I won't, but I can't guarantee we won't kiss during the movie. It wouldn't hurt you to let Murph kiss you." Janet looked at me with her flirty eyes caked with purple eye shadow and thick blue mascara.

"I don't owe anyone anything."

"You wanna bet?" Janet laughed. "Poor Murph. Are you ever going to kiss a boy?"

"Hey Anna," Murph said, handing me a ticket. I glanced at it.

"*Nightmare on Elm Street*? Are you crazy? I'm not seeing that!"

I figured if Murph knew about the nightmares I battled almost every night, he would have expected me to freak out. But how could he know? I'd never told him or Janet or anyone.

"Chicken shit," Anthony teased.

"Shut up, Anthony. Call me what you want. You're on your own for this one," I said, turning towards Murph.

"Seriously . . ." Murph said.

I was about to pounce again, thinking he was mocking me, too.

". . . Anthony talked me into it. That shit freaks me out, too," he said, backing me.

Janet, Murph and I looked up at the screen where the movies and times were displayed above our heads to see what else was playing.

"*Just the Way You Are* starts in ten minutes," Janet said.

"Are you shitting me?" Anthony complained.

"No, we're not," Murph said.

Janet glared at Anthony. He knew Janet was a sucker for romance and keeping her happy would benefit him later that night.

The four of us got into line for popcorn.

"Butter?" Murph asked.

"No thanks. I don't need anything."

When I saw Murph's disappointment I changed my mind. "I'll have a root beer." He smiled, pulling two fives from his pocket.

If someone asked what I thought of the movie, I wouldn't have a clue. Murph reached for my hand when the previews ended and the lights dimmed. From that point forward I could think of nothing but my sweating palm and the itch on the edge of my nose that I desperately needed to scratch.

"Thanks Murph," I said awkwardly, standing behind Janet's car. Anthony and Janet attacked each other with intense kisses, embarrassing both Murph and me.

"No problem. Hey maybe we can go out again sometime. Alone," Murph added, tilting his head in Anthony and Janet's direction and rolling his eyes.

"Maybe." I smiled, returning his gaze.

twenty-six

I checked the name to make sure I'd received the right geography test when I noticed the large C+ written at the top.

"Hey, nice work" Mrs. Fitzgerald said after the bell rang. She saw her students out, standing at the classroom door, smiling and either telling kids, "Way to go, Hawks." Or "Awesome game."

"Thanks," I said, returning the smile. Maybe she had forgotten the F I got on her last test.

When I received a B- on an English quiz the next day I was completely freaked. I had studied just as much for the two previous tests and earned Ds on both. For once, I wasn't worried to be asked how I did. My good grades gave me a confidence I hadn't felt since I was in second grade.

Mr. Simmons was at his desk grading papers and monitoring a study hall during my lunch period. I walked past the classroom, trying to stay calm. I had marked three algebra homework problems that I didn't understand so I could reference them quickly. My chest thumped. *How is this quadratic equation shown as a closed-form expression?* I repeated it again. Once I stepped into his classroom in front of a classroom of juniors and seniors pretending to study, there would be no turning back.

I prepared, like a medieval knight wearing a suit of armor. "Mr. Simmons," I said, reserved. "Can I ask you a question about a problem I'm having trouble with?" I asked, opening my notebook.

Mr. Simmons looked at the problem. "Did you take notes on closed-form expressions yesterday?" he asked arrogantly.

"Yes." *And I looked it up in the textbook and worked the problem about a million times and stayed up late so I wouldn't have to ask your sorry ass.*

"Then you should be able to identify why the equation is tractable and can be expressed."

"Oh, okay," I said, knowing that if I didn't escape soon my chest would explode, possibly right after vomiting all over Mr. Simmons desk. Not that he didn't deserve it. *Breathe.* I stayed calm hoping Mr. Simmons might realize what a jerk he was, or tell me he was just joking and start laughing. Instead he just stared, as if I would suddenly develop a magical understanding of this same problem that I could have hanged myself over last night.

"I get it now. Thanks." I said, choosing the safest way out. Walking away, I recited over and over. *Breathe. Breathe.* When I was home I slid my English quiz and several pages of cryptic algebra notes in between my mattress and box springs, beside my geography test.

I HAD BEEN on my bed for the last hour making flashcards and studying the American Revolution. There were a bunch of tests the second week in November, just before twelve-week grades went home. I wasn't sure what I had done differently to get good grades on the last geography and English tests, but I was hoping for the same results in the next few days.

Boston Tea Party. I flipped over the index card. Political protest. 1773. Key event in the growth of the Revolution. *Yes!* I slide the index card in the pile of cards that I had memorized. I read the next card. Samuel Adams. Colonial delegate. Defended the Boston Tea Party.

But why? I flipped to the glossary of my textbook. I turned over the index card and copied, *because he agreed with the people's choice to defend their constitutional rights. Denounced taxation without representation.*

When I couldn't find the definition for denounced in the glossary, I ran downstairs to the bookshelf and looked it up in our massively thick and heavy Webster's Dictionary. I quickly ran back to my room and continued writing on the index card before I could forget the definition. *Publically declare to be wrong or evil.* By 10:30, I had all the facts and dates leading up to the American Revolution memorized. I set my alarm for five. I wanted to make sure I was ready for tomorrow's social studies test.

During the test, everything I'd worked so hard to learn went blank.

The following week, Mr. Surrick held class in the student library. We were to read quietly until he called us one at a time to confer with him about our most recent test and progress report grade. This had me worried because when Mr. Surrick handed back six-week progress reports, he looked at me in disapproval—like he thought that was the boost I needed to bring up my grade. *What an idiot.* I acted like it didn't bother me, but honestly it did. I hoped today wouldn't be a repeat of six weeks ago.

I found myself reading notes from Samantha and returning responses.

"Look at him flirting with Amanda," Samantha wrote and then snuck the note over to me. Mr. Surrick had assigned seats to keep us quiet. Samantha was sitting at the table next to mine. Passing notes it was just a short throw instead of a long hand-off. We were careful not to get caught.

"Yep. I'll bet she's getting an A," I wrote back and threw the folded paper over to Samantha after waiting for the right moment to avoid getting caught. The note landed on the table and Samantha hurriedly swept it into her hand. She opened the folds and read, nodding yes.

"Should I unbutton one more button?" She wrote, with a smiley face.

"Go for it." I wrote, not caring either way.

She unbuttoned her blouse so that if Mr. Surrick looked, he'd get a peek at her plump boobs.

I mouthed, "No way!" I rolled my eyes and gave her a look of *you're crazy*.

Samantha wrote and sent the note flying toward me.

"Two points away from an A. I'm going for it."

"Samantha." Mr. Surrick called.

I jumped from my seat thinking we had been caught, but Samantha calmly pulled herself from her seat. She walked toward Mr. Surrick with the complete confidence that I so badly wanted.

Their conversation was quick with smiles and a small laugh from Samantha as she leaned toward Mr. Surrick, giving our teacher a quick peek, and back again. Walking back toward her seat, she mouthed, "Gorgeous."

Finally, I was called. Mr. Surrick glanced around the room looking for the face that went with my name, like he'd forgotten what I looked like. "Unbelievable," I mumbled under my breath.

He tapped the table for me to sit. A big sigh came from his entire body and then the dreaded pause.

His words were like fingernails on a blackboard. "These grades are a reflection of your effort." His finger pointed to each test grade, each assignment, each and everything I had done wrong.

"What about the C on the last quiz? And every assignment was turned in on time," I quietly added.

Mr. Surrick looked at me like I was trying to argue with him.

"One C isn't going to change much. Your effort is lacking, Anna."

"You're wrong. I work hard. My assignments prove it."

"They're in on time, but if you tried harder, you'd be

able to get full credit," he said, showing me the column in his grade book labeled possible points and points earned. "This shows a lack of effort."

My heart skipped a beat. *Had I heard him right? Did he just call me lazy? Twice? Did he have any idea the hours I put into homework and studying?*

"I'm sure your parents wouldn't approve."

My response shocked both of us. "Approve of what? Your interest in girls like Samantha?"

"Anna, that's inappropriate."

"Inappropriate? What about your obsession with big boobs and cute girls? Would you call that inappropriate?"

"Our conversation is done here," Mr. Surrick said, pushing my progress report toward me. "You'll need to have this signed by tomorrow."

I snatched my progress report from the table. I should've stopped what I said next, but I couldn't. "By the way, after twelve weeks in your class it would be polite if you pretended to recognize me by name since apparently I'm unrecognizable by cup size!"

I wanted to appear calm, but it was impossible. I was so filled with anger, that there was no chance of hiding it.

My head was pounding by the time Sam and I headed for the lunch table. I had accused Mr. Surrick of something terrible. As much as I wanted to take revenge on him for not noticing me, and for calling me lazy, I didn't really believe his actions went beyond harmless flirtation. Accusing him was wrong and I knew it, plain and simple.

"Mr. Surrick looked pissed." Samantha said. "What the

heck happened?

"I got an F." I figured this was the best way to stop Samantha from further questions. And it wasn't a lie. F stands for failure.

Samantha and I sat with Janet. Five minutes later Murph and Anthony sat down with us like they did almost every day. Murph put his yogurt cup down and took a big swig of Coke, swishing away food that might be caught in his braces and then swallowed. "If I should die before these nasty things come off," he said looking at me, "rip them from my teeth before I'm shoved into a coffin."

"You got it." I laughed.

"Shut up, Murph. Why do you always say things like that?" Janet said, rhetorically.

"Hey, it's inevitable—we're all dying eventually, and I don't want to be nothing but bones and braces in a hundred years."

The image of a skeleton with braces being dug up in a hundred years was absurd and I couldn't keep from laughing.

"Well, at least Anna gets me." Murph smiled.

Anthony picked up his soda, pretending the straw was a microphone and began singing.

"And somethin' tells me we're into something good."

Murph joined in singing his version of Herman's Hermits, *I'm Into Something Good.*

"You guys are idiots." Janet laughed.

"I agree," I said, rolling my eyes at the two of them.

Janet and I picked up our trays and left the table. I

wanted to stay because Murph's sense of humor was the only thing that distracted me from Mr. Surrick.

"He's so adorable isn't he?"

She meant Anthony, but I was thinking of Murph. "Yeah, he is."

After lunch, in Spanish class, I received the *See Me* note that I'd been dreading from Mrs. Avery, the senior counselor.

Breathe. I reminded myself as I walked down one wide hallway after another, pass in hand. I was glad to be called to her office now instead of waiting until my last class or tomorrow morning. Mr. Surrick probably ran straight to Mrs. Avery's office after class to cover his own ass. No doubt he explained everything from his point of view, leaving himself innocent and me to blame for the entire incident.

I mulled over every possible outcome, reenacting what I'd done, thinking how best to answer Mrs. Avery's questions. I convinced myself that taking blame would probably consist of a phone call home. It would be embarrassing, but my mom would take my side even if I decided not to retell what happened. The closer I got to Mrs. Avery's office the worse my stomach felt. I knocked quietly on her office door.

"Enter," she called from inside.

Enter? I thought. *She couldn't have said 'come in' like most normal people? If she thought using enter separated her from being human she was dead wrong.*

She sat behind her desk. I sat in a hard plastic chair

directly across from her. It felt like a huge rubber band was squeezing my lungs. I had to remind myself to breathe over and over. I tried desperately to appear confident when I placed the hall pass on her desk. "Hi," I said.

Instead of returning any kind of greeting, Mrs. Avery continued to look at my twelve-week grades, without so much as a glance in my direction. I quietly cleared my throat. Word around school was that Mrs. Avery was a bitch, but because I hadn't met with her before today, I didn't know for sure.

She cleared her throat. "D. C-. D+." Mrs. Avery read, sliding her bony index finger down a record sheet in a file. She continued reading each letter grade with shock as if she had never met a student with less than a perfect A+ progress report.

Well, at least the rumors were confirmed. She was a B. After a period of intentional disregard, she looked in my direction. Her cold brown eyes, pierced through me. Her face showed disgust more than disappointment. She shifted in her chair, sitting taller like she attempted to give off some kind of *I'm the adult and you, Anna, are the hopeless failure*.

"You need to get serious about these grades. A 1.40 GPA is nothing to be proud of. It shows a very poor work ethic. And colleges frown on a low GPA. If you want to get anywhere in life, you'll need to buckle down."

Mrs. Avery gave me a sharp look that implied she wanted only meek agreement, not an explanation. *You don't deserve what you don't work for.* A flash of my dad standing tall and Tim shrinking ripped through my thoughts. My father and Mrs. Avery were no different. Neither cared enough to understand how hard we worked. Mrs. Avery's message was loud and clear, as it was for Tim at our July Fourth balloon toss, and all my siblings and me, at one time or another. *Mrs. Avery was calling me a failure. She made it clear I was lazy and worthless.*

My head felt light. My heart felt as though it could stop at any second. *I would not slump any further into this chair.* I straightened, sitting as tall as I possibly could. Mrs. Avery's face seemed angrier and her eyes grew colder as though she thought I was playing a game—a game of trying to intimidate her. She had not raised her voice because there was no need. Her body language and facial expressions were loud and clear. *I was a failure!*

"We need to discuss what happened this morning in Mr. Surrick's class."

"What about?" I said defensively.

"That tone stops here, Anna."

I concentrated on the exit door, while Mrs. Avery continued.

"I don't know the details, but Mr. Surrick says you were very rude to him. He deserves a written apology for your misconduct by tomorrow morning. And it must to be signed by your parent."

"Okay," I lightheartedly smiled, dying to ease my swelling throat.

The hallway looked strange. It seemed too narrow for a school hallway with loads of students that pass through easily. The piercing bell sent a sharp pain down my spine. Students flooded into the hall. Nearby noises and voices seemed distant. The exit stretched so far out of reach. Strange looks came from a few passersby. Minutes passed. Everyone disappeared or maybe it was me disappearing—from the hallway, from the entrance, from EC. I walked almost two miles to Yorktown Mall and called my mom.

twenty-seven

"Don't ask," I vented as I climbed in, slamming the car door. "I quit!"

"Mrs. Avery already called."

"Yeah. Did she tell you I'm stupid and a no-good failure? Because that's what she told me. I bet it was all about how she's right and I'm wrong. Huh!" I smirked angrily.

"You're not stupid."

"Really, Mom. You're constantly calling yourself stupid and then you make remarks that I'm like you. What does that make me? Stupid! That's what."

"I do tend to say things wrong."

"See! There you go again."

"Anna. Tell me what happened with Mr. Surrick."

"What does it matter what happened? The guy's a jerk. Everyone at that school is a jerk. There's no way in hell I'm going back."

"Leave me alone," I said when we arrived home. I

slammed my bedroom door and sobbed quietly before falling asleep. The cracked window caught my eye when I awoke a few hours later. I peeled the Scotch tape from it and wiggled a piece of glass loose from the window frame. Cold air whistled through the small opening. *How painful would it be?* I held the glass against my wrist and pressed hard enough to leave a red line with bits of surface skin separating. I jumped at a knock on my door. The glass pierced my skin. A drop of blood rushed to the surface.

"What?" I yelled angrily.

"Forget it!" Bridg yelled from outside my door.

I quietly repositioned the glass and taped it back in place, before taking my journal from my nightstand. I opened to a new page.

November 14, 1984

Dear Journal,

I wish I were dead!

I WAS UP and dressed early the next morning with nowhere to go. I pulled the scale from underneath my bed to see if I'd lost weight in the last hour. I didn't hear my bedroom door open.

"God, Mom! What are you doing?" I yelled, when my mom walked up behind me unannounced.

"Where'd you get the scale?"

"I bought it." I said, shoving it under my bed with my foot.

"Do you weigh yourself every day?"

"What does it matter? It's not like you don't. I guess I

need to watch what I eat every day, just like you!"

"Anna, please. That's not true."

"You're kidding me. I don't think you've ever missed a day without getting on the scale. You've said a million times that you have to watch what you eat if you've put on an ounce. I've heard you say gluttony is a deadly sin so many times it's ridiculous."

"Oh Anna, it's just a saying. I guess I do weigh myself more than I should. It's my problem," Mom said. Her voice was calm, trying to defuse my embarrassment at being found on the scale, but part of me wanted a fight.

"No! It's my problem too. It's everyone in this family's problem. We never had any pop or sweets in the house."

"Anna, you're upset. We didn't buy sugary foods because I didn't want you kids to have cavities. It had nothing to do with weight."

"Oh my God, Mom. Please. It is about weight! Jeez! God help me if I took one cookie too many. Someone in the family was bound to call me a slob. I don't know how many times I heard that stupid song, 'Christmas is coming, Anna's getting fat.'"

"I never realized, Anna. I'm sorry."

Bridgette's bedroom door swung open. "Would you shut up already?" she screamed.

"You shut up!" I screamed back. "You and Marie don't have a clue what it's like. You're tall and skinny. You can eat all the crap you want and still be skinny!"

"Shut up, Anna! You just want attention!"

"What about the meat market candy bars? We got

disgusting Charleston Chews just so they would last! And then we'd choke 'em down before we got home just so no one would call us greedy!"

"You did that! Not me. I got the Marathon bar because I liked it. You're the one with the problem! Not me! Not Mom! You!"

I barged into Bridg's room before she could get the door locked.

"You have no idea!" I screamed into her room, standing tough at the doorway.

"Get out of my room!" Bridg screamed.

"I'm sick of hearing how smart you are and your high IQ! How would you like to be stupid and ugly and fat? Never thought of that did you?"

"You're not even fat, but if that's what you want, be my guest. You're a cow. There. Happy?"

"Fuck you!" I screamed, slamming her bedroom door closed.

"Anna, please," Mom begged. "We have an appointment with Dr. Ellison at nine."

"What!" I screamed, kicking the outside of Bridgett's door. "Why did you call her? You're freakin' crazy if you think I'm going."

"She's expecting us."

My screams become violent. "Us! Now it's us! You plan on holding my hand? We don't even freakin' hug in this family! Out of my way!"

I grabbed a coat off the foyer bench and escaped out the front door, slamming it behind me.

"My life sucks," I shouted into the cold wind. I put on my winter coat and pulled up the hood holding it closed with my bare hand. I walked down the street with nowhere to go. I hid behind two bushes when I saw a car coming down the road. When the driver turned away, I ran across the street, through a couple backyards, and jumped over the ice-covered creek bed. Ahead was nothing but a field of frozen prairie grass blowing sideways in the wind. I reached into my pockets, letting my hood blow off my head.

"Just great," I mumbled. "It's just like me to pick the coldest day in November to take off." McDonald's was less than a mile away. I headed in that direction fighting the wind.

"Can I help you?" The girl behind the counter asked.

"No thanks. Just need to use the bathroom," I replied.

I was a mess. My hair was windblown in ten different directions. My cheeks were beet red and my nose was draining buckets. My eyes were swollen. I washed up in case I encountered someone I knew. *What now? Go where*? I leaned against the back bathroom wall.

Turning back toward home, because I had no place to go, confirmed that I'd been defeated again. My ears stung, and covering them with my hands only numbed my fingertips. As if a violent force controlled me, I hurled my fist into thin air and screamed. "I hate you! I hate you! I hate you!"

MY MOTHER AND I were on our way to Dr. Ellison's by ten-thirty.

"I'm not going back to the fifth floor," I said to my mother.

She stared straight ahead, but I could tell her thoughts were focused on everything but the road.

"You're not," she said, confirming she knew more than I did about today's discussion.

"What's she thinking then?" I asked, keeping my eyes straight ahead, prepared to be a back seat driver. Mom had already gone through two stale green lights without as much as a glance to her right or left. She had me nervous. I completely understood how she must have felt driving with me and my siblings with permits.

"Full-time therapy school."

"No way, Mom! You know what I dealt with last time. I'm not doing it again!"

"Dr. Ellison assured me it would not be the same program. You would be going to an actual school with students who need extra support," Mom said, thinking this might convince me.

"Oh yes, I completely understand—this will be the perfect situation," I said sarcastically like I was agreeing with Dr. Ellison. "She's wrong Mom! I don't need extra support! I'm fine. Get Mrs. Frank to tutor me again."

"It's not all about school work, Anna. It's going to help you talk about what's bothering you."

"Oh God, Mom! You're kidding! I am not doing it. Tell Dr. Ellison I'm not going! I don't need extra support—mental nor school!"

By the time we pulled into the parking lot, I was

hyperventilating so much that my mother stayed seated staring through the windshield.

"I can't do it. Dr. Ellison will say she knows what's best for me, but she's wrong. I can make it on my own without some weirdo therapy school."

We both sat quietly before my mom agreed. "I will mention tutoring," she said.

Dr. Ellison sat far back in her chair thinking. "I don't think it's the best idea, Mrs. Maedhart. I understand that you want for Anna what she wants, but she doesn't know what is best for her right now. It's up to you to know what's best."

"I may not know what the next months will bring, but I'd like Anna to begin tutoring again. If it doesn't work out, we can then consider the school."

"Then Anna is going to need limits," Dr. Ellison said, scooting forward in her chair, making sure she had my full attention. "I need for you to understand Anna, that these rules are non-negotiable." She looked for my response or a nod or something.

"Yep," I said, with a little huff to remain indignant. Secretly I was incredibly relieved that recommitting me to the fifth floor was not an option being discussed.

"One, your grades will need to be a C or better. Two," Dr. Ellison looked at my mom, "Anna needs to return to seeing me three days a week." Mom nodded, indicating this would work. "And three, I would like Bridgett to come to a few of our meetings. If these conditions cannot be met then I'm going to strongly encourage that we make other arrangements for schooling and therapy placement."

"Thank you, Dr. Ellison," Mom said.

Thank you? What the hell?

"Your mother cares about you, Anna. You have a tremendous amount of potential. I believe in you."

I turned away holding my breath tightly to my inner core. I longed to let go and tell Mom and Dr. Ellison how I wanted to die. "Well then, you're the only one," I smirked instead.

November 15, 1984

Dear Journal,

Today was terrible. I hate everyone. I hate school. I hate homework. I hate teachers and counselors. Dr. Ellison implied I might go back to the fifth floor. I will not go. I wish someone could make it better and understand why I'm so lonely. If you're listening God, please send someone to help me. Please. Please. Please.

I sucked in a large amount of air completely filling my lungs and then let it out. I closed my journal and tucked it under my pillow. My chest felt so tight I could barely stand it. Again, I breathed in as much air as I could and then buried my face deep into my pillow.

twenty-eight

Mom and I drove to EC on Friday night when I figured everyone would either be at the Addison Trail basketball game or hanging out with friends. Besides the janitors, the halls were empty, like my insides. If not for the well-lit hallways and Mom walking alongside me, I'd find the nearest corner and cry.

"Don't freak out," I said when Janet answered the phone, "but I cleared my stuff from our locker tonight. I'm not coming back to EC."

Janet freaked out anyway. "What? Why aren't you coming back? I'm heading over right now."

"No Janet. Please don't. I want to be alone right now." I felt truly horrible I didn't tell her what happened because I knew she'd understand. Janet's friendship was the reason I was included in the group of popular kids. Had it not been for her, I would have remained in the slip-through-the-cracks group, like in junior high.

"We'll still do things together though, right? Next

week? How about next Friday since there's no school?"

"Maybe," I said.

When Murph called a half hour later I treated him worse than I did Janet.

"Please Mom, tell him I'm not feeling well. I'll call him later."

"Are you sure, Anna?"

"Yes. Please now before he thinks there's a chance I might talk to him!"

I was enrolled at Downers Grove South High School five days after walking away from EC. Dr. Ellison allowed my mother to request a home tutor instead of attending school and Mrs. Frank accepted the job. We would begin next week, after the Thanksgiving holiday.

FRANCES, MARIE, GABE and their families came for Thanksgiving. With Tim, Bridg, my parents and me that made a total of sixteen. The commotion was a reminder of my childhood and it felt good. The kids played in the basement, Dad mixed drinks, and Mom placed the final touches on the table setting. Bridg and I chose seating arrangements, setting paper turkey nametags on plates. Frances and Marie poured hot and cold foods into serving bowls. And then my father had the honor of cutting the bird.

There was another reason I was glad for the commotion. Priorities like pouring the gravy on turkey and passing the rolls meant I went unnoticed. Today I was free to not eat. I filled my plate and poured gravy over my turkey and potatoes like everyone else, but I moved the food around my plate picking at it quietly. Nobody seemed to notice. For all they knew it could simply have been my second serving that I could not finish.

I looked around the busy tables. *How could ten years have passed with so few mentions of Liz? How did the others survive? How could anyone live through this tragedy without crying or hanging themselves from the garage rafters? I hadn't wanted Liz to return, I had needed her to return. Was I alone in my thoughts or had my family needed the same things?* I wanted to scream my questions, but I didn't. Mom was right. *Live in the present.*

MRS. FRANK AND I met at the Woodridge Library. The apple bag swung from her bent arm thumping against her left hip with every other step.

"Anna, how are you?" she asked, her smile returning like we had seen each other just yesterday, even though it had been almost four months. "So here we are again working together. I'm delighted, but also disappointed that East Catholic didn't work out."

"I'm not."

"Then, this must be the right choice for you. I'm glad I could be part of it."

"Thanks. Me too," I said for lack of a better response.

We got started like we did in the summer by getting acquainted, but today it was more like friends catching up after spring break.

"Some things have changed," Mrs. Frank cautioned.

"We'll meet from eight to one, Monday through Friday. Each class will be fifty minutes long with short breaks in between. Did you eat a hearty breakfast like I suggested?" she asked.

"I wasn't hungry," I honestly told her.

"Well, lunch is a long way off, but just in case . . ." Mrs. Frank looked around like she was up to no good. "I brought energy boosters for us." She smiled. "Ah, sometimes rules are meant to be broken." She placed watermelon and butterscotch hard candies in the center of the table. "Tomorrow, promise me you'll eat before you come."

"I will."

From the look of my schedule and syllabus, I was required to complete everything as if I were sitting in the classroom, no special favors. I looked at quiz and test dates and worried about these the most. Studying had never worked well for me. Even worse, I couldn't figure out why my efforts bombed. Worst, teachers assumed it was because I was lazy. *And best were their incriminating glares, which were somehow supposed to encourage me to do better.* I shook my head to dispel the thought. Crying in front of Mrs. Frank for a second time would prove I was a basket case. *Besides, eventually Mrs. Frank will probably think I'm a lazy failure like every other teacher.*

After five long hours and after Mrs. Frank left, I explored the adult fiction section of the library. "Lad . . . Leb . . . Led." I mumbled, sliding my finger over author's names. Finally, I came to Lee, Harper. T*o Kill A Mockingbird* was on the shelf. It reminded me of kind, gentle Ben—a friend from the fifth floor who understood me better than anyone.

twenty-nine

Shhh! Her head aches," Mom reminded Meg. "Be careful not to sit on her bed. It might wake her."

"She looks so weak and puny. Is she sleeping?" Meg asked.

"Shhh!" My mother said as Marie walked into the hospital room. "Remember, don't wake her."

"Hey Liz," Marie said. "I brought you Raggedy Ann and Andy. Open your eyes."

Meg pulled a plastic-wrapped popcorn ball from her coat jacket. "And we made popcorn balls for you. Please Liz, open your eyes so you can see the dolls and taste the popcorn balls." Meg shook Liz's leg, trying to nudge her awake.

"Shhh! Her headaches," Mom said again.

"I can't wake her." Meg cried. "I can't wake her."

"Is she sleeping?" Marie asked, her voice demanding an answer. "Mom!" Marie screamed, "Is Liz sleeping?"

"No, Marie, she's not."

"What do you mean?" Meg asked. "If she's not sleeping, then what is she—?"

"Dead," my mom said. "Liz is dead."

"Anna, wake up! Jimmy! Come quick!"

Running feet sent Marie and Meg fleeing from the room. In slow motion the dolls fell slowly to the ground. The popcorn balls rolled to the corner of Liz's hospital room.

"I can't wake her!"

Echoes of Meg and Marie's screaming were heard from miles away. The dolls hit the floor breaking into pieces.

My screams exploded.

Nightmares returned fast and furious. Most nights I woke up gasping silently without disturbing my parents. Other nights I had no control over the screams incited by the scariest and most realistic nightmares. These didn't happen as often as before, making it seem my nightmares had almost ceased.

"I'm fine," I convinced my mom. Dad had already returned to bed, but Mom insisted on staying a few minutes longer. She'd stay all night if I asked her. "Really, I'm good now."

I opened my journal after staring at the ceiling for far too long after my mother returned to her bedroom. Tears filled my eyes.

November 30, 1984

Dear Journal,

Help!

MY MOTHER PICKED me up alongside the library entrance,

and we headed to Bridg's school, and then to Dr. Ellison's.

"How was school?" Mom asked Bridg.

"Can I spend the night at Jill's on Friday?" Bridg asked.

"Maybe," Mom said.

Bridg and I both knew that was a yes. Mom's maybe was always a yes.

Bridg had her nose in the latest Sweet Valley High book. I opened up my algebra book and pretended to be studying, but I was only thinking about the test I bombed today. I didn't need Mrs. Frank to tell me I failed. I didn't do the studying necessary to pass, not that it would have helped. I didn't care what difference a lousy grade made. Dr. Ellison would be disappointed. My mother would be unmoved. I would hide it from both of them for as long as I could.

IN DR. ELLISON'S office I watched large snowflakes drift silently outside the large glass window. Bridg and Mom stared outside, too, from where they sat on the leather couch. Soft gray clouds burrowed into each other, making them look like sewer drain tunnels connecting one with another. Not one tree branch was moving, nor was a speck of sunlight in sight. It was an unusual winter day. There was no wind to remind us of Chicago's blizzards and bitter cold.

"Here we are in December already." Dr. Ellison said, breaking the ice when she was seated. Awkward silence filled the room.

"Do you know why I asked for you to be here?" Dr.

Ellison asked Bridg.

"I guess it's because you want to talk about things."

"This is one reason. Do you have an idea about what?"

"Probably Anna."

"If it's okay, I'd like to talk about you first."

"Okay," Bridg agreed with reluctance.

"I'll ask questions that will help me to know you better."

Bridg nodded.

"What are some things you enjoy?" Dr. Ellison continued.

Bridg shifted in the chair, tucking her hands under her thighs, taking them out again, and then crossing them over her stomach.

"Umm . . . I like school and being around friends. I like to read."

"What kind of books do you enjoy reading?"

"I guess anything as long as it has a happy ending."

"Why so?"

"Not sure."

"Do you have a favorite book?"

"I like the Sweet Valley High books. I don't have a favorite though."

Dr. Ellison asked about Sweet Valley High and Bridg gave a quick summary.

"How did you feel about visiting Anna in the hospital?"

"Nervous."

"What made you nervous?"

"What the nurses and doctors thought of me."

"You visited Anna often. Especially the first month she was hospitalized."

She did?

"Chad and Isaac. And Virginia. They all said you were polite. What exactly made you nervous?"

"What Anna might have said about me."

"What did you think she might say?"

"That I was mean to her."

"I didn't say things like that," I blurted sympathetically. "You weren't mean to me."

"Do you know why Anna was in the hospital?" Dr. Ellison asked.

I was truly mortified. My face felt flushed. I wanted to remind Dr. Ellison that in my family we don't talk about things like this. But I was afraid if I did, Bridg would stop talking about things I wanted to know.

Bridg looked to Mom, shrugging her shoulders, wanting to be rescued. She moved her hands under her thighs. Maybe she felt like running away from this place, like I did.

"She knows that Anna was there because she wasn't eating," our mother said, coming to my sister's rescue.

Dr. Ellison looked back to Bridg. "Do you know why she stopped eating?"

"I think she does eat. I hear Anna open the fridge at night when nobody's in the kitchen."

"I thought this meeting was about Bridgett." I smirked. "It was because of Liz, Bridgett!" I hissed, glaring past Mom toward Bridg. Then I glared at Dr. Ellison narrowing my eyes.

"Have you told Bridgett this before today?" Dr. Ellison asked me calmly, ignoring my outburst.

"I don't need to tell her. She already knows. And if you don't know," I said, looking away from Dr. Ellison and toward Bridg again, slamming her with the brutal truth, "I was locked up because Liz is dead and I couldn't handle it, being the idiot I am!" I turned back toward Dr. Ellison, "There—satisfied?"

"Anna, please . . ." my mother began.

I instantly regretted losing control. I looked away, at the wall, and felt staring eyes.

"Is she okay?" Bridg whispered to Mom.

A flash ripped through my head.

BRIDG WAS THREE years old. I was seven. Bridgett lay between Mom and me in my twin bed. Liz was gone, but her bed remained in the room, across from mine. The three of us, side by side like tin soldiers, stared at the blank ceiling. Bridgett hummed and giggled. She lifted her head a few times and smiled at me.

She rolled toward Mom and put her mouth to Mom's ear. In her tiny three-year-old voice she whispered, "I'm trying to make Anna happy because she's sad." She rolled toward me and pulled the covers to my chin. "Sleep tight. Don't let the bedbugs bite," she said, smiling. Then she whispered softly in my ear. "I love you, Sissy."

"I LOVE YOU too." The whisper came from somewhere other

than my flashback.

"Anna. Anna," Dr. Ellison said again. "You're deep in thought about something."

"Yes," I admitted, shaking the memory away. "I'm sorry, Bridg—for being such a terrible sister."

"No, you're not," Bridg responded, sounding more concerned than sincere.

Dr. Ellison stayed quiet. She was waiting for Bridgett and I to talk things out, and I wished I could. I wanted to tell Bridg how much I love her and ask her what I could do to make things between us better.

"I think it's important for everyone in the family to understand what happened."

The way Dr. Ellison phrased her comment toward Bridg made me wonder if she was subliminally trying to tell our mother about the importance of open communication. Everything Dr. Ellison said and did had a purpose.

"Anna was at a crucial age when Liz died. Because she internalized her grief, which means she kept it to herself, handling difficult situations eventually became problematic. To recover from what happened she needed more help than I could provide seeing her a few days a week, so she was admitted to the hospital where a group of doctors and nurses could help her work through Liz's death. Does this make sense?"

"Mm-hm."

"This is a difficult time of year for your family," Dr. Ellison continued looking around at the three of us.

Not really! No, it wasn't! That isn't necessarily true! I

imagined the three of us subconsciously undermining Dr. Ellison's comment.

"Remind me, Mrs. Maedhart, what is the date of Liz's death?"

"January first," our mom answered, clearing her throat between the two words.

Dr. Ellison leaned forward, crossed one leg over the other and clasped her hands over her knee. "What can you tell me about Liz?" Dr. Ellison asked Bridgett.

"I don't think about her. She was . . . I don't know . . ." Bridg hesitated.

"It's okay to talk about it. What do you remember?"

"She was like a fictional character, like from a book."

"What do you mean exactly?"

"When I was young, I wasn't sure if she ever existed."

Bridg was coming into herself, like she was when she was away from this office and speaking with an adult. She has a large vocabulary and was highly articulate, as her teachers were always pointing out.

"Why did you think she wasn't real?" Dr. Ellison said, leaning against the chair's back.

"No one talked about her. Besides, since I was only three, I don't really remember her."

"Can you give me one memory?"

"Mrs. Beasley," Bridg said.

"Who is Mrs. Beasley?"

"She was the doll that . . ."

Instantly, another flash took over my thoughts. Mrs. Beasley. Liz's doll—the one with the blue and white polka-dot dress with yellow trim, and black squared eyeglasses.

"SISSY," I WHISPERED into the dark.

"Yeah?"

"I had a bad dream."

"You can sleep with me," Liz whispered, opening her sheets for me to dive under before something could grab at my feet and pull me under the bed.

"Here, you can hold Mrs. Beasley," Liz whispered, handing me her doll.

BRIDG CONTINUED. "AFTER she died, Mrs. Beasley was hidden away in our mom's closet. Sometimes Anna and I would sneak in there and take her off the shelf and play with her.

"Did this help you realize Liz was real?"

"Kind of. Anna told me that Mrs. Beasley belonged to Liz. I wanted to believe that it was true."

"Do you have any memories about Liz of your own?" Dr. Ellison asked.

Bridg hesitated. "No, I don't" she said. I knew Bridg well enough to know she was hiding a memory, keeping it safe. I understood her motive.

"Did you ever hear Liz being talked about by anyone else in your family?"

"Sometimes, but the mention of her name made me feel uncomfortable, like I shouldn't be listening and the others shouldn't be talking about her." Bridg answered Dr. Ellison.

Bridg avoided Liz's name. I wondered if our mother and Dr. Ellison noticed this too.

"How do you feel talking about Liz now?"

"I don't like it."

"Why?"

Bridg breathed a sign of frustration. "Because we never talked about her until recently and now because Anna needs to talk about her, we're all supposed to bring up the subject every chance we get. I barely know anything about her because I was a baby."

"You're still part of the family." Dr. Ellison confirmed as if she thought Bridg wasn't so sure.

Bridg paused. My ears focused on her shallow breathing. It grew heavier, more desperate than before. I sensed the tension beneath her skin as she fought to gain control.

Dr. Ellison looked to our mom. "Would it be possible if I talked with Anna and Bridgett alone?"

It was obvious Dr. Ellison took Bridg's silence as an indication that Bridgett felt she'd already said too much and she didn't want to hurt Mom's feelings.

"BRIDGETT," DR. ELLISON continued after our mom closed the door. "Do you feel like you're a part of your family or not?"

"Not," she said, her shaking voice barely audible.

"Why do you think you don't belong?"

"I was three when it happened. I wasn't part of Liz's life, so why should I have feelings about her? It makes me uncomfortable to hear her name all the sudden. Like all at once, it's important to bring her memory back into the house. And then . . . while Anna's in the hospital, I'm left thinking about what's happening. One day Anna's fine and the next day she's gone."

"Why were you left alone?"

"If I didn't go with my mom and dad to see Anna then I was at home alone. I did my homework by myself. I ate dinner by myself. I did everything by myself."

"Are you angry at your parents for leaving you?"

"No, it's not their fault." Bridg answered. Her tone sounded like she was annoyed with Dr. Ellison for even suggesting such a thing. "My mom and I have fun together. We sit on her bed at night and talk a lot."

"Are you angry at someone?"

"At Anna."

I wanted Bridg to look at me so I could be included in what she was saying. I wanted her to know I was honestly sorry, but she didn't take her eyes from Dr. Ellison's.

"Why?" Dr. Ellison asked.

"Because it's like she's not even the same person. Sometimes I wonder why Anna is putting our mom and me through all this. I hate it when I come home from a friend's house or wherever and our mom is sitting in the living room by herself eating a whole bag of Snickers looking like she is miserable. It's a constant reminder that something isn't right and it scares me to see my mom afraid. Anna could stop this if she wanted to, but she doesn't."

Our mother? I question. *Afraid?*

"I can see you are frightened, Bridgett."

It appeared that Dr. Ellison regretted her decision to have our mom sit in the waiting room instead of next to my sister. She was probably thinking that our mom needed to hear what Bridg had to say. Not the part about me, but the part about Bridg—that she was scared.

"You have been through a lot with everything that has been happening. You may not remember Liz, but you have as much right to be part of your family, as do your siblings. You also have the right to express your feelings as much as anyone."

I could only imagine Bridg's thinking, hearing things like *express your feelings* and *you have as much right*. She was probably dying inside like me. When would Dr. Ellison ever realize that there wasn't a person in our family who talked about this kind of crap?

"How about you come again next week?"

"No thanks." Though I wasn't surprised at Bridg's answer, I was surprised she'd said it aloud.

"Well, how about we decide later?"

Unlike the pull Dr. Ellison had over me, she would not win Bridg over. Bridg had nothing to fear. Dr. Ellison couldn't send her to the fifth floor.

"Bridgett, how about you join your mother in the waiting room?

Bridg left without a word, but as she closed the door behind her, we looked at each other,

"How do you think it went today with Bridgett here?" Dr. Ellison asked.

"Not good. No wonder Bridgett hates me. I hate myself, so how could I blame her? I've made everything worse." My chest tightened with the thought of facing Bridg when we got home.

"Why do you hate yourself?"

I rolled my eyes in disbelief and gave a small huff of exasperation. "Because I am a complete screw up. I'm supposed to be Bridgett's older and smarter sister and clearly this is not the case. Not that I need to be reminded. She has everything. She's pretty. She's tall. She's smart. She has friends. She doesn't need me or want me." I paused for a few seconds. "She has everything I want. It's completely unfair."

I pressed my chest, hoping to breathe easier. *Breathe. Breathe. Breathe.*

"Anna. You have these qualities too. You are a smart and beautiful young girl. You are clearly well liked. I observed this over and over during your stay at the hospital. And Janet wasn't the only one who visited while you were in the hospital. Several friends came."

"What?" I asked, confused.

"Janet came with a group of friends, twice."

Twice? What friends? "Why didn't anyone tell me?"

"We did, but you were not ready to grasp this idea or accept it. You were only capable of focusing on one person and you chose Janet. This is not uncommon, Anna. You were very ill. Details are often forgotten in cases like these. You hadn't remembered Jim's visit either until you were ready."

"I remember Gabe visiting without anyone reminding me and . . ."

Pictures shot to the forefront of my mind. I pushed my fingertips into my forehead trying to remember the memory before it was gone. Then it came. *Marie and Frances, on the fifth floor, visiting.*

"Marie came. And Frances was there, wasn't she? They came to visit."

"They did, Anna. Marie came several times, and Frances at least twice."

"I remember. They came."

"Yes, Anna, your family visited."

"How often did Bridgett come?"

"Every day for the longest time. Then not as often, but she still visited once in a while."

"Dr. Ellison," I said at the end of my session with my hand on the doorknob.

"Yes," she said, looking up from the notes that she'd already begun to chart.

"The friends that came to the hospital, was there a Murph?"

Dr. Ellison flipped toward the front of the chart that held my life tucked inside.

"It says here Murphy. Same person?"

"Mm-hm," I nodded.

"Why do you ask?"

"Just wondering."

On the way out Dr. Ellison told Mom, "Make a family visit for next week. Perhaps a day when Anna and Bridgett's dad can join us."

Bridg and I quickly glanced at each other, lifting our eyebrows as to say, "Not happening" to each other.

It wasn't that our dad wouldn't come. He would, but Bridg and I would stick to one-word answers. Elaborating was way too chancy. Our dad wouldn't have much to add either, especially to sappy discussions like these. Bridg and I could say just about anything in front our mother. Dad . . . well, it was best to sit back quietly. He got right to the point and was brutally honest in every situation, even if it meant hurting other people's feelings.

thirty

"Where is she?" I asked.

"Who?" Mom questioned.

"Liz. Can't you hear her giggling?"

My mother put her ear to my bedroom wall. "Huh, imagine that," she said, smiling. "Lizzy's come home. She's outside waiting for you."

"Where?"

My mom took me to the window in our dining room that looks out into the back yard from two stories up. "See, right there." Mom pounded on the window glass to get Liz's attention.

"Mom!" I screamed. "You'll break the glass."

Liz climbed on the swing set and stood on the bar that stretched across the top. "Anna, it's me," she yelled, waving.

I stared shell-shocked.

"It's me. Don't you remember me?" she yelled again waving, first with one hand and then two. Then, her waves

became flails. She tried to catch her balance. In slow motion, Liz fell.

I sat straight up in bed panting. *Please God. Not again.*

"HELLO ALLISON. THIS is Mrs. Maedhart." A short pause followed. "Anna will be unable to make her appointment today."

My mother was on the phone with Dr. Ellison's office.

"She's not feeling well," My mother answered.

Allison was on the other end and apparently more concerned than she needed to be. There was a slight pause between, "You'll let Dr. Ellison know then?" and "Thank you Allison," before my mother hung up the phone.

"Any better, Anna?" Mom said, poking her head into my room.

"Yeah, I'm fine, I think. I'm just tired."

"How about some soup?"

"Okay."

Mom left me to rest while she heated the soup, which I could only guess would come with the usual ginger ale and toast to help settle my stomach. I hadn't eaten in a couple of days.

It was almost one in the afternoon. My room was dark from the cloud-covered sky. The constant bursts of wind against my windows rattled my thoughts. *December 12.* In ten days it would be ten years since Liz was taken to the hospital and ten short days after that it would be the day she died. Ten years ago. Ten days. Ten years old when she died.

"Hello," My mother said after the phone rang.

"Yes, this is she."

"Hello Dr. Ellison, thank you for calling."

"She's not feeling well," my mother said into the phone.

There was a long pause and I wondered what Dr. Ellison was saying.

"No, she hasn't. Two days, maybe three. Yes, Yes. To the hospital?"

I jerked my head off the pillow so that both my ears could detect exactly what was being discussed.

"Yes, we'll be there within the hour."

The moment Mom hung up the phone she walked from the kitchen toward my room.

"Anna," she called calmly. "Dr. Ellison wants to see you at the hospital."

"Why?"

"She's concerned about you not feeling well. She says it's important that I bring you now. She will meet us there."

"Why the hospital?"

"She's concerned," my mother repeated.

"It's the flu. I don't need her to tell me what I already know!"

"She's not convinced it is the flu."

My exhausted body jumped to attention. "What the hell, Mom! I'm sick. S-I-C-K! That's it! I'm not going back!"

"I agree with Dr. Ellison, Anna."

"I don't care," I screamed. "You can't make me go!" I picked up a shoe and hurled it at the broken windowpane.

I raced to a fallen piece of glass and held it inches above my wrist. "I swear to God! I will kill myself first!"

The glass cut deep into my palm, but I didn't feel the pain until I saw the heavy flow of blood draining from my right hand. That was when I fell to the floor.

"Anna! Oh Lord!" Mom scrambled down the hall to the phone.

Bitter cold poured into the room followed with a violent blast of swirling wind. The blurred ceiling flashed an image of Meg and Marie lying in their twin beds almost a decade ago, days after Liz's death.

"Marie, are you awake?"

"Mm-hm," Marie whispered.

"Why didn't we make the popcorn balls?"

"Stop! Please Meg, I can't."

"She was there in that bed, lying there—her puny little body and shaved head. She was so weak she couldn't even smile. That's all she wanted were those stupid popcorn balls." A violent gasp gushed from Meg.

"Meg, we are so selfish. Mom was so tired. That's all she asked was for us to make popcorn balls and we refused to do it. I can't stand to think about it, but I can't stop thinking about it."

Meg and Marie's sobs bounced from wall to wall—terrible, horrifying sobs that seeped through to my adjoining bedroom where Bridg and I slept.

"And the dolls," Marie said. "We didn't let Liz see the Raggedy Ann and Andy dolls we made for Anna and Bridg. Liz was so excited. She wanted to peek. She begged us to

see them just once, and we told her no—that she'd have to wait for Christmas Day and now she's never coming back. She's dead Meg. She's never coming home."

thirty-one

The same designer gown, white with faded blue stars provided on the fifth floor, was apparently the fashion rage on Advocate Hospital's third floor as well. White gauze wrapped my right hand and my arm throbbed with pain.

At the slightest movement pulsating throbs of pain shot through my forehead. I lay as quietly as possible and allowed the nurse to take my vital signs. My eyes were heavy. I fought to keep them open, hoping to see my mom soon, but I couldn't. The room went dark as I drifted into sleep.

WHEN I WOKE, darkness filled the room except a dim desk lamp where my mother was reading. My father was slumped in a corner chair near the window, still dressed in his suit and tie. Outside the window it was dark, except for the moon's soft glow pushing through the thick clouds

"Mom," I whispered, giving her a small wave. A wire pulled at my hand. "When did this happen?" I asked wondering about the IV tube connecting me with the bag of liquid above my bed.

"Hours ago." Mom replied, getting up from the desk chair and coming to the bed's side.

"How are you feeling?" Mom whispered.

"Okay. What time is it?"

"Eight twenty," she said.

A gurgling snore came from the corner of the room. My father stirred, leaning his head from one side of the chair to the opposite side. "Dad's here?"

"Yes, and sleeping soundly." And then, "Oh for Heaven's sake, Jimmy," she whispered when another snore erupted in the darkened corner.

"It's okay, Mom. Are you leaving soon?" I asked.

"We'll leave in an hour or so. When you're ready."

"What about Bridgett? Where is she?" I asked panicked.

"She's with Jill. Dad and I will pick her up on our way home."

"Is Tim home yet?"

"No, not for another week. Why?"

"Bridg needs someone home with her."

"She's fine for now."

"Mom?" I asked. "Am I going to . . . God, I can't even say it. You know where—upstairs?"

"I don't know for sure. Your dad and I are going to visit a different facility tomorrow morning. One that Dr. Ellison thinks will be a good fit for you for the next month."

"What about Bridgett? Who will stay with her

tomorrow?"

"Anna," Mom said worried. "She'll be at school."

"Mom. I don't want to be left alone, but . . ." a half-controlled sob came from my chest.

"I know, Anna."

I shook my head indicating I wasn't finished.

"What is it?"

"It's Bridgett. Please don't leave her alone anymore. I'll be okay, I promise. Stay with Bridg."

Three snores erupted from my dad and then a gigantic yawn from his mouth. My dad straightened his slump.

"Marie will be here tomorrow morning to visit." Mom said.

"Did Marie have the baby?" I asked hopefully.

"Already two days late. Babies have a way of controlling every situation," Mom said.

My father agreed. Shrugging his shoulders, he said, "It's time we go. See you tomorrow, Anna." And with that he was gone.

"Wait, Mom," I whispered as my mother switched off the lamp, ready to leave for the night. "The popcorn balls? Did Liz get the popcorn balls?"

"Anna, I have no idea how you know about the popcorn balls, but yes, Lizzy got them."

The hall was quiet, so I assumed I was far from the nurse's station. Thoughts of Bridg being picked up so late on a school night bothered me. She liked being with her friends, but not like this. Just as Liz's death had shattered my life, my absence had upended Bridg's life once again.

Bridg intuitively understood that the Anna she knew was never returning. Bridg and I were not as different as I thought. We were exactly alike.

"I'm sorry Bridgett. I'm truly sorry." My whispered words were swallowed by the dark.

thirty-two

Artificial light flooded the room.

"Anna Maedhart," a woman said, pronouncing my last name correctly.

I shielded my eyes, trying to adjust subtly to the brightness of the ceiling lights.

"You remember me?"

"I do," she said with an Indian inflection, "Anna from two floors up. I do believe the last time we met you complained I was taking too much of your blood."

"Sorry."

"That's all right. My work is one of those jobs where people would rather I didn't show. I don't mind. You didn't mean it."

When she finished taking a blood sample, I closed my eyes hoping to sleep away the day.

"Well, hello Anna. How are you?"

I practically jumped from my skin at the booming voice.

"I didn't mean to scare you," Dr. Pins grinned. "The lights were on so I figured you were awake."

Dr. Pins is the doctor who completed my physical exam when I first arrived on the fifth floor. His hair was a bit thinner and whiter since I'd seen him last, but he was still as jolly as Saint Nick.

"Well, let's see here," he said looking at his chart. "Dr. Ellison asked me to check on you. How are you feeling?

"Fine."

"Looks here like you vomited last night. Still feeling nauseous?"

"No."

DR. PINS LISTENED to my heart. He placed the stethoscope on top of my gown, moving it around to four different places.

"You have a good ticker in there," he said. He tugged at my gown to pull it from underneath me so he could easily raise it to view my middle. He pressed on my stomach in a couple places before he listened to my abdomen as I stared at the ceiling tiles.

"Let's take a look at your hand," he said, unwrapping the gauze. His brown eyes glowed with warmth. His pressed lips and slight smile let me know he was sorry for what I'd been through.

Though only five stitches were required where the glass cut deeply into my palm and index finger, the mounds of bandage made it look like I had a major wound.

"You had quite a tight grip on that glass," he said

pressing the middle of my hand. "Well, the swelling has gone down and there doesn't seem to be any infection. You should heal fine." Again, he softly smiled. "The nurse will be in shortly to bandage your hand. Do you have any questions for me?"

"No. Thanks."

"Well then young lady, I'll pass on the good word to Dr. Ellison."

MARIE ARRIVED BY eleven holding her bulging belly. I made myself as presentable as possible.

"Hey Anna," Marie said solemnly.

"Thanks for coming. Not yet, huh?" I said, pointing at Marie's belly.

"Seriously he or she better come soon because I'm fatter than I can handle."

Marie placed a gift shop bag on my bed. "Here—this is for you. Thought you might like it."

"What is it?" I asked opening the bag. I pulled out a doll made for sitting against the pillows on a fancy bed, not for play. Her pink hair was made from fine yarn and her striped dress was a combination of pastel greens and yellows trimmed with white eyelet ruffles.

"Thanks Marie. I like it. Thanks."

"I bought it downstairs at the gift shop if you want to return it for something else."

I understood what Marie was feeling and I felt sorry for both of us. She protected herself against the chance that I might want to exchange it for something better, like Dad always did.

"No way! It's awesome." I smiled.

Marie sighed as if her lungs just remembered to breathe. Her eyes quickly shifted to my wrapped hand and back. "You okay?" She asked.

"Yeah. It was stupid."

"I brought Pringles. Want some?" Marie smiled, pulling the skinny red can of potato chips from her purse.

"No thanks," I smiled. "I swear, Marie. You have a Pringles obsession."

"Is there anything I can bring you, like homework?" Marie teased.

"You're so lucky you're smart, Marie. Everything comes easy for you."

"That's not true Anna. First of all, you are smart, but you think you're dumb for some dumb reason."

Maria and I both chuckled.

"You know what I mean. And I'm not as smart as you think I am. School was fine until I was fifteen or so, then I didn't give a crap. Smoking outside with the burnouts and skipping classes was more exciting. The only reason I went from a straight A student to a C student, instead of an F student like I deserved, was because I was every teacher's pet. They showed me mercy for some reason. I'm not sure why I suddenly decided one day that pot and beer tasted better than good grades. I guess I didn't care."

I honestly couldn't believe what I was hearing. Everything Marie said was news to my ears. "When?"

"I guess I would say it was soon after . . ." Marie

cleared her throat like it suddenly dried up, ". . . Liz died. I guess that's why my teachers let me slack off." She cleared her throat again. "Whew!" Marie breathed out hard, brushing her hand over her forehead, a potato chip grasped in her fingertips. "It's so hot in this room."

Marie rubbed her throat clumsily beneath her chin. I sensed her throat was tightened, choking the life out of her, like mine used to months ago. It was still difficult, but I had been coerced to say Liz's name aloud on the fifth floor. Unlike my siblings, who still had trouble saying our dead sister's name.

"Can I ask you something? After Liz died?" I cautiously asked. Marie's silence said I'd made the wrong decision in giving her a choice. I should have just asked the darn question.

"Like what?" she said, guardedly. "Nothing deep I hope."

I went for it without a second for either of us to decline. "What was it like when you went back to school?"

Marie gave a half-smile. "Weird. It's too hard to explain," Marie said shifting her eyes down, putting the can of Pringles back in her huge purse. "But on a different note," she smiled, brushing salt from her hands. "I want to ask you something."

"What?"

"Will you be the baby's godmother?"

thirty-three

Dr. Ellison arrived ten minutes after lunch. I hadn't even glanced at the food, but with Dr. Ellison in the room I instinctively straightened to attention, pulling the rolling cart toward me like I was about to eat.

"Hello, Marie." Dr. Ellison smiled.

Marie smiled, like she felt good that Dr. Ellison remembered her.

"Well, I better get going." Marie said, picking up her coat.

"No need to leave. I'll be here for only twenty minutes or so. The three of us can talk," Dr. Ellison said.

My stomach churned. Marie and I looked at each other. Our faces spoke volumes without a word. She wouldn't stay because she was as uncomfortable as I was, probably afraid that Dr. Ellison would bring up things she couldn't talk about.

"No, that's okay," Marie said.

"What a blessing," Dr. Ellison said, gesturing to Marie's

belly as Marie was on her way out.

Now it was just the two of us in this hospital room with my lunch. I prayed Dr. Ellison didn't mention the fifth floor or therapy school.

"Is this Marie's first baby?" Dr. Ellison asked.

"Yes."

She smiled. "How are you feeling?"

"Okay," I lied.

Dr. Ellison pulled the corner chair closer to my bed. "Let's talk while you eat lunch."

There was no point in arguing. I stared at the dry turkey sandwich, lime Jell-O blocks and a small bowl of canned peaches. I took the turkey off the bread and did my best to swallow it bite by bite.

"What happened yesterday?" Dr. Ellison asked.

"To start, I don't need to be here, and you convincing my mother that I did irritates me. Things just went crazy."

My throat tightened, making it even more difficult to swallow the dry meat. I could almost read Dr. Ellison's thoughts. She thinks I tried to kill myself, *and maybe I did or didn't*, but either way I needed to convince her I didn't.

My parents pushed the wide door open. I placed the last piece of turkey back on the plate and decided not to eat another bite.

Dr. Ellison stood to greet my parents and the three exchanged hellos. Something seemed different. My father, dressed in his suit and tie, went to the window and looked down from three floors up. He was contemplating something. When he turned around, he positioned himself with his arms crossed and lying over the top of his beer belly. He leaned back ever so slightly, but still looked intimidating.

Dr. Ellison was speaking with my mother about their visit to the therapy school. My mother didn't say a word but she also wasn't constantly nodding her head like she usually did when Dr. Ellison was talking. Dr. Ellison finished and looked to my mother for validation, but it was my father who spoke.

"Dr. Ellison," my father began. "Anna does not belong at that facility."

"Why not?" Dr. Ellison said losing a bit of steam. She put on a serious face that matched my dad's.

"The patients seemed to be worse off than Anna."

"Much worse." my mother added.

"Some are, but the staff there helps countless patients make significant progress," Dr. Ellison responded, attempting to reassure my parents.

"We consider you an excellent doctor, but we are declining your recommendation." My father said.

Like my father, Dr. Ellison was never speechless and she was quick to reply. "You understand that Anna cannot go home. She attempted suicide, . . ."

"No, I didn't!" I interjected harshly.

". . . she's not eating. She's been vomiting from nerves, not the flu. The anniversary of Liz's death is nearing. Anna is going to need immediate around-the-clock support."

"We completely understand," my mother said, "but

what's wrong with returning upstairs?"

"Nothing. We can definitely readmit her."

"Looks like we have a fair deal then," my father added.

He gave Mom a peck on the cheek and left for work.

I lay back on my pillow, wrapped my arms across my face and began sobbing.

"Anna, I know this is difficult," Dr. Ellison said.

"No, you don't. You have no idea how this feels." I said through gasps for air. My eyes were still covered with my forearms pressed over them. To lift my arms from my face was to accept that I wasn't going home and I couldn't do it.

"Dr. Ellison," my mother said reserved. "Please leave Anna and me alone for a while. She's been through a lot."

"Anna," Dr. Ellison said, touching my arm gently, "you'll be okay. We are here for you."

Her voice turned toward my mother, "Have the nurse page me when you are ready for the paperwork."

Except for my unrelieved sobs, there was no sound in the room. I felt my mother's presence next to me, but sensed her attention was focused elsewhere. Finally she sat on the side of my bed, her hand gently resting on my blanketed leg.

My forehead pounded. I took my arms away from my closed eyes and pushed my fingers into my forehead trying to stop the pulsating pain.

"I feel it won't be for so long this time, Anna," Mom said caringly.

"It's not even that," I choked between sobs.

I covered my face again. A few moments passed

before Mom spoke. For once, she wasn't asking me to be courageous or find the silver lining. Somehow she understood why I was consumed with sadness.

"You poor thing," she whispered. "I am so sorry you are hurting so badly. Get it all out Anna. It's important that you cry. Cry tears for Lizzy."

I never thought I would ever hear these words from anyone in my family. At that moment, I knew that Mom realized that her lack of emotion had become our weakness, not our strength.

For hours I fell in and out of sleep. My mother remained on continuous vigil throughout the day and night and into the next morning.

thirty-four

After three days on the third floor and two bags of IV fluids, I stepped onto the elevator. My parents, Isaac and I rode up to the fifth floor. Isaac had come down to welcome me back to paradise, as he called it with a smile. My father agreed with him, probably thinking of the place he and Mom had visited. Bridg spent the night at Marie's apartment. She and Marie splurged on pizza, hoping the big meal might induce the baby to come.

Unlike the last time when I entered the fifth floor lobby empty handed, I had a bag filled with some essentials. That included my journal, which I asked my mom to pack, but not read. I trusted her completely. No questions asked.

Mom had filled out the paperwork earlier, so Isaac took us right from the elevator to the locked door.

"How about we get you settled in your room and then you can visit with your parents?" Isaac said.

I knew it was his way of easing me back into the strip search. I didn't care though. I simply accepted it.

I was grateful it was Saturday. Many of the patients were away on family home visits. I wouldn't have to face Chad or Carol because they didn't work weekends. They'd be here Monday and so disappointed in me. *With any luck, by then, I'd be dead.*

We passed my old room. I was thankful I wouldn't sleep there again because listening to the locked door snap shut a hundred times a day, reminding me that I was imprisoned, would be too much to take. Isaac walked to the last bedroom door on the hallway. My parents waited in the hall.

"Anna," A nurse named Holly said as I enter the room. "How are you?"

Fucking perfect! I recognized Holly from my first trip to the fifth floor. "Okay," I said instead.

"So you haven't lost your voice," Isaac said, smiling.

The room had bare walls with no pictures and there was no sign of a roommate.

Isaac left the room and Holly peered inside my paper bag for contraband.

"Sorry Anna, but the spiral notebooks have to stay in the nurse's station."

Yeah—because if I decided to kill myself I would start by poking out my eyeballs. Whatever.

"Which side of the room would you prefer?" Holly asked.

Eenie, meanie, miney, neither. I chose the bed by the window. I placed my clothes in my nightstand drawers. My journal, pens and extra paper went in the top drawer of my desk. Schoolbooks and other items went in the bottom desk drawer. I placed paper bag of toiletries underneath one side of the bathroom sink in case I found myself living with a roomie.

There was a note from Marie. "Hey, things Bridg and I know you'll need."

Inside were the feminine products that all girls need, but I kept them hidden, embarrassed.

thirty-five

"Everything okay?" Isaac asked the next morning, when I placed my breakfast tray in the return cart.

Isaac was a teddy bear kind of guy, not fat—more like plush. His brown wavy hair matched his dancing brown eyes. He's easygoing. Once I thought he would let me get away with anything. Then I had decided that taking advantage of his genuine niceness was wrong. I probably could have eaten a single bite of food and he would have let me off the hook because today was Sunday or my first day here, or whatever, but I was not playing a game. I would do what was expected to prove to Dr. Ellison that I should be at home.

"SORRY I'M LATE. I had to get the kids fed and in their pajamas before I left," Frances said when she arrived closer to seven than six that evening.

"It's okay."

I was glad someone was here to make this Sunday

night go by faster. My parents and Bridg traveled to SIU in Edwardsville for Tim's graduation.

"Marie wanted to come, but didn't want to chance it. How was your day?" Frances asked.

"Good. How was yours?"

"Busy. Kids take a lot of time."

"Is here okay?" I asked pointing into the room from the hallway.

"Sure."

"Um. Do you want coffee or something?" If Frances asked what something was, I had nothing to offer except water. But it sounded better than mentioning only coffee, like we should be best friends chatting over a cup, instead of sisters who were thirteen years apart in age and had little in common.

"No thanks," she said.

Frances looked around the room. "At least it's a nice set up," she said.

"Yeah, I guess."

"Anna," Frances finally said looking at me, "Do you remember the matching dresses I made for you and Bridg for Christmas Day, the white dresses with dark blue lace around the neck and the bottom hem line?"

"Yes," I said. "Mom has them in her cedar chest."

"Oh, so that's where they are," she said, like she had just solved a lifelong puzzle. "I racked my brain trying to remember where Mom had stored them. Are all the Christmas dresses I made in there?"

I thought back to when I last looked through the cedar

chest years ago. "I don't think so. Why?"

"I don't know. It just comes to my mind occasionally."

"Do you still sew?"

"No. Those dresses were the last things I ever sewed. Life happened, I guess," Frances breathed out forcefully. She looked off into the distance, like she was remembering every last detail of those dresses. "About everything that's been happening to you. It's so . . . well, anyway," she sighed. "I'm sorry for your loss, Anna."

Your loss? Didn't she mean our loss?

Frances sighed again as if holding in thoughts too painful to say out loud.

"It's okay, Frances" I said.

thirty-six

I woke when the first light of dawn entered my room at 7:05. I stared at the digital clock, which was how I had spent most of the night. The digital clock was a new addition since my last confinement here. I listened to the faint sounds of nurses coming and going as the shifts changed. It was only a matter of time before a nurse was in my room, introducing herself as my shadow.

I wondered if it would be Carol or someone new. I didn't know which was better. Having Carol and Chad again would save me the trouble of talking and telling things I didn't want to recall. They already knew as much as I could offer. But maybe that was too much like a defeat, to be right back where I started.

I was still lying in bed when Carol walked in. Before I would have been up and ready for the day, striving to look respectable to cover up my screwed-up life. Today, I simply didn't care who saw my pajamas or the rat's nest on top of my head. I'd taken a quick shower last night and though I hadn't washed my hair, it was wet when I crawled into bed, which straightened the side I slept on and left the rest frizzy.

"Hi Anna," Carol said. I was grateful that she left out all the typical greetings: how are you, it's good to see you again, welcome back. Because on the fifth floor none of those remarks made any sense.

I smiled weakly, trying but failing to hide my misery with a cheery smile.

"I'll be your nurse again during your stay. We've got lots of catching up to do."

Carol was plump, but it definitely looked like she had lost weight. Maybe it was the fine lines around her mouth and on her forehead that made it more noticeable. She'd added a little makeup since last time, too. Lightly pinked cheeks and full eyelashes brightened her full face. She kept her curly brunette hair moussed, leaving it with a wet look. Now that she was here, I was glad she'd be my nurse. With all the chaos in my head, it felt good to have some familiarity.

"Chad also?" I asked.

When Carol said yes, I felt differently. Chad held me accountable to high standards—so different from being the ninth child who faded into a crowd of siblings at home. When I was released, I had hoped to make Chad proud. Returning to the fifth floor for round two meant I had failed.

"Dr. Ellison wants us to weigh you," Carol said. "Afterward we'll go through your daily schedule before breakfast arrives."

In the past, being weighed pissed me off. This

morning, I didn't fight it. I wasn't sure if it was because I'd lost the fight or I'd accepted that there was no such thing as winning on the fifth floor. Whichever it was didn't matter. My job was to prove to everyone I was good to return home. When I got there it would be up to me if I should live or die.

"Hello Anna." Dr. Inkblot said as Carol and I passed him in the hallway.

"Hi," I said.

I called him Dr. Inkblot, because he gave me the Rorschach Inkblot Test the last time I was here. I looked away quickly, remembering the juvenile stunt I'd pulled. No matter what inkblot he showed me, I claimed it looked like an eagle. Carol and I continued down the wide hallway to the locked entrance. The scale was at the end of the hallway directly across from my old room. I took a quick peek inside. I wanted to cry right there on the spot. *I shouldn't be back here*.

I stepped onto the scale without complaint. "Carol, I'm seventeen. Can I please weigh myself?" I asked. "I don't need to be treated like I'm two years old."

"Of course." She smiled.

I read the doctor's scale quickly. I had added the two numbers together so many times the sums were etched in my memory. *Ninety-seven.*

"Ninety-seven," Carol said, charting my weight, "that's a great beginning."

And end if I was in control, but I'm not—not here anyway.

Although the weekend had passed, the locked ward was not nearly as busy as it was six months ago.

"Why does the place seem so empty?" I asked on our way back to my bedroom.

"December mostly. This time of year varies considerably." Carol remarked.

"How many patients are here?" I asked, knowing that this place holds twenty-two patients—twenty-four if the locked rooms in the way back, reserved for crazy people, were used.

"Thirteen."

"You're kidding! I'm number thirteen? That's never good."

"Depends on who you're talking to. I see it as lucky thirteen," Carol grinned. "However, this does change our routines and schedules a bit."

She unclipped a form from her clipboard and handed it over. I took a look at the dreaded schedule I'd be expected to follow. It listed meals and therapy times, visiting hours, and the usual quiet time, which was code for "stay in your room and get out of our way."

The only differences from last time were Study Hall/ Tutors and Physical/Occupational Therapy so I asked about both.

"What do we study at study time?"

"The other teens who are here work with their school tutors so they can keep up with their schoolwork. We've already scheduled Mrs. Frank. She will be here tomorrow through Friday of this week. Next week is Christmas break so then it becomes more of a study hall for reading or schoolwork. We'll probably change it up a few times during the holiday week. We'll have to see."

"What about Physical and Occupational Therapy?"

"OT is the same as arts and crafts, just a different name for it. Physical therapy—you'll like this, Anna. You'll work downstairs with a physical therapist starting Wednesday, and after that whenever it's needed. You'll be stretching and working on some relaxation exercises. It's good to leave the unit and learn something new."

There was nothing more I needed to ask. I knew the drill all too well.

"How about you get ready for the day?" Carol pointed to the chart, "Breakfast at eight." She smiled.

"Thanks for the reminder," I half-hearted smiled back.

A FEW MINUTES after eight that morning, I joined the others in the dining area, but sat at a table by myself and by nine I found myself following Dr. Ellison into a small conference room.

"Why did you sit alone at breakfast today?" she asked, closing the conference room door.

"I guess I wanted to be alone, that's all."

"Have you met the other teens yet?"

"No."

"Why not?"

"No reason. I didn't feel like it."

"I know it's not easy being here."

"Why am I here?" I asked, trying to hide my

indignation.

Dr. Ellison leaned back in her chair thoughtfully. On the third floor, Dr. Ellison had convinced my parents that the next month would be tough to get through. But to me it seemed no different than November or October or last year.

I pulled my feet up to the chair's seat and brought my knees to my chest, pulling my large hooded Chicago Bears sweatshirt, handed down from Tim, over my legs.

"I want you to have extra support over these next few weeks. Liz's death . . ."

I interrupted. "Forget it. I don't need to know."

"It's important that you are clear on why you are here."

I could list all the reasons why it wasn't important, but I had been through them all before. Dr. Ellison had a *why it was* for my every *why it wasn't*.

"I feel fine. I'm no different from before." I complained.

"You are not well. You attempted suicide . . ."

"Quit saying that! I did not. You're always telling my mother what you think is best for me and it drives me crazy."

". . . You vomited from anxiety. You stopped eating again. You've experienced uncontrollable bouts of crying. According to your mother, nightmares are keeping you awake at night. And let's not forget school. One day, you simply decided to walk away from it all? Something happened that you haven't been able to share. Whatever your reasons, this sort of behavior is alarming."

Dr. Ellison definitely had one thing right. I couldn't stop crying. She barely begun her statement when I lowered my head onto my knees, my tears and runny nose soaking my sweatshirt.

"I've always been honest with you. I believe you need to know exactly why you are here. This way we can focus on what caused those changes. I suspect if we can do this from the start, your time here will be short."

"Whatever!" I said into my sweatshirt, embarrassed to show my reddened face.

"You'll be happy to know that I'm not going to prescribe any medication for you yet."

"Are you serious?" I asked, lifting my head.

Dr. Ellison smiled, "When have you known me to joke?"

"How about we track your weight on Fridays, like we've done? As long as you maintain your weight."

"Sounds fair, I guess." I agreed reluctantly.

thirty-seven

It was almost three in the afternoon. Chad would soon come on duty and see that I was back on the fifth floor. I pulled out my textbooks and thumbed through pages to occupy my mind, though I couldn't focus. I was simply killing time and avoiding thoughts of all the things that had gone wrong to get me here for the second time.

Three twenty. Three thirty. I stared at my schedule, but the words and numbers blended into a blob of black ink. I picked up the jigsaw puzzle my parents brought yesterday, but when my fingers shook trying to open the box, I gave up. My journal was the last resort. I took it from the bag under the sink. I didn't want Chad to see it or that I'd been writing things down because it would lead to questions I didn't want to answer. I gave myself fifteen minutes to write.

My mind jumped from one thing to the next like I was born yesterday, reacting to every sound. Chad would be here soon. I grabbed for a pen and pleaded with my thoughts, *just one sentence*. Nothing happened. He would be so disappointed I was here. *Kill me now. That's what I should write.* My mom's words cut through my thoughts like always. *Don't write what you don't want others to know.* "But I do write, Mom," I whisper. *I fight your words every time I write in my stinkin' journal.*

Sometimes writing how I felt scared me so much I fought a horrible urge to erase every word as soon as it was down. Many times I scratched over and rewrote the first few words two or three times before I either decided to continue or close my journal with nothing but scribble marks on the page. Three forty-eight and I had nothing written. *Oh my god, I can't take this.* I anxiously walked to the bathroom, closed the door and tucked my journal away. My entire body shook. The morning shift was leaving one by one. Chad would be here soon.

Back at my desk, I pulled out a piece of paper and pretended I was about to write something. I began to doodle strings of letters on the white paper. I decided it shouldn't be the string of cursive b's and y's that I had written in last year's notebooks. First, Chad might ask why I was writing the two letters over and over. *Oh no reason, Chad. I was only thinking I'd say good-bye to the world and you'd never guess what happened? It turned out I used the incorrect spelling of such a simple word.*

I began stringing letters together. *abcdefgh*—

"You're back." Chad said.

"Yep," I nervously replied.

His concerned blue eyes were just as I remembered.

His smooth face and enticing aftershave, his grin, and his short blonde hair that he'd eventually push to one side were exactly the same. He stood tall in the doorway with his fist near the door frame like he was about to knock.

"What are you writing?" Chad asked.

"Doodling," I said, scrunching the paper into a wad and throwing it in the trash.

"How are you?" he asked.

"Fine."

"Have you forgotten that I'm not big on one-word answers?" Chad smiled. He pulled the chair from the other desk and moved it a bit closer. "So tell me. What do you mean by fine?" he asked.

I wanted to smile back, but I couldn't seem to force a grin. I was so embarrassed to be here, with Chad sitting a few feet from me, and on the fifth floor, again. "Sorry."

"For what?" he asked.

"You know, things not working out. Being back here." Heat radiated up to my face.

"Anna," Chad said, "Just because you've returned doesn't imply that things haven't worked out. You're here because a lot to people care about you and want what's best for you. If you're going to place blame for being here, then we will need to work extra long to get over this before we can move on. Or you can decide right now that you are here, where you need to be, in order to get help."

I couldn't bring myself to look at him, but looking from my lap toward the wall and back again was ridiculous.

"Which is it going to be?" Chad said. "Are we going to

make this hard or easy?"

"Easy, I hope."

"Okay then. I'll be back in five minutes so we can start over. There will be no hard questions tonight."

I watched the clock. Four minutes. Three. Two. "You're early," I said, making eye contact.

"I'll ask again. How are you?"

"Chad—I am sorry."

"For what, Anna?"

"I don't know. I feel like I've let you down."

"I'll tell you what. I'm proud you're being so honest and upfront with me. It suggests that you've improved since I saw you last. I'm not sure if you recall, but when we first met, you barely spoke a word. Seems to me, you're not giving yourself any credit for a tremendous amount of progress."

Chad leaned back in his chair and crossed one leg over the other, resting his ankle on the other knee, giving a relaxed feel to the conversation.

"How's school?" Chad asked.

I would guess Chad knew about me going AWOL from school, yet I hoped by some chance he didn't.

"It's okay," I said, figuring it was the truth since I had been working with Mrs. Frank.

Chad eyed me with a serious look. He knew what I'd said was only a half-truth. "What was so bad that you couldn't return?"

"I don't know."

"You don't know or you don't want to say?"

There was no getting around Chad's questions. It would be ridiculous for Chad to believe I walked away from school without a reason, but I held out anyway. It was embarrassing enough to be told I'm a failure, but to spread the word was worse.

Chad rested his chin on his tented hands, supporting his head. He looked to me for an answer. His patience was greater than mine and we could be here all night.

"Please say something, because this is torture," I said.

"I did. I asked what happened to make you leave school."

"Oh God, Chad. It's really hard to talk about."

"All right. Now we're getting somewhere. So something happened, but you won't tell me. Does this sum it up?"

"Yep!" I was exasperated at Chad's assumption that if I said I can't, I'm indicating that I won't. "Not every little thing has to be picked apart, you know," I huffed.

"Walking away from school is not a little thing. Wrapping your hand around a piece of glass and threatening to kill yourself is not a little thing."

I wanted to argue this point like I had with Dr. Ellison, but I couldn't. I was not sure what my intentions were less than a week ago, but now, in this room on the fifth floor, I wished I'd sliced my wrists and finished the job.

"Wonderful! Another thing I can't do right." Blood rushed to my cheeks. I pulled at the neck of my sweatshirt.

"What can't you do right?"

Never say or write what you don't want the whole

world to know. "Crap, Chad! Can we please change the subject?"

"Nope." Chad maintained his position. "I know this is incredibly hard for you, but you'll need to trust that I will help you through this."

"Hard?" I mocked, realizing I'd gotten Chad on a technicality. "You said tonight would be easy."

"Anna, you know the answer to my question."

"I don't want you to help me through it!" I yelled from pure torment. "You can't force me to tell you!"

I looked away from Chad, but his eyes remained steady. I hated that I couldn't tell him. I hated Mr. Surrick and Mrs. Avery for putting me in this position in the first place. I hated everything about this moment, this day, this stupid, hellish life of mine.

"You're right. I can't," Chad said, pulling himself from the chair.

I watched him leave, silently begging him to stay.

"PLEASE STOP. YOU'RE burying me alive." I screamed.

"Did you read her obituary? She killed herself. Sliced her body in half with a piece of window glass."

"I'm here!" I screamed from far below. "I'm still breathing!" I begged of the onlookers.

"Stupid girl! She even misspelled bye."

"Let me out! Somebody! Help me! Please help me!" I sobbed.

I woke in a cold sweat at 2:35 a.m. Seconds later, vomit came spewing from my mouth. By the time I made it to the bathroom and threw my face into the commode, I was covered with vomit. Trudy, one of the night nurses, rushed into the bathroom.

"You hang in there, sweet thing. Let it all out," she said, sweeping my hair away from my face.

I waved her back indicating she should leave, but she didn't. She stayed, waiting for the last of what was inside to work its way out. I sat back against the wall, drained. My T-shirt was soaked through.

"You wait right here. No need to make a move."

Trudy was a large black woman with a bright disposition. She sifted through my drawers looking for a change of clothes. She returned with another T-shirt and pajama bottoms, underwear and two towels.

"Dear Jesus—I do believe they need to make these bathrooms larger. I'll be lucky if I can turn around from here," she said after turning on the shower and backing out. "Get yourself cleaned up. I'll be right here if you need me."

She closed the door, letting me recover from this embarrassing situation. Trudy, or someone, had changed my sheets and cleaned up the mess in my room by the time I was showered.

"Feeling better?" Trudy asked.

"Yes, thank you."

Trudy sat on the side of my bed, like my mother would if she had been there. The bedroom door was open so that the hall light brightened a small portion of the room.

"Trudy?" I whispered, looking at her silhouette.

"Yes," she whispered in a gentle voice.

"Why can't I control my nightmares?"

"Is that how you look at it?" Trudy whispered.

"Look at what?" I asked.

"Your nightmares. You said you couldn't control them."

"You know what I mean, Trudy. I want to stop them from happening."

"Anna, you can't control your nightmares any more than I can stop the earth from spinning. You need to face your nightmares—deal with them head on—figure out why they're controlling you."

Trudy settled in a little more, like I was a grandchild she was about to tell a bedtime story to. I felt childish at first and wondered if I should act tough—say I was tired and needed to sleep. But having Trudy there was comforting, like nothing could harm me at this moment. No nightmares. No memories. No self-destructive thoughts.

thirty-eight

"Here they are," Carol said, handing over my notebooks when Mrs. Frank arrived.

"These are the wrong ones," I said.

"They are?" Carol said, taking one back to look at it.

"No, I mean they're mine, but they're from last semester. I checked all of them and confirmed they were last semester's classes that I used through summer. "My mother grabbed the wrong ones."

"We can still use them. There's plenty of paper. We'll keep them here until your mom can get the others to us," Mrs. Frank said.

The hour passed quickly. I headed to lunch after returning my books to my room. *Yes, Mrs. Frank had betrayed me to Dr. Ellison about the obituary, but I like her anyway.*

Virginia, one of the older nurses, with a southern drawl and a very sweet personality, wrapped her arm around my back and squeezed me into her ribs when she saw me. "Hi darlin'," she smiled. "Looks like we'll be together sometimes."

"Hi Virginia. How are you?"

"Wonderful. Now let's see here," she said, opening the second steel door on the rolling lunch cart before she found my tray. "Anna Maedhart. Here you are, darlin'."

When I met Virginia, I assumed her wrinkles and gray hair meant she was old. She is, but the last time I was here, she practically lifted me from the bed and helped me to the bathroom.

If given the choice I would eat alone in my room at every meal, but this wasn't an option. I sat down at one of the four tables, beside Laura and across from Cate. I met them both yesterday during group. They seemed close, although they were very different from each other.

"Hi," I said, feeling awkward.

Laura smiled and replied, "Hello."

Sixteen-year-old Laura talked with her hands and smiled a lot. Everything was happy, happy, happy. It seemed so fake. Nobody this happy would be celebrating the holidays locked up like a prisoner. Laura's perfectly straight hair hung halfway down her back. Thick bangs covered the tops of her perfectly-shaped eyebrows. She had a friendly smile, I guess, despite the braces on her crooked teeth. Her eyes were very pretty. They were olive green without a touch of brown, so impossible to characterize as hazel. They were simply green, and it was easy to get caught staring at them. Just as I had once wished for blue eyes like Frances, I now envied Laura's green eyes.

I wanted to stand out in some way other than the girl from the psycho ward.

Cate wasn't much taller than I but definitely weighed more. Her short, dark brown hair fell in ringlets, tightly held back with a headband. A few curls sprang out alongside her face. Her appearance was that of defiance. Even though it was winter, she'd worn shorts and a sweatshirt since I'd been there, and probably long before. She was even feistier than the typical fifteen-year-old.

"Hey," Cate said without looking up. She gripped her spoon with her fist, instead of properly resting it on her middle finger, as she piled a heap of SpaghettiOs into her mouth. "This stuff tastes like shit," she mumbled around a mouthful.

I immediately lost my appetite and considered changing seats, but stayed, mainly to avoid what Cate might say. I didn't want only issues with her — she just seemed like she was looking for a fight.

I only needed to choke a few minuscule portions of food down my throat and no one would complain. Unless my stinking weight bottomed out. I blew on a spoonful of lukewarm chicken noodle soup. I tried to force a rubbery piece of chicken down my throat but picturing the mashed-up SpaghettiOs in Cate's mouth made me gag. I was furious at Cate and her disgusting table manners. I plunked my spoon into the bowl and pushed my chair away from the table.

"Sorry, Virginia," I said sliding the tray into the lunch cart. "I don't feel good."

"What is it?" Virginia asked.

"Nothing. I just don't feel good."

CAROL AND I met for one-on-one therapy. The day before, there had been nothing I could tell her that she didn't already know, but she wanted updates anyway. She asked about Bridgett and my other siblings, my parents, and summer vacation. She even asked about Oreo—twice.

Now Carol had an agenda. She expected more of me, but I had nothing to give except for my horrible mood and gagging thoughts of Cate's sickening table manners.

"Are you feeling okay?"

"I'm fine."

"Are you looking forward to PT today?"

"Anything's better than sitting in group with Cate, so I guess I am excited," I remarked snidely.

"Did something happen with you and Cate?"

"I don't like her."

"Something must have happened."

"Well, so you know she's the reason I couldn't eat my lunch. Chewed food was practically falling from her mouth."

"So why not change seats?"

"Because Carol . . ." I shrugged with my palms up and fingers spread. How could she possibly wonder why I didn't change seats instead of simply agreeing that Cate was horrible?

"Are you kidding? Anyone can see she could beat the hell out of someone double her size."

"This is why you didn't eat or move elsewhere?" Carol said, like she found my reasoning pathetic. Her elbows rested on the table. If not for Carol's intrigued look, I might have thought she was mocking me.

"You don't get it!" I huffed, slamming my body against the back of the chair.

"You have choices. If you couldn't eat because you were not feeling well, I would understand. But if you decided not to eat because of Cate's manners, than you should have sat elsewhere. You didn't. It isn't Cate's fault you didn't eat. You decided that on your own."

"Great! It's my fault. Let's move on," I said sarcastically.

"How is your schoolwork coming along?"

"It's okay," I said, shrugging my shoulders to suggest I didn't care.

"Mrs. Frank said you're quite the writer. I didn't realize that. Have you always liked writing?"

Part of me wondered if Carol was referring to the obituary. I didn't see why Mrs. Frank would mention it, but then again she had completely blown the whole obituary thing out of proportion. Even if Mrs. Frank hadn't mentioned it, it could be in my file somewhere.

"Are you asking because of the stupid expository essay I wrote?"

"No. Though to be honest with you, I do know about the obituary, if this is the expository writing you're referring to."

"Yeah it is," I snapped. "Can we pretend I never wrote

it?"

"Mrs. Frank speaks highly of you. One thing she mentioned was your writing. I thought we could try writing instead of talking." she said, bouncing the word *writing* like this might help convince me to give it a try

"How does it work?" I asked.

"However we want it to work, but basically instead of discussion, we write. It's worth a try, don't you think?"

"It sounds okay. What happens to our writing when we're done?"

My mom's adamant motto of *don't ever say or write anything you don't want the whole world to know* drowned out Carol's explanation. "What? I'm sorry," I asked, embarrassed.

"That's up to you," Carol repeated. "We can tear out the pages and throw them away or keep them."

"Throwing it away sounds good, I guess."

"We'll give it a go tomorrow."

"Okay."

"Where are you going?" Carol said when I stood up like we'd finished. "We have plenty of time to talk."

"Oh, sorry," I said with a slight chuckle at my optimism. "Like what?"

"Your mom mentioned to Dr. Ellison that your nightmares have returned."

I sighed heavily, wanting to give these nightmare discussions a permanent rest, but Carol wouldn't let it go. "They're terrifying, Carol. There's nothing else to tell. I can't stand to think about them. And please don't say that talking about dreams in the conscious world—blah, blah, blah—will help, because it doesn't."

"So you talked to your parents about them?" Carol asked.

"No way! I'm talking about the last time I was here." I said. "Dr. Ellison said it would help if I talked about my dreams, but it didn't."

"Maybe it did. You were having fewer nightmares by the time you left here."

"Who says?" I asked more sarcastically than I meant.

"That's a good question. I don't know. I guess I assumed. So, are you saying they didn't get better?"

"No, that's not what I'm saying."

I knew darn well Carol was gathering information for Dr. Ellison and I didn't care. Maybe because Chad was right—if I didn't talk, my chances of getting home soon would be ruined.

"Then what are you saying?" Carol continued.

"The nightmares never stopped. They changed."

"In what way?"

I adjusted my position in the chair, trying to scratch at an itch that all the sudden seemed to encompass my entire body. I leaned back in the chair knowing I hadn't accomplished anything that would help me get off the fifth floor sooner rather than later.

"They're just nightmares. Everyone deals with bad dreams once in a while. I'm not anything special." My breathing was a series of heavy sighs.

"Is it that you don't want to talk about these episodes

because you're scared to think about them? Or is it that you're afraid I might think less of you because of what you dream?

"Both."

"Anna," Carol said. "Your nightmares don't define you. They may sound crazy to you, but it doesn't mean you're crazy. They exist because you're still suffering from years of suppressed memories."

"She calls for me. That's what I dream sometimes." I said quietly.

"Who is she?"

"Liz."

thirty-nine

By the time Chad came by my room at four o'clock for our one-on-one, I was working on my homework. I had been scratchy all over for hours and it was driving me crazy. Algebra demanded my concentration, but so did the tiny bumps all over my skin. I had hoped they'd disappear before I had to ask for help, but I couldn't hold out a second longer.

"Hey, how about some chat time?"

"Chad I have a problem. I seriously need your help."

Chad smiled. "Whoa, asking for help. I like this idea. What is it?" Chad asked, looking at my textbook, "Algebra? Sure, I can help."

"Chad . . . um . . . I . . . I mean something is wrong with my skin." I rubbed my thighs with the heels of my hands to get at another itch. "I'm so itchy," I contorted, trying to scratch my back.

"C'mon," Chad said, motioning with his hand. "Let's see."

I pushed my sweatshirt sleeve up to my elbow. We both looked at hundreds of little bumps all over my wrist and forearm. We looked at the other arm and then my legs.

"Let's get you in a doctor's room," he said, concerned. "And don't scratch at it."

"Please not there, Chad. Can I stay here? Please."

He understood my dilemma. I couldn't bear to go in the back room, where I once screamed out my childhood nightmares and an entire day vanished to memory loss. Just the thought intensified my urge to scratch. Chad left and Virginia came in to inspect my rash. She had me take off my shirt and pants to see how bad it was. I was so willing to get these clothes off I didn't even care that I stood half-naked in front of Virginia.

"Virginia," I whispered, pointing toward the open bedroom door.

"Oh darlin', of course." She smiled. "Actually, let me get you a gown."

She returned with two.

"Put these on." She looked again at the bumps. "It could be from the detergent on your bed sheets or the soap you're using. I'll put in a call to one of the doctors."

"No, I just need to take a shower. I won't use soap or anything."

"There's more to it than a shower, honey."

When Virginia left I hopped into the shower using nothing but hot water. The minute I turned the water off the itch returned. Except now the bumps were bright red and the itch was three times worse.

Virginia knocked on the bathroom door before I was dressed. "Darlin'? Dr. Pins is here."

I wanted to absolutely die right there on this floor. I hadn't taken Virginia's advice and now I was worse off than before. I grabbed my underwear and pulled it up quickly before realizing it was on backwards. I stood blocking the bathroom door in case either one decided to barge in. There are no locks on the bathrooms, which struck me as ironic because everything else was locked up tight. I stepped out of the leg holes, twisted the underwear around and stepped in again.

"C'mon already," I whispered under my breath, trying to untangle the twisted bra straps.

"Well, you girls sure do need plenty of time," Dr. Pins said to Virginia.

"We sure do," Virginia replied.

I threw on the two gowns, one facing front and one facing back so all private body parts were covered. I opened the door, sweating bullets, causing the bumps to rise another inch off my skin.

"Well young lady—let's see what we've got here." Dr. Pins said, holding my hands in his and turning them over and then back again, inspecting my skin.

I lifted my gown above my knees so Dr. Pins could look at my thighs. Then he wanted to see my middle. I had no good option here. I could raise it up so my underwear was showing or pull it down so my bra was exposed. I reluctantly chose to lift up. After my middle was inspected, Dr. Pins inspected my back and chest.

"Well young lady. You are loaded with a rash, but something tells me a smart girl like you already figured that much."

He turned to Virginia giving an order for some type of medicine. I stopped listening after the word injection.

forty

By Wednesday afternoon the itch was gone and only a few red spots remained on my wrists and behind my knees. I headed to lunch and sat at a table, away from Cate and Laura.

"It's Ann, right?" The lady sitting across from me asked.

"Anna."

"I had a cat named Ann. I lost her a long time ago. Oh, Ann—I wonder where she is." The lady began to cry. I kept my eyes on my plate and poked at the radishes in the salad with my fork.

"Ann is such a beautiful name. Oh my poor Ann."

"How's your lunch, Marla?" Virginia asked.

"Delicious." Marla smiled. Her tears vanished.

"This is Marla." Virginia said.

"Hi," I gave a weak smile.

"Hi, I'm Marla. What's your name?"

Virginia had moved on to someone else. I had no idea

how to get out of this situation. "Bridgett," I finally said.

"Bridgett is such a beautiful name."

"Thank you."

As soon as a man sat down next to Marla, I knew it was either bail now or never. I stood quickly, pushing my chair backward. It slid right into Cate. Her face twisted as she massaged her left thigh.

"Are you okay?" I asked.

"Idiot!" Cate sneered.

"Cate," Virginia said firmly.

Isaac put himself between Cate and me. "Hey, settle down," he told Cate

"Whatever," Cate huffed as Isaac followed her from the room.

"Are you okay, Anna?" Carol said, coming into the dining area.

Embarrassed at being called stupid, I walked past Carol without a word.

"READY?" CHAD SAID.

"Can I finish this last problem?" I asked.

"Sure." Chad pulled the empty chair from the other side of the room closer to my desk. "Any homework you want me to look at?" he said, looking over my shoulder.

"You can check this sheet if you want." I handed him my first page of solved equations.

He glanced through a couple problems. I closed the book hard enough so a puff of air blew a few strands of my hair. "Done."

"Let's talk in the dining area to give us a change of scenery," Chad suggested.

We walked across the TV room, through the wooden double doors and into the dining area or group therapy room depending on the time of day. We sat opposite each other at one of the tables. Chad tilted back in his chair so it rested against the wall. I looked around the all-too-familiar room. Not so long ago, I sat in a circle with six other teens hashing out problems here five days a week.

"Hmmm," I joked. "This is a great change of scenery—the same four boring white walls and the same digital clock—exactly like the bedroom we left."

Chad smiled.

I liked the way he understood my dry sense of humor.

"I'm sorry to hear what happened at lunch." he said. He pushed the top of his short blonde hair to one side, but it sprang back. "Do you want to talk about it?"

"Nope."

Neither of us said anything for a few awkward seconds.

"This place is so different from last time."

"How so?" Chad probed.

"Remember my roommate Betsy the last time I was here?"

"The two of you were like two peas in a pod." Chad chuckled.

I smiled. "My mom always uses that expression. Anyway, how do you figure?" I said lightheartedly. "Betsy is pretty with her red curly hair and amusing giggle. And," I pointed out strongly, "she made everything fun and interesting."

"You exactly," Chad said. "Minus the red hair."

"Anyway . . ." I rolled my eyes dismissing what Chad said. "I miss having her as a friend, you know. It was kind of like she didn't judge me. I don't know . . . I felt I could be seventeen around her. Does that make sense?"

"It does. Does it make sense to you?"

I laughed. "It does and it doesn't.

"In what ways?"

"Growing up, it seemed that I was expected to know everything without experiencing it. So when I experienced something new, I felt embarrassed because . . . Ahh! It's hard to explain," I huffed, frustrated.

"It might help if you give an example."

"I can give you a hundred examples. I specifically remember feeling so proud I learned to tie my shoes. But tying shoes had already been done eight times before me, so nobody cared. Here's another one. Why should I be afraid to swim across the pool for the first time, right? Or why is it impossible to return from the dead, when clearly people in the Bible did it all the time? Or why should I be expected to stop referring to Liz as Sissy because I turned four? Here's a good one." I said, realizing my voice had become louder. I sucked in needed air and quieted down.

"My father walked in from work and accidently threw the newspaper onto the dining room table where my paint-by-number project was drying. I had worked on it for days and within seconds it was completely ruined. Here's the thing, Chad. I get it was an accident, but there was no 'I'm sorry' or 'let's try to fix it.' I'm supposed to get over it right then. Oh well, his loss, not mine," I sighed. "Sorry. These examples are going nowhere."

"That's not true. I'm getting a clearer picture."

"Then explain it to me, so it makes two of us."

"You're that confused, huh?" Chad lightheartedly laughed.

"Anyway, we were talking about Betsy, not some dumb paint-by-number painting. I miss her because she seemed to get me."

"Did you try calling her?" Chad finally asked.

"I left here before she did. She said she would call when she was home for good. Since I haven't seen her hiding anywhere nearby, I'm kind of guessing she had better things to do."

"Well, when you get home, you should give her a call. Maybe she's lost your number."

"Nah, not Betsy. Besides, she's twenty. I'm sure she doesn't want to hang around with a seventeen-year-old."

"The painting. It was for your Dad then?" Chad asked.

"It doesn't matter who it was for."

"It does matter."

"Actually Chad," I said defensively. "Yes, his dad died and I wanted to do something special for him. Not that it matters, but I . . ." The sting in my eyes and nose intensified with every passing second. "I wanted him to be proud of me, not that I did anything to deserve it, or maybe I had. I don't know what the heck is admirable."

Chad righted his chair and leaned forward on the table. "It can't be easy to return here, but considering the shape you were in the first time we met, I'd say you're doing quite well. I'll tell you what, I see you as an intelligent and inquisitive young adult who has a lot to offer."

"Please Chad. Let it go." I sucked in a salty tear trying to get rid of the evidence. "I'm . . ." I began, but Chad quickly interjected.

"Something positive better come past those ruby red lips of yours," he said rolling his eyes. "I mean it."

I tried to laugh, but it came out as a sob.

"I'm . . . what," Chad said, coercing me to finish what I started.

"I'm scared." I covered my face for what seemed like eternity.

"Anna," Dr. Ellison said, touching my shoulder, suddenly standing beside me. "Why don't we let Chad get to his other patients and we'll continue back in your room before dinner?"

I shook my head, still sobbing. "Everyone . . . will think . . . something's wrong."

"How about you go on your own and I'll meet you there in a few minutes?" Dr. Ellison suggested.

"We're okay here." Dr. Ellison said to Chad.

"I'll be around in a little while, Anna." Chad said, touching my shoulder on the way out.

forty-one

I immediately went into the bathroom, away from everything, and turned on the shower to mask any sound. I pounded the fake-mirrored glass hoping it would break. "Stupid! Stupid! I'm the one in the hospital. Not Bridgett, not Marie, or Frances. Me!" I wiped away fog on the steamed mirror. "You don't get it, Chad! Look at me," I yelled into the mirror. "This is not something to be proud of!" I lowered my head to the countertop and hid my face on my arms. *I wish I could run from myself.*

Dr. Ellison opened the bathroom door without knocking. My first reaction was to push against it, closing it tight, but I would not win against Chad's strength if he needed to be called. I didn't need to be reminded of his skills in taking down a resistant teen.

"Please Dr. Ellison. I'm not done yet. Can I wash my face? I'll come out right away."

"Sure, I'll wait."

My face faded into the steam again. I turned off the

shower, watching the water gurgle down the drain. I hurried from the bathroom to my bed, throwing myself flat on my stomach.

Dr. Ellison worked at the empty desk. I heard charts being opened and closed, papers being ruffled, and the same scribbling several times, probably her signature. I turned my head toward her to get an idea of the time. It was 5:32 p.m.

I sat up with my back against the wall. "Dr. Ellison?"

"Yes," she said, turning toward me.

"Why don't you have me on medication?"

"Because I believe you need to get through this trauma without being medicated. It may or may not work, but I want to give it more time before I decide."

"I won't need it."

"Medicine is a great help for people with many different conditions. Why do you despise it so much?"

"It didn't do any good for my sister." A huge sigh came from my insides. Relief flowed through my lungs.

"You're right. In Liz's case, medication could not save her."

"It can't help me either," I said.

"Is this what you think? That you don't deserve to have what Liz couldn't? Anna," Dr. Ellison continued. "Liz's death was not your fault. It wasn't your parents' fault or anyone's fault. Depriving yourself of medication in retaliation for Liz's death will not help you heal. It will only make matters worse. If you need medication, you deserve to have it like any other person. You need to recognize this."

"I do."

"Do you? You don't sound sure of yourself. You cannot take away your rights because Liz died."

"It's not that."

"What is it then?"

"It's all so confusing. I don't know what's normal." I said in frustration.

Dr. Ellison pulled her chair over to my bedside. "Normal for what?"

"For everything."

Dr. Ellison's eyes focused on mine, urging me forward, listening to my every word.

"It's like the medication thing—I'm scared of being considered weak if I need help from meds or even need help from anyone, for anything. I'm scared to ask for help. Here it seems normal, but at home it seems like being a baby. It's confusing to know when it's okay and when it's not."

"I understand. Your family does seem to have a hangup about asking for help."

Dr. Ellison had hit a nerve, but she was right. If she had said this months ago, I would have accused her of not understanding the family that I was so proud of. After the past six months, I could see her point. But I still couldn't stand that she was insulting my beloved family.

"It's not all true, you know," I said abruptly. "Tim asked Bridg if she needed help. My sisters and brothers visited me here. My mom and dad refused to send me away to that weirdo school."

"Your family cares."

"Then how can you say we have a hangup with helping each other?"

"That's what you heard, but that was not what I said. There's nothing wrong with asking for help, Anna. But in your family it's traditionally been viewed as a sign of weakness," Dr. Ellison said.

She continued, "I believe your family is trying desperately to change. What's happened to you has happened to them too. I don't believe one person in your family mourned Liz's death properly, mostly because nobody felt they could show deep emotion or ask for help. Nobody knew how to support each other. Your parents expected each of you to work out your emotions on your own, but processing such a profound loss alone is impossible for anyone —a child or an adult. There are times when people need help sorting out their experiences. They need emotional validation."

Dr. Ellison searched my face, checking for understanding. She reached for a pad on the desk and moved the chair closer to the bed. She sat back in the chair in a more comfortable position than a moment ago. She clicked her pen and repositioned her crossed ankles.

"What makes you sad?"

I brought my fingertips to my forehead and exhaled a quiet snort.

"What makes you sad?" Dr. Ellison asked again.

"Animals dying."

"What makes you angry?"

"Oh my God," I said embarrassed. "We don't use sappy words like angry,"

"Anna, what makes you angry?"

"It makes me mad when you use the word angry." I said seriously.

"What makes you happy?"

I struggled. I didn't want to look totally pathetic. "I know what could make me happy." Maybe . . . if I made someone . . . you know . . . like . . . proud of me."

"How about now?"

"Good memories, I guess."

"What frightens you?"

Nightmares. Asking questions. Ridicule. "Nothing."

"What frightens you?" Dr. Ellison asked again.

"Being thought of as stupid."

Dr. Ellison quietly looked over what she'd written. She ripped the paper from the pad and handed it over. She had written my answers next to her questions. "I'll keep it in your file," she said, reaching out so that I could hand it back to her. I'd rather not have junk like this in my file, but I handed it back without complaint.

Dr. Ellison looked at her watch and I looked up at the clock. It was 6:22 p.m.

"My parents are probably here," I said, wondering how it was possible that Dr. Ellison allowed me to miss dinner.

I hopped off my bed. Overcome by a wave of dizziness, I stumbled to one side.

"Careful," Dr. Ellison said.

She apparently thought I'd tripped over my own two feet and that was fine by me.

In the lounge, my mom sat on the couch with her eyes closed and my dad watched the news, drinking a cup of coffee. Cate's mom was also in the lounge. Cate was screaming in the back room, and I wondered what had happened now. This was the second time Cate's poor mom had sat alone while Cate remained in back. Last time, she hung around until visiting hours were over. Cate took her sweet time, torturing the one person who seemed to like her. I wondered if this is how Bridg felt—that I tortured her and Mom on purpose.

"Hey Mom," I said. "Hi Dad."

"Oh, Anna," my mother said, startled. "Are you finished?" she asked.

"Hello Mr. and Mrs. Maedhart," Dr. Ellison said. "We're a bit late." Dr. Ellison turned back to me. "I'll make sure your dinner gets to you."

My parents stepped into my room and sat in the two desk chairs. I'd been sitting for too long so I stood, rocking slightly from side to side to loosen my muscles, and maybe knock off a few calories. My dad sipped on his coffee.

"Is Tim home with Bridg?" I asked.

"He is," my mother said, handing over a baggie with three Christmas cookies inside. "Bridg packed these for you. We decorated them last night."

For as long as I could remember my mom has made sugar cookies from her Betty Crocker cookbook every Christmas. Bridg and I loved pressing Santa, reindeer, angel and tree cookie cutters into the rolled-out dough. We'd frost them with homemade icing made from confectionary sugar, almond extract and milk, and top each one with red or green sprinkles. Last night Bridg and Mom frosted without me.

"I'll be glad to have dessert tonight," my father said, smiling like the Grinch.

"Jimmy," Mom lightheartedly scolded, "They are for the party."

Dad looked at me, his grin still as wide. He probably planned on hiding a few for himself in the far back of the freezer like he did the Hostess Suzy-Qs he bought himself every Saturday.

"Also Anna, Tim took a job in Seattle. He's going to be leaving after the New Year."

"Really? Then what about Bridg?"

"She's fine," Mom said.

"You can't be leaving Bridg to come here every day. Someone's got to be at home with her."

"We'll cross that bridge when we come to it."

"What about Christmas Eve and Christmas Day? Don't come here. Please stay home."

"Anna, we've already worked it out. Bridg is going to spend the night at Frances's house. We'll pick her up in the morning and the two of you can open your gifts here together."

"That doesn't sound fun at all! So Bridg has to come here for Christmas? Now, she's really going to hate me."

"She doesn't hate you. She's actually excited to go to

Frances' house."

"She's just saying that!" I huffed in frustration. "I am to blame for this whole mess and everyone knows it." My insides quivered and I felt sick to my stomach. "Seriously Mom! There's got to be a way you can get me out of here."

"Dr. Ellison is here late tonight."

"Nice one!" I huffed, not letting my mom off the hook for changing the subject. Another wave of dizziness had the room moving. I stepped toward my bed to sit down, but it was too late. An echo ripped through my head.

"Anna! Jimmy!" A voice yelled.

My father swayed to the left and then the right as he jumped from his chair in slow motion. A splash of coffee leapt upward and then recoiled, spreading droplets in all directions. My father lunged toward me, his hands reaching. Then, complete darkness.

"Get up, Sissy! Please, get up!" I yelled, pushing at her limp body.

Liz slowly rolled from her front to her back. She groaned. "Agkh."

"I thought you were dead!" I said.

"She is dead!" Frances screamed angrily. "She's underground, covered in smelly dirt!"

A pungent odor filled my lungs causing me to cough. Chad and my parents stared down at me. Virginia was waving something under my nose.

forty-two

My fainting spell had everyone fussing. I had my blood drawn by five the next morning and blood pressure taken, twice, by eight o'clock.

Carol stayed by my side in case I went down right here in the hall on the way to breakfast. And Dr. Ellison wanted to be assured I ate breakfast. When that was confirmed, she moved on to my blood pressure, iron level and fainting spell.

"I am going to start you on iron tablets. One of the side effects is constipation."

My eyes left hers. "Oh God!" I huffed.

"I want you to know what to expect. If you feel constipated, let one of us know."

The thought of my cramps while camping were bad enough. Letting someone know would be humiliating. Not again, I prayed because constipation is a crap load of horrible.

MRS. FRANK HANDED back my algebra homework from Tuesday. *Great Work* was written in purple marker on the top of the loose-leaf paper. She had obviously gone back to her elementary school habits, using bright colors and stickers.

"I'm impressed, Anna. There were a couple problems I had to double check to make sure they were right. Math has never been my strong suit, but I can see it is yours. Twenty problems and every one is correct. Excellent."

Mrs. Frank raised her eyebrows and smiled at me like I should be proud. I actually did feel proud but it was too awkward to admit. I gave her a half smile, but only because I had no idea what else to do.

"Well, this homework shows you'd pass a test with flying colors."

My blood pressure rose and my heart thumped through my chest. "What test?"

"There isn't a test. I meant that you'd do fine if there were a test, even if it was right now. Anna," Mrs. Frank said, possibly noting my deep breath, "You'd do fine."

"It's never fine. I have always done my homework. It doesn't make a difference when I take the test. Seriously, every time, I get a fat red F for Anna is a failure!"

My hands began to shake. The round table seemed to be spinning. "I need help," I whispered. Telephone wire buzzing filled my ears. "I'm going to faint."

Mrs. Frank immediately jumped from the table and leapt outside the conference room door. "Could I get a nurse in here?" she yelled in a panic.

Holly must have been nearby because she darted into the room in an instant followed by Carol a moment later. Holly took my blood pressure with the cuff Carol brought to her.

Dr. Ellison showed up. "She's on bed rest for the day," she said.

Mrs. Frank came by after I was settled. "How are you feeling?" she asked.

"I'm okay."

"That was scary. I've never seen anyone faint before."

"I didn't faint," I said.

Mrs. Frank chuckled. "You were close to it, and I've never seen that before either."

"Thanks for helping me."

"Sure. I must admit, when you said you needed help, I thought you meant studying for tests. I was about to walk you through it."

I smiled at the comical scenario. Mrs. Frank grilling me while I was passed out on the floor. My smile grew into a huge grin. I laughed aloud.

"What's so funny?"

"I don't know," I laughed lightheartedly. "A funny thought, I guess." I told Mrs. Frank what I pictured and she too laughed.

"Tomorrow's our last day together for two weeks. I hope you're feeling better. I'll call in the morning to see if I should come or not. If I'm not here, I want you to have a merry Christmas and happy New Year. Will you do that for me?"

"I will, but I should be okay by tomorrow."

"Be good." She smiled.

"Mrs. Frank," I said before she left.

"Yes."

"I could use your help. On taking tests." A bubble burst in my throat.

"I'm here for you, Anna. See you tomorrow."

When she left, I couldn't hold back a second more. I cried into my pillow.

THAT AFTERNOON, CAROL came to my bedroom with two spiral notebooks for our writing experiment. She placed her notebook and pen on one of the desks and sat in the chair.

"We begin by writing a question that requires more than a simple answer. For example," Carol said. "You can ask something like . . . Where's your favorite place to visit? But the answer can't be a one-word answer. You have to elaborate. Tell why it's your favorite place. Then we'll exchange notebooks, write our answers, and then end with a new question. There is no time limit. We'll switch notebooks when the two of us are finished. Ready?"

I nodded my head. We both looked down at our notebooks. Carol began writing immediately but I lingered tapping my pen on my upper and lower teeth. The pressure was intense. I had no idea what to ask Carol. If I used her idea of where to visit I'd look like I didn't care about this assignment or worse I'd show her I was too dumb to think for myself. I looked over at Carol, her pen moving quickly over the notebook paper. She would be done before I'd thought of anything to write. My breathing became labored.

"Carol, I can't do this! I have no idea what to write."

"There is no right or wrong way to do this."

"There's no right and it's all wrong. I'm such an idiot! I don't have a single idea."

"Hey, wait a second. Calm down. You were willing to do this. What's happened in the last few minutes?"

"It feels like I'm taking a test. My brain goes blank. I've had questions to ask you before today, but now they're completely gone. It's like I become a basket case or something, and suddenly I can't think."

"Is this how you feel when you take tests at school?"

"Yes. When I look at the page I can't read a word of it. The words blend together in one big gray spot on white paper."

"Have you mentioned this to Mrs. Frank?"

"No. I thought about it, but . . ."

"But what?"

Carol's eyes looked into mine and something told me it was okay to say it. That she'd understand.

"I know she's my teacher and everything, and she's not supposed to think . . . but . . ." I let go with a big puff. "I don't want Mrs. Frank to think I'm stupid or not trying or can't read."

Carol smiled. "Well then, I'll help you."

"BASICALLY THAT'S WHAT happens," I said to Mrs. Frank the next day shortly after we were seated in a small conference room. Carol eased my anxiety by helping me explain what happened the day before.

"Anna mentioned you might be able to help her learn some skills that might help her with taking quizzes and tests."

"You bet I can." Mrs. Frank said looking at me. "You'll be a great test-taker in no time," she added in her elementary teacher voice.

"Yeah, right."

"And here's your first lesson. No more condemning yourself. I've wanted to ask you and now it is the perfect time. Why do you insist on calling yourself stupid?"

"Because I am." I said, slightly backing down.

"This has to stop. You are not stupid. Look how well you did this past summer. Your homework was done neatly, on time and correct. You have a talent for writing. You are good with numbers. Give yourself credit, Anna. You even finished a week earlier than expected."

"But I didn't have to take the final exams either. Those were sure to be Fs."

"Change your thinking right now. Say, I could have gotten As on my exams."

"That's not true. I've taken many tests and they were never As."

"I didn't ask you to say 'I would have gotten As.' I am asking you to say, 'I could have gotten As.'"

"I guess it's a possibility, but it's not probable."

"Say it, Anna." Mrs. Frank continued. Her voice changed from the sweet tone of a teacher handing stickers to third graders to that of a high school teacher giving a tough new assignment.

"I could have gotten As." I said exasperated.

"Now say it knowing that it is possible."

Mrs. Frank is right. *Everything is possible.* I tried again. "I could have gotten As."

"Perfect." Mrs. Frank said. "No time better than the present."

Mrs. Frank pulled out an algebra test. "First, read through all the questions answering the ones you know for sure, the easy ones. Then go back and begin with harder problems."

"I've tried this a hundred times."

"What happens?" Mrs. Frank wanted to know.

"My insides shake. Then my hands tremble. Then I concentrate only on the clock, every second bringing me closer to a time bomb ready to explode. Sometimes I erase an answer, over and over because I didn't write a number or letter perfectly. It sounds crazy, but I'm telling you, it's not crazy, it's torture."

"All right. Let's say you allow yourself the first two questions to panic all you want, but then stop fretting and move on."

"How?"

"Erase the answers for the first two questions ten times if that's what it takes, but once you move to question three, panic mode is turned off."

I read question one. *Factor the algebraic expression* $9x^2 - 21xy + 8xz - 28yz$. "God! This is not working," I huffed, already in panic mode.

"Anna, get up."

"Why? I scoffed.

"C'mon. Get up. I want you to walk down the hallway and back."

I returned to my seat a few minutes later.

"Tell yourself, I can do this."

"I can do this," I repeated sarcastically, feeling ridiculous.

"Now start again."

I panicked through question one, but eventually got it solved. Question number two threw me overboard. "I'm done."

"Walk."

"No teacher is going to let me leave the classroom to walk the hallways."

Mrs. Frank points to the hallway. "Walk."

When I returned, I get through the second question.

"Say to yourself, 'I've already finished two problems and I'm doing fine,'" Mrs. Frank said. "Then move on to question three."

I panicked on the next four questions. Mrs. Frank required that I walk the hall. When I returned, I repeated the same words. "I've already finished two problems and I'm doing fine." By the time I practiced on a mock geography quiz, repeating the strategies I used for algebra, there was only one obvious difference. I didn't need to walk the hall—not even once.

forty-three

Carol took her title charge nurse seriously, especially during group therapy.

"Christmas is around the corner," she said. "Let's talk about holiday traditions, memories, or plans for home visits." She looked around at the four of us wondering who would be first.

"I'm taking off at eight this evening," Jeff said.

Jeff was quiet. He wasn't a shy quiet or a defiant quiet. He was more like a guy who was quiet because it was in his nature. Tall with an average build, his voice had long changed, I suspected. He was seventeen, but I only discovered this yesterday by listening to Laura and Cate talking in the lounge while I pretended to watch TV.

Jeff's arms were crossed with his left ankle resting on his right knee. His blue eyes were distant and his pale skin was speckled with a few freckles across the bridge of his nose.

"We're seeing Jake. Maybe he'll recognize me this

time," Jeff continued without a change of expression.

Who's Jake? I considered asking. Then I saw Laura tear up at the mention of him.

"Hell! Not this lame shit again," Cate said. "Is there anything else in your life besides Jake?"

"Cate," Holly cautioned, "everyone here is free to talk as long as it's respectful."

"Respectful, my ass! I hear one more thing about Jake, I'm going to be sick."

Jeff looked hurt.

"Shut up, Cate!" I sneered, giving her a dirty look.

I barely had the words out of my mouth and Cate ambushed me like a windstorm. She flew out of her chair, kicking and punching. I was quick to react, trying to shove her back with my foot, but her extra weight kept her coming.

"You shut up, bitch! You think you're the only one with problems! Not even!" She dug her fingernails into my neck and sent a violent kick to my shin. "Talk to me again, and I'll knock you flat on your back!"

"Get your hands off me, you freak!" I screamed. I pushed back as hard as I could. "I said get off her!"

"Her?" Cate smirked, pushing me up against the wall. "What! You got multiple personality disorder?!"

BRIDG AND I walked up the street mid-morning, away from our home. We were headed to the pool for swim lessons. I was eight years old. Bridg was four. Twelve houses away, where Jim's friend Bob once lived, two mean boys had moved in. They were bigger and older than Bridg and me. We skipped about on the sidewalk nearing their house. Rustling from behind the bushes caught my attention.

Two mean boys burst from the evergreens. They ambushed us, knocking Bridg off her feet before bolting toward me like lightning. The fat kid jumped me. The taller younger kid threw himself at Bridg. She began to cry as though she'd been injured. I clawed at the fat kid's face and attempted to kick him. My fingers dug into his cheeks sending him screaming, both hands covering his face. I kicked his chubby legs off mine and before I was completely untangled, I sprang towards Bridg. I grabbed the tall kid's shirt and pulled as hard as I could. I almost had him off, when the fat kid pounced again, knocking me off my feet and onto the sidewalk.

"Liz!" I screamed, looking around frantically.

My right leg found its way between my stomach and the fat kid's chest. The power behind the kick was so violent he was thrown to the grass, holding his ribs. The tall kid, holding Bridg facedown, screamed when the bottom of my sandal repeatedly kicked at his side. Bridg immediately jumped up and we both began to run back towards our house. A blue station wagon pulled to the curb.

"Hey, what's wrong?" Marie yelled from the driver's seat through the rolled-down window.

Bridg and I stopped running, realizing we'd been saved. We ran toward the car and hopped into the back seat. Bridg was crying. I cried too, telling my older sister, in between sobs, what happened. Marie peeled into the driveway where the two boys lived.

"Stay here," she said, slamming the car door and heading to the front door. She rung the bell and waited.

Bridg and I watched from the backseat, through the open window. The front door opened slightly.

A lady dressed in a housecoat and slippers with her hair up in bobby pins smiled, embarrassed. "Can I help you?"

"Yeah," Marie said. "Your kids just beat up my sisters!" Marie yelled accusingly, standing tall and brave.

The door opened to its full extent. "Hey punk, don't you dare yell at me!" the lady screamed at Marie.

"Don't call me punk! You're the punk. And your bratty kids are punks! My sisters are little girls. They're in the car crying hysterically and scared to death because your bully kids attacked them."

"Scott! Pete! Get up here!" the lady screamed.

Bridg and I slunk a little lower so the two boys couldn't see us staring.

"Are you pickin' on a couple of girls?"

"They were teasing us," the boys lied.

"What's wrong with you!" Their mother screamed, hitting both the kids several times on their shoulders and the backs of their heads. "Get to your rooms! Now!" She screamed louder. Then she slammed the door in Marie's face.

DANIEL, AN MHT of average height but surprisingly strong, rushed in and took Cate to the floor in a death hold right in the middle of the room. His quick movements and the sun shining through the window sent flecks of light bouncing across my eyes from his diamond stud earing.

"Liz?!" Cate screamed at me, struggling against Daniel's hold. "You're the freak, not me!"

Almost as if it was uncontrollable, my right leg propelled violently towards Cate just as it had the fat kid. I was able to stop the kick just before it connected and ran from the group, right into Isaac.

"Let go!" I screamed, when he caught hold of my arm. Isaac fumbled. I twisted from his grip, ran to my bedroom and slammed the door.

Holly knocked and opened the door. "Are you okay?'

"What a freak!" I shouted in anger. "What is her problem?"

"Let me look at your neck," Holly said, coming toward me.

"It's fine," I said, rubbing my hand against the sting. A small amount of blood stained my fingers. "God! She's a major jerk!"

forty-four

Last night, Laura said she was *stoked* about her home visit on Christmas. Dr. Ellison had already left for the night so today was my last chance to ask her before the weekend. If Jeff and Laura were going home for Christmas Day, then I figured I had a good chance too. Cate was so volatile I totally understand why she was stuck here for the holiday, and probably why we don't meet often as a group. But I'd done all right.

By eleven thirty, I was seriously worried because I hadn't seen Dr. Ellison all morning.

"Do you need something honey?" Virginia asked when she saw me eye the staff through the glass of the nurses' station."

"Is Dr. Ellison here?" I asked hopefully.

"She's been tied up, but she'll be around soon."

"I need to ask her something."

"I won't let her leave, darlin' without seeing you first." Virginia smiled.

"Thanks Virginia."

Dr. Ellison entered my bedroom during shift change. "Virginia said you have a question."

"Um, Laura and Jeff are going home for Christmas. Am I?"

"No."

This was not the answer I expected. But then, maybe I should have. If I was going home for Christmas, I would have known about it already. But Dr. Ellison's direct, my-way-or-the-highway tone infuriated the hell out of me. She didn't even mention why I couldn't go home.

"Why?" I snapped.

"You're not ready for a day pass."

"Yes I am. Besides, it's Christmas."

"Anna, I'm not sending you home."

"How ridiculous! It's Christmas and you're keeping me locked up in this prison!" My anger made me forgot my mother's number one rule. *Never say or write anything you don't want the whole world to know.*

"Besides, it's not your choice," I smirked, reacting like a brat. "The doors can't be watched every second now, can they?"

"Are you thinking of running from the unit?"

"You'll know soon enough." I said.

Within fifteen minutes I was in the locked back room under a twenty-four-hour watch.

forty-five

Chad came strolling into the back room from the nurse's station only a few steps away.

"Not a good day, huh?" Chad said, pushing a rolling swivel chair into the room.

"Nope." I replied sitting cross-legged in the middle of the bed.

"Do you want to tell me what happened?"

I answered sharply, partly because I was sure Chad already knew every freakin' detail of what happened. This was formality. "Nope!" I replied quickly and then changed my mind. "Actually, I do. I don't need to be here! It's ridiculous! All I asked was to go home for Christmas! And because Dr. Ellison thinks she has the right to trap me here, I'm stuck in this dump!"

My yelling could probably be heard through the glass and into the nurse's station, but I didn't care. Chad let me vent and I allowed myself to do it.

"Hmmm," I voiced sarcastically, looking around the

room purposefully at the four boring walls. "Where are the chains?" My eyes pierced through Chad. I continued on my rampage, holding back tears. "The ones you and Dr. Ellison used the last time I was here. Remember? The ones that strapped me to this bed so I couldn't move a fucking muscle! Remember that, Chad? I had to depend on everyone but myself! Sitting and waiting, like Liz's bear—depending on the world to take it away from its suffering! So where are the chains, Chad?" I blasted my rage towards him. "When is Dr. Ellison going to chain me down to the bed like Ziggy was chained to a wall? Well, I'll tell you something right now! I'm not going to be trapped like Ziggy."

I sounded like an insane person, spewing nonsense into thin air. It was no longer possible to control the tears that I held back a second ago. Streams of tears dropped onto my lap.

Chad leaned back in his chair, his linked fingers resting on his stomach, and his elbows supported by the chair's arms. He let me cry without interrupting a single tear finding its way from deep within me into the open, as if he understood I had no option but to let the tears flow. I wiped my nose on my sleeve, not caring how I looked. I moved to the head of the bed and lay down to sooth the pounding in my head and the aching in my chest and let my crying turn into sobs.

"Please leave," I whispered. I needed to rethink everything I had said.

"Well, that's not fair. You do all the talking and I don't get to say a word?" Chad said.

"My head hurts," I told him.

Chad left. I barely had my eyes closed and he was back with Virginia.

"Take these, hon," she said, holding out two pills. "It'll help that headache of yours."

I repositioned myself and downed the aspirin with water.

"Thanks." I said, laying my head on the pillow. Chad sat down in the chair.

"That should help." It was apparent Chad was back for the duration of our one-on-one. I was glad he was here because I didn't want to be left alone. Although I would never let him see that.

He didn't wait for the aspirin to dull my headache. "Ziggy, I believe I know and we'll get to him in a bit, but first I want to know about Liz's bear."

"Actually, I'm not sure what I meant."

"You said, like Liz's bear . . ."

"I know what I said, but I have no idea why I said it."

"Nothing?" Chad asked.

"I have no idea what I meant."

"Let's talk about Ziggy then. Can I assume you're talking about the elephant at Brookfield Zoo?"

Since anyone who's ever been to Brookfield Zoo knows Ziggy, it's not surprising that Chad recognized his name.

"Yep."

"What's upsetting you about Ziggy?"

"He was chained to a wall," I sneered. "This poor

elephant, who probably fought to stay in the jungle or savannah or where ever he was from, was captured and chained to a wall for thirty years." Hearing the words and picturing Ziggy chained had me upset again. "God! This is getting embarrassing. Are there tissues anywhere?" I asked, swiping my nose across my sleeve.

"There is no shame in crying Anna. Neither is there shame in hurting for Ziggy. He didn't deserve to be mistreated. Ziggy definitely received the attention of many people who rallied for his release. People learned a lot about animal behavior because of him."

"He shouldn't have suffered for the benefit of others," I said, tears silently falling. "His death was the only good thing that happened to him." I gasped. "It was so unfair. He suffered so much, chained to that wall. It wasn't his fault a person died because of him. He was doing what he thought he should do."

"You're right, Anna. It wasn't your fault Liz died."

"What! I'm not talking about Liz!" I snapped.

"Yes, you are."

"Chad!" I snapped louder. "I am talking about Liz, not Ziggy. I mean . . . God! You have me so confused! I'm talking about Ziggy, not Liz!" I slammed my fists against the mattress. "Why are you doing this to me?"

"You have suffered enough Anna. Let her go."

"You let it go! She's dead!" I screamed. "D-E-A-D!"

I flopped down on the mattress. My legs stiffened as straight as arrows trying to shoot the pain from my pointed toes. My arms bent fastened to my chest. My tight fists began to shake from the intensity of insane rigidness. I couldn't breathe. My head felt like it was about to explode from suffocation. I could not breathe. My arms flailed about rigidly fighting for air like a diver who'd waited too long to resurface.

I was pulled to a seated position. Someone whacked the crap out of me with a hard blow on my back, practically knocking me off the bed. The trapped air immediately rushed out. Then fresh air was pulled into my lungs just as rapidly. Chad, Dr. Ellison and Dr. Inkblot were standing around the bed.

If Dr. Inkblot was here to give me another Rorschach test, I would give the same crazy answers I gave him last time. *"It looks like an eagle. Eagle. Hmmm. Definitely an eagle. Yep! That one too. An eagle."*

forty-six

Twenty-four hours later, on Saturday afternoon, I was released from the back room into the locked ward, much like Ziggy was released from his three-foot chain into a secured enclosure a few years before he died. A letter was on my pillow with a larger white envelope that had my name written in bright blue marker. I pulled out copies of my tests. The algebra test had a pink A- written on the top of the page. In lime green marker a B was written on my geography test. A note was attached. *Keep up the great work. From, Mrs. Frank*. With no one around, I smiled hugely.

When I saw who the letter was from I shoved my tests back into the large envelope and tore at the envelope from Jim.

Dear Anna,

Hello from Carbondale. I received a call from Dad that you were back in the hospital. I hoped to make it home closer to Christmas, but unfortunately it's not going to work.

I'm sorry to hear you're struggling. You may not want to hear this, but I think you are in the right place. I was impressed when I met the staff the last time you were hospitalized. Since I won't be able to see you for Christmas, I thought sharing some of my memoires with Liz might be helpful. Dad agreed.

I was twenty when Liz died, in the Air Force over in England. I'll never forget when I received word that I needed to get home because Liz was sick. I was in the mess tent eating dinner and talking to a buddy of mine, Charlie is his name, about a trip we were going to take when we earned our leave a few months later.

I flew in the back of a WWII vintage cargo plane that was making its way to the United States. It was a strange feeling being alone with hours to think about Liz being sick and what was happening back home. Liz always had such a glow about her that I couldn't imagine her lying sick in a hospital bed.

When we lived in Ohio, Liz and I used to build forts with blankets over chairs and then lob rolled socks across the room trying to hit one another. She laughed all the time—even when I nailed her. Other than sock wars, there's not much more I can remember. Liz and Frances were very close, but I was more interested in girls and hanging out with my friends so I didn't do too much with Liz by the time we moved to Chicago.

I will mention one regret I have. I hope you don't mind, but it's something I have thought about often and it might be helpful to you, especially if you think you are alone in this area of regrets. When I got back to England after Liz's funeral, my buddy Charlie (the one who was with me in the mess tent) and I met up with each other. Immediately, I started talking about our upcoming trip. Charlie looked at me strangely, "Jim—your sister just died, man. Why are you talking about travel?" I thought it was strange he said that, but when I thought about it later, he was right. I had treated Liz's funeral like it was one more thing in life to tackle and move on from.

Even today, I tell myself that I was twenty and it was normal to react that way, but in truth maybe it's far from normal. I looked at death differently than most people, even when I was a late teen. I remember thinking it's just a part of life.

Well, Anna. I hope this letter finds you well. Make the most of where you are. I hope you have a merry Christmas.

Your Brother, Jim

HOW EXACTLY WAS I supposed to make the most of today? Jeff and Laura were gone on weekend visits and I was stuck on the fifth floor with Cate. She was so unpredictable—the way she mouthed off whatever was on her mind. The few times we were about to cross paths, I turned and went a different way, which was almost impossible on a unit shaped like a capital H.

I was in the TV lounge watching anything to keep my mind occupied until visiting hours. Mom and Bridg were Christmas shopping today and then they would be coming by afterward. I was worried about Bridg coming. She didn't want to be here, but maybe since it was Saturday and most of the patients were away and no one was acting particularly weird, Bridg would feel better about it.

"Hey Anna, there you are," Isaac said.

"Was it hard to find me?" I said jokingly. "I take it back." I grinned. "I probably get around to more rooms in this place than anyone else."

"Aw! You're doing all right. Hey, your mom called. She and your sister will be about thirty minutes late. They're finishing up their shopping." Isaac looked like a small child hiding a secret.

"Your mom wanted you to know that somebody else was going to visit."

"Who?" I asked, interested but cautious. I searched my brain. *Tim. No. He's too busy with friends. Marie. No.* She was still waiting frantically for her baby to come. Twelve days late now. *Frances. Not with three kids at home. Oh God, Janet. Please don't let it be Janet.* I didn't want to see her, but to turn her away again would be unforgivable.

"Is it Janet?" I asked hesitantly.

"No. Hmmm . . . should I tell you or should it be left a surprise?"

"Jim? Kyle?"

"Nope. Nope." Isaac loved this back and forth guessing game. "Five letters. Starts with an M."

My eyes opened wide with excitement and then it hit me like a bomb. *No way.* I raised my fingertips to my temples trying to calm the chaos in my head. *Murph cannot see me here.*

"Call my mother and tell her he shouldn't come here. Please hurry before it's too late."

"Too late. He's already here, Anna. I've been talking with him for the last five minutes. He seems like a good guy. Why don't you want to see him?"

"I can't do it." *It's not that you can't . . .* I desperately drowned out the memory of Chad's words.

"How about you give yourself five minutes to think about it? I saw your smile. You might regret it if you turn him away."

"No, Isaac. I'm not changing my mind."

Isaac looked disappointed with my quick decision. He strolled down the hall, probably hoping he'd find the right words to let the nicest guy in the world down easy. *How could I be so awful?*

"Isaac," I yelled before he reached the exit door.

"Have you changed your mind?"

"Can I talk to him in the waiting area?" Somehow it

wouldn't be so bad meeting with Murph outside a locked ward.

"Sure. As long as you don't mind me hanging around."

"It's okay."

"Hey Murph," I said.

Murph greeted me with a full-face silvery smile. "Hi Anna. I wasn't sure you'd want to see me, but it's awesome that you did."

I couldn't help smiling. "Thanks for coming."

"Phew! Isaac said it was a fifty-fifty chance that I'd get to see you tonight."

Isaac shrugged his shoulders and gave me a quirky look. "Girls."

"Whatever." I rolled my eyes.

"Trust me, Murph," Isaac said, "Girls are a lifetime of work."

They both laughed like they were having a grand ol' time. Murph seemed taller and more muscular than last time I'd seen him. And as Samantha would say, *he's adorable.*

"So you didn't turn me away," Murph said, grinning.

"Well, here's the thing. We can talk out here, but Isaac . . . I pointed to Isaac with my thumb ". . . has to be our chaperone."

Isaac shrugged his shoulders and lifted his eyebrows like he didn't mind being the third wheel. "Hey, the more the merrier, right?" he said.

We sat on the two couches across from each other chatting. Isaac propped one foot on the coffee table and placed his hands behind his head, like he was swinging in a hammock without a care in the world. He and Murph hit it off right away, starting with football.

"You a Bears fan?" Isaac asked Murph.

"Of course, ten and six. Who isn't?" Murph said.

Umm. Me. I knew nothing about football.

"How do you think the Bears will do in the playoffs?" Murph continued.

"Well, got an NFC central division championship with last week's win. Hopefully, this is the year we get to the Super Bowl." Isaac said.

"Yeah, but McMahon's got to stay healthy." Murph said.

Dad and Gabe had talked about the Bears. There had to be something I could say that wouldn't be totally pathetic. "No doubt," I said, referring to the McMahon comment. I felt like a total idiot. *No doubt? God—kill me now.*

To my surprise, Isaac and Murph didn't make fun of me. "What do you think about the Giants and Rams tomorrow?" Murph asked, looking at both Isaac and me.

I shrugged my shoulders. I was a complete fake.

"I hope the Giants beat the Rams so we play the Redskins on the thirtieth cuz I think we can beat 'em," Isaac answered. "What did you think of the Lions game last week?

"Man, the Bears hammered them." Murph exploded. "Never easy to beat Barry Sanders in Detroit!"

It was obvious Isaac sensed my suffering because he

changed the subject. "Oh well," he said, "We'll see what happens.

About five minutes before Bridg and Mom arrived, Isaac asked Murph about his college plans.

"You'll like Purdue," Isaac said. "It's a great school. What's your major?"

In all the time I'd known Murph, I'd never asked him this. He talked about college, but never stayed on the subject more than a couple seconds.

"Aeronautical engineering."

"Space?" I asked.

"Somewhere up there. I haven't decided between the space program and commercial flying."

"Neil Armstrong went to Purdue," Isaac said.

"Amelia Earhart taught there," I said, realizing I shouldn't have. "But she— sorry I brought it up."

The three of us laughed. "Well, that makes my decision easier, then. The moon it is!"

"That would be awesome," I said.

I was happy for Murph and miserable for me. He was going off to college. I wasn't. He was so lucky to be leaving.

When Mom and Bridg arrived, I formally introduced Murph.

"Isaac?" I asked. "Can I stay out here?"

"Sure." He looked at my mom. "You can sign her out, but she's not allowed to leave the waiting area. Anna, I'm trusting you won't ask to leave." He grinned.

"Thanks for coming, Murph," I said.

"Don't worry, I'll be back."

"Ummm, any chance you can wait 'til I get home?" I asked shyly.

Murph smiled. "I'll be there the same day."

Isaac and Murph shook hands. When it looked like Murph considered hugging me goodbye, I looked away.

"Merry Christmas everyone," he said when the elevator opened. He stepped inside alone. I wanted to be there with him. *You're gorgeous, Murph Izak.* The door slid closed.

forty-seven

"Soooo," I said, stretching out the anticipation, "What did you buy me?" I chuckled hoping to keep the mood light.

"We didn't buy you anything," Bridg said, amused.

"I kind of wish it was true," I said to Bridg. "Because I won't have anything for you until later. I hope you don't mind."

"I don't care," Bridg said.

I regretted my decision to avoid occupational therapy. I could have made her something, though it would probably have been a crummy gift, since we'd only had OT once since I'd been here.

The three of us worked so hard at keeping the conversation light that time dragged. I wanted to let Bridgett off the hook and send them both home, but I couldn't make myself do it. Since Bridg was thirteen years old, the four-year gap in our ages made us worlds apart, but I didn't care. Having Mom and Bridg here made an evening on the fifth floor tolerable.

"WHAT BOOK ARE you reading?" I asked, remembering Bridgett's willingness to summarize Sweet Valley High for Dr. Ellison. It felt completely odd to ask this basic question, but Bridg responded so I went with it.

"The Pigman." Bridg smiled.

I knew about this book, but acted as though I didn't. "Seriously, that's the title? The Pigman?"

"Yeah, it's good."

"Would you bring a pile of books you've read, only the good ones, on Christmas? Maybe I'll have time to read them while I'm here."

"Man, I have a ton," Bridg said with so much excitement that I knew we had finally made a connection.

"I'll bring some magazines too if you want." she gleamed.

"Yeah, that would be cool."

When Isaac came for me I couldn't believe visiting hours were over. We said our good-byes and turned in different directions.

In bed, I opened my journal. The pen clicked between my teeth as I mulled what to write.

Anna Izak. Anna Izak.

I wrote it in print and cursive across the line to see which looked more sophisticated. I added my middle name. I created different styles of letters and viewed my name from different angles by turning my journal a little to the left and then the right.

Anna L. Izak. Anna Leah Izak

"Lady Anna Leah Izak," I whispered in a formal

aristocrat tone. Then in a priestly wedding day kind of voice. "Anna—Leah—Izak, do you take Murph . . ." I laughed. On the next line I wrote my name in a string of cursive letters.

Annaizak. Annaleahizak. Annalizak.

Admiring the perfection behind every letter's precise curve, a burst of light like a flashbulb snapped a picture of the journal page and sent it racing through my brain.

"What the . . ." I stopped. Then stared. I threw the covers off and dashed to the nurse's station. "Isaac," I said abruptly, standing in the doorway.

"Hey, what's wrong?" he said, surprised to see me at this hour, wandering about in my pajamas.

"Nothing. Where are my notebooks? I need them."

"Whoa! Slow down. What notebooks are you talking about?"

"My spiral notebooks from last semester's classes. Holly said they'd be in here. Well, I need them."

"Now?" Isaac looked at the clock. "At this hour?"

"Yes, Isaac. Please."

"Anna, you know you can't have them in your room?" Isaac said, phrasing it like a question.

"I know. Please. I just need a page from one of them. Any one. I don't care. It's important."

"Okay." He sighed. "How you talk me into things I haven't quite figured out, but let me do some looking. I'll bring one to you."

Isaac looked on shelves. I stood in the doorway with no intention of leaving.

"It might take a while," Isaac said, indicating I should

wait in my room.

"They're over there . . . on the right . . . behind that . . . that . . ." I shook my head trying to figure out what that thing was called.

"That pencil sharpener," Isaac chuckled. "What has you so flustered?"

I grabbed for the purple notebook and flipped through the first few pages until I came to a page with strings of cursive doodling. I ripped it away from its spiral. I took another from the yellow notebook. "Thanks Isaac." I smiled and turned to go.

"Should I come with you?" Isaac asked behind me.

"No. I just want to check something out."

I walked back to my room casually to disguise my urgency. When I disappeared from Isaac's line of sight, I jumped into bed, pulling the covers over my lap.

"Crazy!" I looked at the notebook paper and then my journal in disbelief, making sure my eyes were in perfect focus so not to make a mistake in what I was seeing. The string of letters that I had written last semester, weeks before my mother dragged me to Dr. Ellison's office for the first time, spelled out Liz. I hadn't been writing a misspelled version of bye. I had been doodling my dead sister's name. Over and over in a string of cursive letters, I had written liz. There was no capital L or a dot above the lowercase i, like there should be, but then again I hadn't stopped to pick up my pen to separate the words either. I had just kept writing her name.

"Anna."

"Ahhh!" I gasped. "You scared me."

"Is everything okay?" Isaac asked.

My journal was right here in plain view. There was no hiding it now. Even if I didn't say a word about this, Isaac would ask Chad or Carol about my journal. Not that I'd be forced to share it, but what's the point if even one person knew my secret. If one person knew, then basically the whole world could know. *My mother was right. Be careful what you say and write.*

Come look at this," I said. "Promise me you won't look at anything else."

"I won't. What?"

Instead of handing it over, I placed my journal on my lap and covered the top portion in case Isaac's eyes glanced upward.

"Don't laugh. Look at the three middle letters," I said pointing underneath the middle of *annalizak*, the last string of letters I'd written tonight.

"Liz, he said."

Okay, now look here," I said, pointing to the long string of cursive letters on the notebook pages. "Notice anything?"

Isaac looked back and forth a couple of times. "A page full of your sister's name?"

"Totally crazy. I thought I had written the word by—please don't ask, but all along I had been writing Liz's name."

Isaac took a closer look at the notebook page's, *bybybyby* and my journal's *annalizak* "Yep, looks the same," he said.

After Isaac left, on the bottom of the journal page I wrote, *tonight gave me goose bumps*.

I placed my journal under my pillow and snuggled under the blanket.

forty-eight

"How do you feel about Jim's letter?" Dr. Ellison asked, after I read it to her during our Monday therapy.

"Hmm," I tucked my lips into my mouth. "He reminds me of my mom more than anything. You know, the way he handled Liz's death. They reacted the same way, without crying or carrying on about it. It's like life went on. Maybe it's a genetic thing or something. Whatever it is—I hope I don't have it."

"What do you mean?" Dr. Ellison asked.

"I'm just sayin' the next time someone dies, I hope I don't stare all stoned-faced like I did after Liz's death. My mom said I didn't cry and wouldn't talk about it. Obviously Jim didn't talk about it either. I wonder if it's some weird gene or something."

"You'll be fine, Anna." Dr. Ellison said genuinely.

I paused, not sure how to ask my next question. I didn't want Dr. Ellison thinking that I used my weight to get attention. I had denied this many times, but now I wasn't so sure. Losing weight was becoming less of an issue for me and I wasn't sure why. "Do you think I use food . . . I mean, use my weight . . . to get attention?" I took a big breath, glad it was out, and yet nervous.

"It's never about the food, Anna. Using food or controlling weight to gain attention is considered abnormal behavior. Sometimes people stop eating to feel a sense of control or to revert back to a childhood weight when their life seemed simpler. In your case it was about being deprived of emotional outlets. So to answer your question, you did not use weight or use food to gain attention. You used it to escape from emotional trauma and deal with critical stressors. Does that make sense?"

I nodded. "I think so." I didn't need to rethink what I said next. I trusted Dr. Ellison. "I want you to know I used to take Ex-lax. Sometimes eight pills a day. I thought it would make me lose weight, but it didn't. It just gave me diarrhea."

"Unfortunately, many teens think this true, but it just isn't so."

Dr. Ellison apparently noticed my hesitation. She probably thought I was still on the food thing, but I wasn't. I had another question, a much bigger question. And because Dr. Ellison wouldn't be here tomorrow on Christmas Day or for the next few days after, I couldn't wait.

"Is there something else?" She asked

"I'm not sure how to ask this without being embarrassed," I said.

Dr. Ellison didn't try to persuade me to talk. Instead

she waited patiently.

"How do I know if I love someone?" My face reddened. "I mean what does love feel like? Real love."

"Anna, this isn't an embarrassing question. What is it about love you want to know?"

"The actual feeling I guess. I can tell you that I like my siblings. I can say I like Murph. I can tell you I like my moth—my parents. But when it's about Oreo or Ziggy or any animal it feels different. I can't stand to see them hurting or suffering. I avoid stepping on ants or killing a spider because they have the right to live. Is that love? Or just weird?"

"Well, it's not weird."

I knew how sappy this all sounded, but I didn't want to stop. "When an animal is suffering, like Ziggy . . . remember Ziggy?" Dr. Ellison nodded. ". . . Or a stray cat or a lost dog or a spider missing a leg, I take on the suffering of that animal. I need to save them, or at least help them."

"Listen, Anna. You have a tremendous amount of compassion. It's one of the many reasons Liz's death affected you so strongly, besides being at a tender age when it happened. Growing up in a family that showed little emotion is a tragedy way past Liz's death. You didn't know whom to turn to for comfort.

"Jim's letter tells a lot about him and how he handled the situation. He turned to travel for his comfort. Bridgett reads books with happy conclusions to avoid any kind of sadness, I suspect, because too much sadness lingered around your family.

"You are able to find comfort in Oreo's loyalty. Your

sorrow for Ziggy or any animal, I imagine comes from your own sorrow for Liz. You were unable to express your pain without fear of being different from your siblings and parents, so you shifted your emotions onto protecting animals in order to cope. You were seven years old. There was no way you could have understood how to handle Liz's death on your own."

WAKING ON CHRISTMAS morning alone, with an empty bed across the room was lonely. I deserved to be alone. I remembered Bridg trying to cheer me up when she was only three years old. Last summer, our camping trip teetered on my decision. If I had not wanted to go, Bridg would have lost her anticipated vacation to Devil's Lake. Now she was waiting for my parents to arrive home night after night after they were here with me. She had been unselfish and not once had I ever heard her complain. She couldn't. She had to hold it together—to waver even slightly might change bad to worse. Bridg was playing it safe.

Kids everywhere were waking early. Parents were crawling from the warmth of their beds tired from the late night of assembling bikes and dollhouses and placing gifts underneath the Christmas tree. When I was younger, Christmas morning was a mad scramble, with squeals of delight as ribbons and bows were tossed aside. This was how I remembered Christmas before Liz died. The Christmas Liz spent in the hospital was a mix of scattered memories. The Christmases after Liz's death were peculiar.

Today brought a sense of disconnectedness much like the last nine Christmases. Bridgett was only three years old when Liz died. I wondered if Bridg ever truly experienced Christmas morning as a magical, dreamlike day. She would have never known the difference, I suppose. We still woke happy. We still opened gifts. Paper still went flying. My parents pretended everything was as it should be. They were never sad, not when I was eight years old. Not when I was nine or ten or any age. They never acted any differently from the magical years when Liz was with us, but there was a difference. I sensed it. I felt it. I lived it. Bridgett simply didn't know any different. In a way some might think she was lucky, escaping a tragic end to happier days. I didn't, though. Bridgett, I thought, was the unluckiest of us all. Like me, my older sisters and brothers would remember Liz's smile. Bridgett never would.

Bridg was a late sleeper, but today I wondered if she had awakened early with our nieces and Frances. I suppose it was important for Bridg not to be home on Christmas morning. Maybe my parents didn't want her to stare at my wrapped Christmas presents sitting on the chair where they were last year and the year before that, and the year Liz died. Bridg was spared staring into the living room at wrapped boxes, wondering what went wrong in the last year. Just as I had tried desperately to understand why Liz hadn't returned home on Christmas Day ten years ago.

Our gifts, like Liz's, would be bagged, but Bridg and I would unwrap our presents here on the fifth floor. Liz's packed presents never made it to the hospital where she died. Her presents were taken down to the basement to collect dust and eventually be given away.

The mystery of Bridg's dislike for me came together piece by piece. Over the years, I had faded away after Liz's death, slowly. The kind of slow progression that goes unnoticed, like a child growing from an infant to six feet tall in a mere fifteen years. I once thought Bridg and I dwindled to a separate family of two after Liz's death. I was dead wrong. There was, and is, my absence—not only today, or the past month or even the past year. My inner child had died with Liz. Maybe it had been this way for the others, too. For the past ten years I had not been the sister to Bridg that I should have been. Bridg was raised as if she was an only child, by older parents, and siblings who barely existed. She hadn't escaped anything. Her tragedy was simply a different sorrow.

BRIDG, MOM AND Dad arrived at two. The others would visit in the afternoon on New Year's Eve to celebrate. Even Meg would be here. She was flying in from Dallas to help with Marie's baby for a week, if it ever decided to be born. I opened a first aid kit from Bridgett. Inside were bandages, gauze, medical tape, a pair of tweezers and an Ace Bandage for wrapping sprained wrists and ankles.

"Just in case," Bridg said, smiling.

Bridg and I thanked our parents for our gifts. We received fuzzy slippers (red for Bridg and green for me), striped leg warmers, puzzles and packages of gum. I also opened a rose-colored cloth-covered journal with a small flowered pattern, a boxed pen and pencil set and Reebok high-tops that Bridgett said she picked out. Bridgett unwrapped Michael Jackson's Thriller album that she went crazy over, feathery hairclips and two *Sweet Dreams* books that she immediately turned over to read the back cover.

We piled our new gifts onto one of the desks and slipped into our fuzzy slippers.

"Are those the books and magazines?" I asked Bridg, pointing to the large brown paper bag on the floor.

"Yep." Bridg took out four books from the bag. She had them in order, from top to bottom, of her favorites. *The Outsiders* by S. E. Hinton, *The Princess Bride* by William Goldman, *The Hobbit* by J. J. R. Tolkien and *Anne of Green Gables* by L. M. Montgomery.

Bridg gave a short summary of each and why it was a favorite. Dad sipped at his coffee, and Mom leaned back in a chair watching her two youngest daughters together. Bridg returned each book carefully into the paper bag, careful not to mess up the order.

"Smells like a good dinner," my dad said, as we heard the meal cart roll by.

"Well, this was such a nice Christmas," my mom said, giving a single clap while my dad stood to throw away his coffee cup. "Everything worked out just perfectly."

It was obvious how hard it was for my mother to leave. She was caught in a difficult choice—Bridgett or Anna.

"I'm exhausted," I said, trying desperately to give Mom an out.

Chad came into the room. "Well, Anna. How 'bout we

put that puzzle together?"

For someone who didn't have kids, Chad intuitively recognized my mother's rock and hard place. He was there to ease her agony.

CHAD AND I laid out the three hundred puzzle pieces. There were only about seven people on the unit tonight and it felt lonelier than usual. The picture on the box was of a decorated Christmas tree backed by several other pine trees on a dark and starry night.

Chad left me to work on it alone every so often so he could get back to other patients. My goal was to get ten or more pieces connected before he returned. I accomplished this twice in his five absences. I liked it best when we worked quietly. Chad liked it best when we worked and chatted.

"Favorite Christmas memory?" Chad said. He focused on the puzzle piece he'd repositioned in four ways trying to squeeze it in to the wrong spot. He picked up another and tried again.

"You first," I said, also trying to squeeze pieces into the wrong places.

"My first bike. I can still see it today, leaning on its kickstand in front of the Christmas tree. It had a banana seat and long handlebars. More recently, my favorite Christmases are time spent with my wife and family."

"Sorry you're stuck here."

"Don't be. We celebrated last night."

"Isaac told me. It's cool you guys switched."

"So now you. Name a favorite?" Chad said.

"The commotion. Oh, yes! Got another one," I said as a puzzle piece easily locked into place.

I sensed Chad's glance and looked at him. He lifted one eyebrow. "Spill. Isn't that the word Betsy always used?"

I couldn't help but laugh. "I miss it—all the commotion of a big family, especially around Christmastime. It was crazy at our house when it was all twelve of us. There was tons of food. Paper flew everywhere. Basically, imagine paper from piles of gifts times ten."

"It sounds amazing."

"It was."

"How about your favorite childhood present?" Chad asked.

"Hippity Hop." I cleared my throat.

"Hey, what's up? Talk to me. What about the Hippity Hop?"

Christmas tree light puzzle pieces blurred. Bluish colors glowed like streetlamps on a foggy night.

"It's not so much the Hippity Hop, it's the year I got it. Liz got a Pogo Stick. We spent Christmas Day out in the garage hopping and bouncing. I had completely forgotten about it." I alternated between a frown and smile, not sure of how I really felt. "I'm not kidding, she learned that thing fast, and once she got on she didn't get off. She bounced circles around the garage. I followed her on my Hippity Hop."

"How old were the two of you?"

"Probably five. Liz would have been eight. Seriously,

Chad." I smiled. "When the snow was barely melted, she was outside pogoing up and down the sidewalk. And out back we have a cement porch with one step that leads to the yard. Liz could pogo up and down it. That's how good she was on that thing. When we played hopscotch, she pogoed the squares, sometimes so quickly she looked like Ricochet Rabbit." I lightheartedly laughed. "But I decided it wasn't fair because she never picked up her hopscotch rock."

"I'm sure you have hundreds of great memories of Liz."

"I don't, actually."

"How about your family? They probably have tons of stories."

"We don't talk about these things—especially on the subject of Liz. It's like her name is taboo or something. Kind of stupid, I guess."

"You could change that, Anna," Chad said. "Take a risk. Ask questions and see how it goes. Did you ever think that maybe your siblings and parents want to share memories of Liz?"

"I would guess they don't. Besides, I wouldn't even know where to begin a conversation like that."

"Simple. Hey Gabe. Tell me what you remember about Liz."

"In what world?" I rolled my eyes.

Since we were on the subject of Liz, I didn't care if it sounded pathetic or cliché or downright stupid. I spoke the truth, in defiance of my upbringing, "I loved her, Chad."

SLEEP DIDN'T COME easily on Christmas night. I lay in bed, thoughts bouncing off every brain cell. There were so many unanswered questions that I was going crazy. Ever since Chad mentioned taking a risk and asking questions, the idea kept creeping back into my head.

What do you remember most about Liz? What fun things did you do together? I wanted to know all her favorites. *Color. Book. Friend. Teacher. Food. What were her likes? Dislikes? (Besides practicing the piano.)* I giggled at this afterthought.

And questions I probably shouldn't ask, but badly wanted to know, like *who visited her in the hospital? Who was at her funeral? What was the casket like? What was she wearing? Was it scary to see her dead?* I wanted to know how my siblings handled these things. *How did they find out she died and what was their reaction? Who told them? Who told me?*

I thought of Frances' visit. *What was it about the dresses? What did she mean, "I'm sorry for your loss?" Why was my loss different from her loss?* How could I manage to get answers to questions when I wasn't sure how to go about asking? When I asked Marie about Liz, she wouldn't answer, or maybe she couldn't. Jim shared his memories without being asked. *Write a letter to Kyle*, I thought. This was the safest way to take a risk.

Kyle lived in Fort Worth. He lived far enough away to discourage a sudden visit and was probably poor enough to prevent a long distance phone call. Kyle could decide to write back or not. If he didn't, I figured I was no worse off.

This way I didn't have to face it head on, even though Trudy said that was the best way to deal with things. *It had to work.*

Two things happened by early morning the day after Christmas. One, I wrote a letter to Kyle and two, my godson Joseph was born.

forty-nine

I dressed and headed to breakfast unusually early. There were only three patients in the dining area. Jeff was one of them. I went over to where he sat.

"Mind if I sit here?"

"No," Jeff said. "How was your Christmas?"

"It was okay. How was yours?"

"Not so good."

I wanted to ask him about Jake, but his bummed look and slumped shoulders told me I shouldn't.

Laura and Cate came into the dining area together and sat at our table.

"How'd it go it with Jake?" Laura asked.

Cate got up. "I totally can't deal with this lame crap," she pouted.

She slid her tray off the edge of the table and carried it to a table away from us. Part of me hoped Jeff spoke loudly so Cate could hear every word he said about Jake. I wasn't totally sure, but it seemed Laura had given up on

Cate. Cate didn't seem to care either way.

"Don't worry about her," Laura said.

"I don't," Jeff replied.

"How is he?"

"He doesn't remember me."

"Is he still at Marianjoy?" Laura asked.

"He's still there," Jeff said, his eyes going distant, like he'd been hypnotized. "According to my parents, there's hope he'll recover. But who knows how much?"

"Is Jake your brother?" I asked cautiously, unable to take the suspense any longer.

"My twin brother," Jeff said.

"Identical twin brother." Laura added.

"Not so much anymore," Jeff responded to Laura. Then he looked at me. "He's in rehab learning how to walk and talk again. Drugs screwed him over. He tried to step in front of a train. I pulled him away, but his head got bashed in first. Not even my own brother recognizes me," he said, pushing his tray away and getting up to leave. "What's the dif anyway? I barely recognize him. Haven't for a long time."

"Sorry you missed Christmas at home," Laura said immediately after Jeff left, like she was afraid if she was silent, I'd get up and leave too. I supposed she read my thoughts, because all I wanted was to be alone in my room.

"It's okay. Did you have a good Christmas?" I asked.

"Yes, I'm going home for good on Saturday."

"Cool." *She had to be kidding. Why her and not me? She obviously didn't have Dr. Ellison as her doctor. If she did she'd be stuck here for the duration like me.*

"Thanks for sticking up for Jeff. He's a major cool person. He's messed up because of his brother."

My nervousness caused my palms to sweat, but I asked anyway. "Do you know what happened?"

"Jeff said that Jake got messed up with drugs and the wrong people. The worst part is that Jeff blames himself. He tried to help his brother on his own. He feels guilty he never told his parents what was going on with Jake, and now both of them are basically basket cases. Jake told Jeff that he was going to kill himself. Jeff didn't believe him until he woke up one night to find his brother's car leaving the driveway. Jeff followed and caught up with him right as a train was coming into the station. Jeff pulled him back, but the train hit him anyway."

"Oh, okay."

How stupid am I? I finally had the courage to ask what happened and I followed through by responding, *oh, okay?* Just as I answered Mr. Simmons when I hadn't a clue about an algebra problem.

BACK IN MY room, I pulled the books Bridg brought from the bag. There were actually five. *Where the Red Fern Grows* had a note attached to a dog-eared page.

Hi Anna, This wasn't one of my favorites, but I thought you might want to finish reading it. From, Bridg.

From the bottom of the bag I pulled out several shabby looking *Teen* and *Bop* magazines from the last couple months. Each had obviously been read through umpteen times. I smiled. I used to read these magazines too. My friends and I couldn't get enough of them.

I skimmed more than half way through *Where the Red Fern Grows* to refresh my memory of the story and then began again where I left off. Thirty minutes later I was bawling so hard that I could barely see the words as I neared the end of the book. I could neither move to close the bedroom door, nor stop from painfully reading on until the end. I lay on my stomach, my head hidden in my pillow.

"Hey," Chad said softly. He picked up the book. A chair was pulled toward my bed. "I read it back when I was a kid. Sad, I know."

My voice cracked. "Little Ann." I sobbed, resting my chin on the heels of my hands and plugging my ears with my index fingers. There was no way I could look at Chad while I explained myself. "She loved Old Dan so much that she died. She starved to death, Chad." I thought of how Little Ann crawled agonizingly toward Old Dan's freshly dug grave, barely making it there before she died. I began another bout of hysteria, wailing for Billy's beloved coonhounds.

"Anna. C'mon."

"How could . . . someone . . . write something like this?" I gushed. "I loved Liz. I would have . . . died for her . . . just like Old Dan died to save Little Ann." My throat opened a sliver. *Breathe, Anna!* I reminded myself, crying hard between my breaths.

I pounded my fist into my pillow. "God doesn't give a crap! No matter how many times my mother goes to church! I begged Him to bring her back. Yeah, it was impossible, or whatever, but do you think someone could have clued me in that it wasn't fucking possible for someone to rise from the dead? Like Lazarus did in the bible? Everyone went on living like nothing stinkin' happened! Something did happen," I yelled into my hands, like I was yelling into a houseful of my siblings and parents. "Liz is dead. D-E-A-D!" I looked at Chad. "Dizzy Lizzy is never coming back."

I tucked my arms under my pillow and plunked my face deep into its softness. I whispered softly, like Bridg whispered in my ear almost ten years ago. "I love you too, Sissy."

"Anna, are you asleep?" Chad eventually asked. "It's five o'clock."

No," I said, opening my eyes.

"I'm on dinner duty. C'mon."

We walked across the TV lounge. "Thanks, Chad."

"For what?"

"For what." I half-heartedly smiled. "You know very well."

fifty

Thursday, two days after Christmas, I spent time in occupational therapy making a leather belt for my father and a leather coin purse for Bridg.

I stamped DAD in large uppercase letters in the middle of the belt, which went under the back belt loops of the pants. I hammered six holes for the belt buckle and then chose a dark leathery stain and rubbed it over the leather, making the letters barely visible. I rummaged through the box of buckles and chose one of rustic gold suitable for a guy. When I was done it looked good, not great, but for a first try it wasn't a major failure. Anyway, my dad would never wear it. He had his favorites and I was sure this wouldn't be one of them. At least I had made it for him and even if he never wore it, I would be reminded that I tried when I saw it hanging from a hook in his closet.

The coin purse for Bridg took longer than I expected. By the time we were asked to *close up shop*, I had about fifty holes hammered around the perimeter that needed to be threaded with a leather shoestring. I put the materials in a bag and left it for next time, if there was a next time. If not, I'd gladly leave Bridg's gift behind and buy her a few books and magazines instead.

CAROL RAN GROUP at two o'clock sharp. The four of us, Cate, Jeff, Laura and I sat at a table instead of pulling the chairs out into a circle.

"It's been days since we met together so I'm sure we all have things to share." Carol said.

I wished Carol would change her wording because it felt like I was back in kindergarten for show and tell. The only difference was that we all sit and stare at each other instead of raising our hands shouting, "Me first!" like we did when we were five.

"Are you ready to go home?" Carol asked Laura.

"Yeah, pretty stoked about it," Laura said, giggling like a schoolgirl.

"Why were you here?" I asked.

Laura looked at me smiling like I'd told her she'd won a million bucks. "My father," she said, her smile disappearing, "died on October 23. Dr. Nix said I was depressed and all."

"At least your father's dead," Cate said. "I wish I could say the same."

"Cate," Carol said sternly.

"What the fuck." Cate laughed. "Ironic isn't it? Fuck. Yeah, that's what my father did to me. Yep, I wish he were dead."

I was completely mortified. I had heard of things like this, but never met anyone who had experienced it. "That's awful, Cate," I spurted sympathetically, like I was some forty-year-old.

"Yeah, whatever. That's what my dad said too. 'I'm sooo sorry, Cate.'" She said, using a deep sarcastic voice. "Whatever. It's not even worth talkin' about. He'll get his in jail." Cate sat back in her chair, her arms crossed with a fierce look.

"It is worth talking about," Carol said. "Your father denied you the right to live your childhood. He abused your trust. You have every right to be angry—furious— with him."

Cate hadn't moved, but I could tell she listened.

"What he can't take from you are the choices that you make. You can decide to fill your life with anger and resentment, letting your father control your life or you can . . ."

"Blah, blah, blah." Cate cut Carol off mid-sentence. "You don't know shit! If I forgive him, then I will be a better person—that's what you're going to say. Well, I'm not forgivin' the jerk. If it were up to me I'd kill him!"

"Then what? Go to prison?" Carol began again.

"I'm in prison," Cate interrupted.

Carol didn't miss a beat. Her voice was steady and calm. "And spend the rest of your days wasting away. How will that help, Cate? You can change who you become."

"The mockingbird," I whispered to myself.

"What?" Cate leered, her eyes drilling holes through

mine.

"Nothing," I answered.

fifty-one

Dr. McKenna, Jeff's psychiatrist, was there for me while Dr. Ellison was away. He was short and looked a little like Al Capone with his dark eyes, bushy eyebrows and big head, but I decided to give him a chance since he and Jeff seemed to get along.

"So . . . you're number nine?" Dr. McKenna asked as the door closed behind him.

"Uh-huh." An only child or someone from a small family would not have understood Dr. McKenna's question, but I did. Dr. McKenna was from a large family like me. He'd been referred to as a number from the day he was born.

"How about you?" I asked.

"Number eight of twelve. Six girls. Six boys. And in that order.

"Awesome. That makes it easy. You know, equal playing ground."

"How many in your family?"

"Six girls. Four boys. Not in that order." I smiled.

Growing up in large families seemed to separate Dr. McKenna and me from the rest of the world. I definitely liked the connection we had.

"Do you like it?" I asked. I sat taller in my chair, focusing on Dr. McKenna's every word.

"I do. It has its pluses and minuses, but you already know that. For me, the pluses outweigh the minuses. I appreciate having many siblings." He smiled. "And you?"

"Sometimes yes. Sometimes no."

"I know the feeling," he admitted. "I remember when I wasn't content with answering one way or another. After my dad died, I thought being part of a large family was horrible. My mom had twelve mouths to feed. She went back to work and depended on us to take on more responsibilities. I guess I was one of the luckier ones. I was eight. My oldest sister Peg—boy, she had a tremendous amount of responsibility. I was in charge of changing Danny's diapers. Can you believe it, an eight-year-old, changing his eight-month-old brother's diaper?" Dr. McKenna chuckled like he was jokingly reminding Danny of his diaper changing days. "Honestly Anna, those were the days when I hated being a number instead of a name. I hated sharing less food. I hated the anger we suffered with my dad's death."

Dr. McKenna paused. His eyes brightened, implying there was more to his story.

"Eventually, time passed. We learned to pull together as a team to make it work. It took time, but today I wouldn't change being part of a large family for anything."

"Being one the younger ones wasn't easy," I admitted. "I never liked being picked on. Especially after—I mean everyone had someone. Gabe had Jim, Tim had Kyle, and Marie had Meg. They all had an unfair advantage."

"I know your older sister Liz died when you were seven. Dr. Ellison asked if I could take you on while she was gone because of our similar experiences. She thought I could help in a small way."

The knots that usually tightened in my stomach from conversations like this had yet to surface. There was so much I wanted to ask Dr. McKenna. Could he explain how this number order thing was supposed to work when an older sibling drops off the face of the earth? Am I number nine or eight? And is it crazy to love a sister who is dead and is no longer my unfair advantage? I wanted to ask Dr. McKenna how I could possibly let go of someone I love. It kind of felt like Dr. McKenna and I had been lifelong friends—so shouldn't I be able to ask him these questions?

In the distance I heard, *pluck up your courage, Anna.*

"HOW DID YOU let it go, you know, your dad dying and all?" I asked Dr. McKenna when he came to my room to get me for therapy the following day.

"Well, now, no need to meet in the conference room. We can stay right here." He pulled out the chair from underneath the empty desk. I turned my chair toward him.

"Before I answer, it's important that I understand exactly what you are asking."

"Everyone keeps telling me to let her go, referring to

my sister Liz. But no one explains how to do this. Like a priest, you know what I mean? One who says, love your neighbor. What if your neighbor's a serial killer? What then? No priest ever explained how to love a mass murderer."

"Yes, I can see this could be troublesome." Dr. McKenna chuckled. "Let's get back to you. Anna, you are asking two very different questions. First, you asked how to let it go. By it, I believe you are referring to Liz's death. Second, you asked how to let her go. By her, you are referring to Liz."

"Yeah, I get that. Let's say both then."

"Not possible. You are talking about a person and a thing.

"Dr. McKenna, please. How did you let go of your dad's death?" *Unbelievable. The once in a lifetime I had a billion questions. And I got the doctor who took his sweet time in answering.*

"I didn't let go of my dad's memory, Anna. However, I did let go of the sadness surrounding his death and my loss. It took time, but our family eventually began to celebrate his life—the good memories. I only had him for eight years, but it seems more like a lifetime because my siblings tell their memories too." Dr. McKenna paused. "You don't have this memory sharing in your family. Is that right?"

"Right." I said, figuring Dr. Ellison had filled him in on my family's life story.

"Yesterday gave me some insight to what you're experiencing. You seem to perceive your family as separate entities—divisions, is that right?

"Every family fights, if that's what you mean," I said in defense. "Besides we didn't fight really, just teased a bit."

"You're misinterpreting what I'm saying. We had our fights. Of course, I can't say I'm as close to Peg as I am to Danny. Danny and I could throw a mean snowball," he said, like he envisioned it at this very moment as the snowball sailed through the air toward one of his siblings. "But when we needed to come together, like in the event of my father's death or helping my mother support a large family, then we did it. These are times we came together."

"Just great," I moaned.

"Whoa! Hold on. Don't assume you're out of luck. You can change this at any time."

"Yeah, I guess."

Dr. McKenna did not understand that we weren't a kiss-kiss, love-love, pat on the back kind of family, but to make him understand that in less than ten years would be impossible.

fifty-two

When Mom and Bridg were about to leave after Saturday night's visit, I picked up *The Outsiders*. "I'm almost finished, but really, Bridg?" I said. "Happy ending?"

"I know. Just finish it. The Princess Bride is next, right? You'll love that one, too!"

"Okay," I said, holding up Bop teen magazine. "Who's your love?"

"Simon," Bridg said, pointing to Simon LeBon.

I FINISHED *THE Outsiders* that night. I loved it and hadn't shed a tear. There were times I could have. Maybe even should have, but I hadn't. The next day, I started *The Princess Bride*, giving it every possible chance so I could talk to Bridg about it, but before lunch, I finally gave up.

After dinner, I was sprawled out on the lounge couch, my feet propped up on the couch's back, reading *Anne of Green Gables*. I skipped over *The Hobbit* because the *Green Gables* cover looked more appealing.

Cate plopped down on the end of the other couch. "There's nothing on TV but shit. I hate Sundays," she said, exasperated.

It was only the two of us in the TV room and since I was reading, facing away from her, I assumed she was talking to herself— at least I hoped so. She went to the TV and switched the dial quickly like she could break it right off, turned up the volume and plopped back down, mumbling under her breath.

What the heck? She was purposefully annoying me. *Okay Isaac. This would be a good time to wander out from the nurse's station.*

Cate got up and again nearly broke the dial from the TV before she plopped back down. "Nothing but shit!"

I turned a page in the book and pretended to read. I wanted Cate to know I didn't like her as much as she didn't like me.

I turned another page trying to concentrate on the words, but it was impossible. Cate was behind me, huffing and puffing like I had done too, many times. I seemed like I brat, I suppose, but really I was just so angry about so many things. I imagined Cate without a cover—without skin, trying to understand only the emotion behind what had happened to her, but I couldn't.

I shifted my eyes to the left, trying to look at her behind me and figure her out. I turned a page and wondered how best to handle this situation. My head shouted *get up and leave*, but my mind tried to understand her resentment. I was furious that my dad fell asleep in my air-conditioned room, but Cate's dad probably hopped into bed with her. *Sick bastard!*

"Yeah, Sundays are boring. There is nothing on TV. Want to play a board game?" I said, pointing to the cabinet stuffed with games, while swinging my propped feet down to a cross-leg position on the couch.

"Only if you want to," Cate said.

"I do. You choose."

fifty-three

"This is for you," Chad said, handing me a letter.

I looked at the envelope. It was from Kyle. "Already? How is that possible? It hasn't even been a week."

"Something special I hope." Chad grinned.

"Not if it came this quickly," I said disappointed.

Chad sat in one of the desk's chairs. "Who is coming to visit you tomorrow?"

"My parents and Bridg, Meg and Marie, Tim, Frances, and maybe Gabe.

"Big crowd. Sounds fun. And the anniversary of Liz's death? Have you been thinking about that?"

"Sometimes."

"Anna?" Chad said a look that begged for elaboration.

"I know." I smiled. "It seems like I should have so many more good memories of Liz than the bad ones, but it's the bad ones I remember. I get why you and Trudy and Dr. McKenna say it's important to let go of the bad memories, but it's like . . . crud! I don't know." I sighed in frustration.

"Because there's nothing else," Chad said.

"Yeah exactly, take away the terrible memories and I might forget Liz all together. I know it sounds crazy."

"That's far from the truth. You're sorting the last ten years of your life. It's going to take time. You'll get there."

"Yeah, that kind of worries me too. I'll be eighteen in less than a month."

"Is this about Dr. Ellison?"

"Yeah, her being a child psychiatrist and all."

Chad laughed. "Dr. Ellison understands that turning eighteen doesn't mean that all of a sudden you don't need help. It will be up to you. If you want to continue to see her, she'll be happy to meet with you. In fact, I'm sure she'll be talking to you about it soon."

"Oh shoot, Chad, please don't write anything about this in my chart," I pleaded, embarrassed I'd admitted that after months of wanting to rid Dr. Ellison from my life, I was now worried I might lose her. "Please Chad. Don't."

"I won't."

"Do you think I'll go home soon?"

"It's not my decision, Anna".

"Ahh!" I scowled exasperated at his answer. "You have an opinion, don't you?"

Chad leaned back in his chair. His elbows relaxed on the chair's arms. "Why did you walk away from school?"

Chad had always challenged my thinking, and I liked this about him. Whereas Dr. Ellison pushed my limits, Chad encouraged me to explore my limits. But this, the Mr. Surrick and Mrs. Avery situation, was ugly.

I let out a long-drawn-out sigh. Telling Chad what I hadn't wanted the whole world to know was the adult thing to do. Chad's hands were now behind his head like he had all the time in the world to relax and wait for however long I needed. I looked into his clear blue-sky eyes—ready to empathize with my every word.

"Mrs. . ." I stopped myself.

"I listened. I mean, I believed . . ." I struggled terribly trying to find the perfect words that would best explain what I think happened. Since I had misheard Chad say, "Let go of it," when he actually said, "Let go of her," I had been wondering. Had I misheard Mrs. Avery and Mr. Surrick, too? *Could they truly have said what I thought they said?*

Chad leaned forward. "Anna, say what comes to your mind. Don't overthink or analyze what happened. We'll organize your thoughts when we both hear what you have to say." He said the word *both* with an elevated tone. "Yes," he said when I looked at him, my eyes questioning his words, "you need to hear it to understand it."

"Basically, my history teacher Mr. Surrick made me feel stupid. He called me lazy. And then Mrs. Avery the bitchy counselor agreed. Except she added that I was a failure too."

Chad's position changed from relaxed to listening intensely. He leaned forward, resting his forearms rested on his thighs.

"Basically it comes down to that I'm a failure," I said matter-of-factly. "I believed Mrs. Avery's words were something like my grades reflecting the kind of person I am—like grades are the end-all to what defines a person."

"You don't believe it then? That you're a failure?"

"I did. Actually, I still do sometimes. Not only a failure at school stuff, but also at other things like being a sister and a daughter." My eyes shifted down and then back to Chad. "You want to know the worst thing about the Mrs. Avery situation?" I asked rhetorically. "It was something I said, not Mrs. Avery. I said, 'Okay.' After she basically left me for dead I freaking thanked her. *'Oh Mrs. Avery, how kind of you to inform me of my failures. I will improve this very minute.'"* I taunted, using a high-pitched squeaky voice, repeating the humiliating incident.

"Misery loves company. My mom used to say that about bullies." I used a motherly tough love kind of voice, "Stay away from them, Anna. They're miserable people." She's right, you know. Mrs. Avery is miserable. I could tell she hated working in her office as much as I hated being there."

"A smart person, your mom." Chad said. "Surround yourself with good people."

"Shoot," I giggled. "I hope I'm good people."

Chad smiled. "You are."

It was an awkward moment. I wanted to tell Chad I was kidding, but in truth, I felt a deep need for the confirmation.

WHEN CHAD LEFT, I opened Kyle's letter, wondering what he had written. It didn't take three pages to tell me nothing. My hands shook uncontrollably. *Dear Anna*, it began and by the time I finished reading Kyle's letter quiet tears streamed down my face. I cried for Kyle and for Liz's black and white bear. For her bike and our rusting swing set that died the same way, in the garbage and alone. I lay down on my bed, huddled in the center with my knees tight against my chest and the letter gripped in one hand. I closed my eyes, giving myself a moment for yet another connection in my broken memory to heal.

"Chad," I called from down the hall when I saw him leaving the unit.

"What's up?" he answered.

"Where's Dr. Ellison? I need to talk to her."

"In the nurse's station," he chuckled, "right behind you. Everything okay?"

"Yes."

"Dr. Ellison?" I whispered into the nurse's station so not to make a spectacle of myself.

She looked up from charting. "Yes?"

"Please, can we talk?"

It seemed like everyone stared.

"Now darlin' that's what we like to hear," Virginia said.

"Of course," Dr. Ellison said. She didn't finish or close the binder in front of her, she just set it down.

We walked to my room together.

"Anna. You look upset about something."

"I am, kind of. Can I read you something?"

"What is it?" She asked sitting in one of the chairs.

"A letter from my brother Kyle." I unfolded the three pages again and read them to Dr. Ellison.

"It's a beautiful letter." Dr. Ellison said. "Will you share it with your family today?"

"I don't know. I don't think I should."

"Why not?"

"For a couple reasons. Kyle put real feelings into his letter. I'm not sure he'd want everyone to hear it. He's probably trusting that I keep it secret, between him and me."

"You know the terrible consequences of keeping feelings bottled inside. I think your family could benefit from a letter like this."

Before I was imprisoned on the fifth floor, I would totally disagree with Dr. Ellison. But then, if I hadn't come to the fifth floor I would also probably be dead, one way or another.

"I guess, but it's kind of like the old adage 'never say or write anything you don't want the whole world to know.' Well, that's what our mom says anyway," I said. "This is why Kyle trusts that I'll take his letter to the grave."

Dr. Ellison stared. "Say that again," she said.

I'd told Dr. Ellison before, hadn't I? Her expression and dropping jaw said I hadn't, but what the heck, she should know this about me, right? Dr. Ellison's shock suggested that though she might have recognized that I didn't like to share personal details, she hadn't known this was a motto I was taught to live by.

"Well, another piece of the puzzle fits into place," she said.

"What do you mean by that?" I grumbled.

"Share truths, Anna. I believe this is what your mom meant. Keep rumors and gossip to yourself, but share the truth."

I felt different about Dr. Ellison at that very second. She could have easily said my mom was wrong but she didn't.

"I'll let you decide how to handle Kyle's letter. But don't forget, another memory —the one of Liz's bear— was restored to you. There could be a connection for one of your siblings tucked inside Kyle's letter. The fact that you've started asking questions has been a benefit not only to you, but also for your family. Imagine all the things that haven't been shared because as a family you consider keeping secrets a strength, when in truth it has proven otherwise."

"But how?"

"Read it to them like you read it to me a moment ago."

"It's not that easy," I complained.

"I didn't say it would be. In fact, it's going to be difficult, but I know you are more than capable of doing this."

"Dr. Ellison, I can't." I covered my face and then slid my hands down pulling my cheeks downward. "Aghk! This is so confusing."

Dr. Ellison was right, but how could I manage to take what I'd learned about Kyle and what he shared about Liz and tell my family about it with my mother's words pounded into my head? But then again, my mother liked to say, it was the calm before the storm. The calm before the storm was often frightening, knowing something bad was about to happen, but the calm after the storm, when the dust had settled, was what I'd been longing for—for almost a decade. I sighed from pure exhaustion. My head hurt. My heart ached. My senses were in overload.

fifty-four

My parents and Bridgett were the first to arrive at two o'clock. Bridg carried a brown grocery bag with potato chips and Doritos. Dad had a cooler.

Isaac unlocked a large conference room down the hall. "How about here? That way you have plenty of room to move about and tables to put food on."

"That'll do fine, young man," my father said.

Marie and Meg came about fifteen minutes later, followed by Tim, Frances, and Gabe. By two-thirty we were all there. My sisters and I put out the chips and dip, coffee cakes and leftover Christmas cookies, a frozen fruitcake that would not be touched, a crockpot of Swedish meatballs that Frances brought, Mom's ring salad, hors d'oeuvres and a few two-liter bottles of pop. I couldn't help but watch my family as a stranger instead of a member. Seeing these people come together, I'd consider them a close family who shared their innermost thoughts and feelings. I saw their laughter as a sign of confidence and leadership. But I knew better because I belonged to this group of people. Within these four walls was something an outsider could never uncover. Inside this room, beyond the laughter and the usual conversations were self-doubt, loneliness and the one thing that had kept each of us striving—an undying fear of failure.

We filled our plates with food and poured drinks. Everyone sat around two tables pushed together to form one. No one seems to notice or care that we were in a room on the fifth floor of a hospital. Conversations about the weather, New Year's resolutions, and the new baby flowed just as they would if we were seated around the dinner table at home for someone's birthday. The real reason we were celebrating in a hospital instead of at home, where my siblings could be with their own families, was ignored. Part of me wanted to scream, "Hey guys! Did you hear? I threatened to kill myself!" Instead I silently began to repeat a simple question. *What was she like?*

Conversation now sounded muffled, as if I was underwater. My palms were swimming in sweat. Trapped air begged to burst from my lungs. *Pluck up you courage, Anna.* Rising to the surface, simple angelic words rested peacefully in a memory. *Let go, Anna. You can do it.*

"What was she like?" I launched the words as if I had pushed off a cement wall, looking directly at our parents.

The room stilled except for heat pushing through air vents, like water falling over cliffs from a thousand feet up. Tomorrow was New Year's Day, the day Liz died. Everyone around this table knew what I meant.

"Lizzy?" Mom asked. She faintly smiled. "Happy and vivacious. Always happy. She loved to laugh."

My eyes swelled at Mom's obvious struggle. I prayed for control, embarrassed in front of everyone, but by the looks on their faces they too were fighting for control. I wanted to be rescued, but there was nobody. These people, who sat around this table, were not Chad or Carol or Isaac or even Dr. Ellison. These people were my family. We all needed rescuing.

"What else?" My voice cracked.

"Are you sure, Anna? You're upset."

"Because it's upsetting, Mom." I said, urging her to continue.

"I will never forget her smile." Mom's eyes shifted up, like she'd already said enough, but I needed more.

"Liz," I said louder than I meant or needed, "she got the popcorn balls." I barely got it out.

Meg and Marie stared at me with ghostlike blank faces. Their mouths gaped open. The others looked about the room, then at Marie and Meg, then to me.

"Liz got the popcorn balls," I said again.

"How do you know about that, Anna?" Marie's voice cracked.

"I heard you and Meg talking about it. After Liz died. I could hear you through the bedroom wall. You were both crying."

"But she didn't, Anna. That was the problem. Meg and I never made them." Marie said.

"But Mom made them," I said.

We turned towards Mom.

"When?" Meg questioned.

"I came home late. When I realized they hadn't been made, I threw a batch together."

"Oh my God. This regret of mine is getting worse by the second," Meg replied.

"Lizzy got the popcorn balls. That's what matters." Mom smiled. "You might like to know that when she saw me coming with the bag, she knew right away what was inside. She started laughing. She decided to eat them right then, before breakfast."

"No. What matters is that I've just spent ten years thinking Liz didn't get the one last thing she asked me for." Marie burst into tears.

"Mom, we're sorry we didn't make them. You were probably so tired. Marie and I didn't have a clue."

"Ignorance is bliss," Mom said.

"Seriously, Mom. Ignorance is bliss? Are you implying Meg and I should be happy we didn't make the popcorn balls or happy we didn't know Liz was dying?"

"Of course not, Marie. I meant that not knowing is sometimes better than knowing. It would be terrible if we had known what was about to happen."

"Not in this case. I wish I had known Liz was going to die then maybe I'd be living without this horrible regret for the rest of my life."

"I'm truly sorry this is so difficult." Mom said, looking around at us. "But we can't erase what happened."

"Erase what happened? It's exactly what we've done.

For cripes sake, I don't even know what the heck happened. The last ten years has been one big blur." I huffed in frustration. "Liz was my sister too, but for some reason, I was left in the stinkin' dark about it."

Nobody moved to get food or drink. They barely breathed. Bridg was in the corner chair, pushed back from the table, with her knees bent up to her chest with her arms wrapped around her legs. Her chin rested on her knees like she was contemplating her next move. She didn't want to be here any more than the rest of us, and I felt bad I could not save her from this awkward conversation. She should be having fun with friends, but instead she was stuck here with us. I wished I could stop to save her, but I couldn't. She was family too.

"It's been ten years, Big Rat. There's not much to talk about," Gabe said lightheartedly, cautiously trying to steer the conversation in a different direction.

I was nervous, but I had started this and now there was no turning back. There was no reason I couldn't ask him the one question that has worried me since reading Kyle's letter.

"Gabe, do you mind if I ask you a weird question?"

"How weird?"

"Actually, seeing that we've all forgotten the last ten years, I guess it's going to sound weird. It's about Liz's funeral."

"Not sure I'll have the answer, but okay."

I had to choose my words carefully. I couldn't bombard Gabe or anyone in this room with something so terrible. "When you were carrying the casket down the church stairs, you said to Jim that if Tim wasn't able to hold the casket, then you'd pull up and Jim should push down."

"I carried Liz's casket? I don't think so."

"You were one of the pallbearers, weren't you?" I asked, looking around to my parents.

Gabe paused, "Wait. I guess I was. Man, I had forgotten about it."

My nerves were on edge. "Gabe," I said, rethinking what I should ask next. "What do you remember most about Liz?"

"Anna, I have to be honest with you—very little. I put it out of my mind years ago. I do remember she laughed a lot and had a lot of energy, but that's about it. I don't remember the funeral or anything that happened afterward mainly because I didn't want to remember. I hung out with friends a lot more after it all happened. I wish I could answer your questions, but I don't remember much of anything during that time."

"I can't believe this," I shouted accusingly toward everyone. "I'm in the hospital, guys. Locked up behind the doors you came through less than an hour ago. Does this seem normal or absolutely insane? It's like when bad things happen we decide to follow Mom's words of advice and live in the present." I looked at Mom. "Sorry Mom, but why didn't we live in the present the day Liz died, or every day after? Because if we had, maybe I wouldn't have spent the last ten years living in this nightmarish world?"

"It's not Mom's fault!" Bridg burst out.

"I'm not blaming Mom, Bridgett," I said trying to calm myself, "But c'mon, you grew up not knowing if Liz was some fictional character or your sister. That's insane."

"Oh Bridgett . . ." Mom began.

"So what, Anna! It doesn't matter anymore."

"It does matter, Bridgett. It matters to me." I looked around at everyone. "You can't tell me you all didn't suffer. I mean c'mon Gabe, how can you not remember being a pallbearer at your own sister's funeral? And Frances, you seem to think Liz wasn't your loss. And Marie, you could barely say two words when I asked you about Liz. I might be the only one here who actually thought Liz could be brought back from the dead, but I cannot be the only person affected by Liz's death. Or am I completely wrong?" I sat back heavily in my chair. "Just forget everything I've said. I'm sorry I've ruined this party." I looked at Bridg. "And Bridgett, you probably hate me right now because I'm talking about Liz and worse, brought you into it, but hate me all you want if that's what you decide. But know that I liked growing up with you. I liked sharing a room with you. I like having you as my younger sister."

Bridgett seemed to sink back into her chair a little farther. The room was still except for plates and cups being fidgeted with. Napkins were lifted to already clean faces. Eyes shifted to the walls.

fifty-five

Frances spoke calmly and carefully, always taking the lead for her younger siblings. "When Liz was in the hospital before she died, I had come home for Christmas. When I planned the trip, Liz hadn't been diagnosed. It happened by chance that I was home. I visited Liz in the hospital only once. I wanted to be there every minute of every day, but my inability to show emotion in front of Mom and Dad was so intense that I couldn't stay.

Later I regretted my decision, that I hadn't spent every possible moment with her. But I couldn't keep from crying and I couldn't bear to let anyone see that I was weak. I missed the signs of why I had possibly been brought home. But even worse, I didn't want Mom and Dad to know that I cared about Liz. Mom was at the hospital every second so I was not."

I couldn't bear to look at our mom. I knew her heart must be breaking to hear this.

"The only conversation I remember was with Dad,"

Frances continued. "He told us that Liz was to have an operation and if they couldn't do the surgery *'it would be curtains for Liz.'* When I learned that Liz died I cried and cried, but not near anyone. There was no consoling, no hugging and no family togetherness because that was how we were raised."

Frances reached inside her purse. "Look, Anna."

I took the photograph. It was of the dresses Frances made for Bridgett and me to wear on Christmas Day when we were small.

"I found them in the cedar chest, where you said they were. The midnight blue lace trim is as vivid as the day I bought it," Frances smiled, pointing to the dresses in the photo. The blue lace on the collar, cuffs and hemline stood out. "Do you remember wearing it?" she asked.

"Not really Frances, but it was the Christmas after Liz died, right? What is it about these dresses? You seemed . . . so sad when you asked about them. Was it because you were only making dresses for me and Bridg?"

"Anna, I made three dresses that year. Liz was buried in hers."

Glassiness covered Frances' eyes. My burning eyes released a single teardrop. Our strength, our silence, I understood now, was our weakness. But I followed Frances' lead anyway, forcing myself to hold back the tears.

"Her little head was wrapped in a white bandage. The white dress was trimmed with midnight blue lace. She looked like an angel. It was surreal. I wanted to cry, but I wouldn't allow it. I stared at Liz lying in her tiny casket."

"Frances. How could—I'm so . . ." My voice struggled to remain as composed and calm as Frances'.

"I'm not wanting to cry on your shoulder, Anna. I can't change what happened. But you . . . maybe I can help you . . . your stays here at the hospital . . . should have never happened . . . you didn't deserve any of it. I am so sorry for your loss." Frances covered her face, breathed deeply and composed herself.

"You didn't deserve it either, Frances," I said, frustrated at her own disregard. "None of us did. Liz's death is your loss too. You loved her as much as I did."

"I did. I loved her with all my heart and to think I didn't spend every minute possible with her is something I've come to accept, but I'm not talking about Liz."

Frances looked at me like she had finally accepted a fate that had troubled her for years. Her blue eyes softened with such calm it was almost eerie. Her cheeks sagged like waterlogged clothing. A redness that had spread over my sister's neck wilted to no more than a patch of pink. Heavy tears streamed down her cheeks. Sobs were heard from around the table.

"Do you remember who told you Liz died?" Frances choked.

I shook my head no.

"I did, Anna. It was me who gave you the news."

The back of the chair caught me as an image of Frances walking up the stairs from our foyer flashed before me. Kyle and Tim followed behind, and behind my brothers was a figment of my imagination—Liz. More than a decade of this reoccurring dream remained airborne, bouncing and dancing along airwaves before it fixed on my memory. A rush of relief surged through every cell of my body and then it drained quickly from every pore.

My hands tightened around the chair's arms in preparation for the violent storm about to occur. Frances' voice boomed like thunder. Her words from when I was seven pierced my heart at lightning speed. Before Frances could utter another sound it erupted from deep within my memory and out into the open room. "Liz is dead! Don't you get it? They're going to throw her in the ground and cover her with dirt!" I winced, as the words repeated like a broken record.

"Yes. That's what I said. My words took everything from you," Frances slumped in the chair next to me, her sad eyes never leaving mine. "Then I staggered to the couch and you came and sat next to me. I didn't know what to do or say to make it better for you. The wind was blowing hard against the living room windows, shaking them so terribly that I thought a window was open by the way the drapes rippled. I wanted to scream to make it all stop. When I looked at you, your little face was all swollen. I will never forget your words. *Frances . . . If you only cry when it's stormy, no one will hear you.* Oh God, Anna . . . your voice was so innocent. Then you laid your head in my lap and cried. I wanted to console you, but I couldn't. I am forever sorry."

I reached for Frances' shoulder, nervous she would be unable to respond to an affectionate gesture, just as I could not the first time Carol consoled me.

"Frances," I whispered. "It's all okay."

Frances placed her hand on top of mine. I felt her body heave and then let go as she breathed. "She was going to visit me in Maine that summer. She was so excited." Frances swallowed hard, choking on her own swollen throat. "She never made it. I abandoned both of you."

"Hey Frances." Marie anxiously gave a half-smile. "You were really a good sister to Anna and Liz. The whole thing was terrible." Marie continued after a long, heavy breath. "Returning to school after Liz died was the worst. Everyone was talking about Christmas break and all the fun they had. I had to go comatose so that I could get through it. I couldn't listen to anyone—not friends, not the priest at her funeral, nobody. I told myself to go numb."

Marie put her hands in front of her like she was pushing a heavy piece of furniture. "I can't . . . I can't."

"A bouquet of flowers is my memory of Liz." Timmy said.

"Marie," he said. "I can tell you what the priest said if you want."

Marie nodded. "Yes. I want to know."

"A bouquet of flowers," Timmy said, looking up and then at Marie.

"What?" Marie asked.

"A bouquet of flowers."

"It's what I remember most. Of all the commotion and sobbing, and carrying the casket down the stairs and in to the church, the only thing that kept me going since that terrible day was something Father Ivan said."

"What does it mean?" I asked, afraid Tim would stop if I didn't.

"We were in the first rows of pews. Liz's casket was up front by the altar. Father Ivan was giving the eulogy. He said God was creating a beautiful bouquet of special flowers and only one more flower was needed to complete the bouquet, but it couldn't be any flower. It had to be extraordinary. So when God looked from the Heavens down to Earth, He chose Liz, the most beautiful flower among all of His creations. Ever since that day, I think of Liz when I see flower bouquets."

Had Tim not apologized for his quivering voice, I wouldn't have noticed he was crying.

Marie wiped away tears on her left cheek. "I carried Liz's obituary in my pocket so when my friends asked what happened, I could show them the paper."

"You want to know something strange?" Timmy said, looking around the table.

I didn't fake that what he had said was enough. "Yes, what?"

He looked at Dad. "I don't know if you remember, but when you came home and told a few of us that Liz died I started crying. Just me. Not you, Frances. Not you, Gabe. No one. I felt like a fool. Like something was wrong with me for crying. I wanted to get back to school and away from home. I hoped someone at school would tell me the pain I felt was normal because I'll tell you—my gut was a mess. It felt like my intestines were tied in knots."

"But school was just as bad." Tim raised his hands in disbelief. "Not a single teacher asked how I felt! I couldn't believe it! It was like the whole stupid thing never happened!" Tim's attitude changed. "Then, I think it was the third day back, my class had art. The one teacher I didn't want to see was Mrs. Lynch the Grinch. On my way in to her classroom, she stopped me. 'Liz was a special girl. I am so sorry, Tim.' I couldn't believe what I was hearing. After that," Tim continued. "I defended her whenever I heard anyone call her the Grinch."

"Thank God," Mom whispered. "She may have saved you."

"I'm not saved Mom. I'm as hurt as everyone here."

"Your mother and I . . . what can we say?" Dad breathed.

"How about something, Dad? Anything." Tim said.

Our dad shrugged his shoulders. "What I'd thought was impossible happened."

"Dad," I said hurriedly before I lost my nerve. "What was it like for you?"

He stared with wide eyes like I had two heads. I imagined it's the same look Liz had when her brain tumor caused her to see double, and my expression when I was crippled with quadruple vision the last time I was on the fifth floor.

"On January third, two days after she died, there was a call from the dentist's office to confirm Lizzy's appointment for the following day. I could barely hold the phone. When I hung up . . . oh how God-awful" Dad said clearing his throat. "Meg was in the kitchen."

"I remember," Meg barely whispered.

Dad continued. "I barely made it down the hallway without falling to the floor. I closed my bedroom door and sat on the bed. My head felt unusually heavy and it hung like I had not an ounce of strength. When I told Dr. Painter's receptionist that Lizzy had died, everything immediately went from surreal to real—painfully real." Dad shook his head and looked at all of us. "Kids . . . I'm sorry. *Curtains for Liz*—I remember saying that to you, Frances. Not much of a father, I guess. I'm not trying to make an excuse, but I was raised with few words. After that phone call, I thought about myself. How was I going to get through this? Call it selfish because it was."

"It was terrible," Meg said. "The house was dead quiet after that phone call. And it only got worse. None of us talked about what happened. We all walked around like zombies. When I returned to school, I didn't know what to say or how to act. I was a senior, old enough to figure it out, but I couldn't. It became the worst experience of my life. My friends wanted to know what happened, but every time I tried to say more than two words, my voice would crack and then nothing would come. It took everything I had to control my emotions, to keep from crying. I didn't want my friends to think I was some kind of baby. Stupid, I know, but I couldn't see it back then."

Our mom looked at our dad. "Jimmy, we've done some real damage."

"Aw, c'mon Mom. Don't worry about it," Gabe said.

"No, Gabe. I've done some terrible damage. Anna asked me about Grandma Peet a while back. Basic questions that she should have known as a kid, not at seventeen. It's because your dad and I never shared anything with you kids. My mother was a very good person, but she was very strict. Her rules were followed, no question about it."

"I remember a long time ago, I was watching all you kids crowded at the kitchen table eating, Dad was at work. Jim and I ate standing with our plates. The commotion was out of this world. I was so happy. My brother and I were taught manners at our kitchen table, nothing else. And here I had kids with manners and conversations. I'm not blaming my parents for how I was raised. Part of it was just their English culture and generation. My brother and I were dressed meticulously, we went to good schools, and we were expected to be seen, not heard.

"When I was only ten, I was reading about World War II in all the newspapers and praying my four uncles would come home safely. I was so scared, and had no one to turn to because my mother had an expression for everything. 'Don't put the cart before the horse, Betty,' she'd say when I asked what would happen if they died. Unfortunately, I've realized too late that just like my mother's use of clichés weren't helpful to me, neither were they to any of you.

"I'm truly sorry kids. I wanted things to be different for all of you, but when push came to shove, I suppose I failed. I should have known better when Lizzy died, but I didn't. I did the best I knew how."

Meg cried. Then Marie.

"Mom," Marie whispered, trying to control her voice. "You must have been so exhausted." Meg nodded, agreeing with Marie, and wiping away her tears that continued to roll down her cheeks. "We should have helped."

"And Raggedy Ann and Andy," Meg sobbed, "Liz wanted a peek. Just a stupid little peek and we told her she had to wait until Christmas. Every time I see those dolls, I want to throw up. It's just so awful."

Sniffles came from around the room. We worked persistently at wiping away our tears, all of us looking away from each other. Learning to cry as easily as we laugh would take time. I looked over at our mother. Her eyes were wet and swollen. She looked longingly at each of us, like she was trying to take our pain away and make it her own. Our eyes caught. She shook her head as if to say, *I'm so sorry*. I smiled, wanting her to know. *It will be okay.* At that very moment I realized our mother was no failure. She was and always will be our constant, for Bridg, for all her kids and for me.

fifty-six

"I have one memory of Liz," Bridg said.

I look over my shoulder at her. "What is it?" I asked.

"When she was sick, she was lying on that gold-colored couch we used to have. Remember?"

We all nodded.

"Oh, do we ever," Mom said.

"I lay next to her on that couch. I remember she held my hand. That's it. It's the only memory I have of her. My childhood memories are of growing up with Anna, not Liz."

Bridg continued "But what kept Liz real for me," she said to everyone before looking directly my way "was the way you talked to her, Anna, when you thought I was asleep. Then when you stopped eating and quit school, it terrified me. I thought you might disappear like Liz did."

"I am so, so sorry Bridg." I said.

"I got news for you Anna," Bridge smiled. "Liz is my sister too."

"Wait," I said. "Please nobody move." I got up, ran to

my room and grabbed Kyle's letter from my desk drawer.

When I returned I unfolded the letter much differently than I did yesterday when I received it. My hands were steady this time because I knew I must get through this for my family.

Dear Anna,

I hope you are well. I started to read your letter more than a dozen times before I could bring myself to finish it. I will do my best to answer your questions.

Liz didn't have a mean bone in her body. She was always bouncing around. Everywhere. She ran around the house and neighborhood always laughing and playing. She had a real zest for life.

Liz had this rickety old bike. Literally Anna, this bike was put together with crap. It didn't have any fenders and the seat was twisted off center, but she loved it. When she was about seven, she heard about the Memorial Day parade starting down at the baseball diamond on 63rd Street (the one we all played at) and Liz decided she was going to be part of the parade.

I gave her a deck of cards and she clipped the entire deck onto the spokes of her bike's wheels with clothespins and rode her bike as fast as she could to the baseball diamond and somehow wormed herself in as part of the parade. She was so happy riding her bike alongside other kids, the cards clipping along noisily.

Later on, after Liz died, I remember her bike rusting away in the basement, like it was fading away piece by piece. I was glad when mom finally threw it away. I remember seeing it lean against the metal garbage can. As if it was possible this inanimate object could be lonely for Liz. The black and white bear, too. I think of that bear sitting on top of Liz's gifts the entire week she was in the hospital. It sat there with a smile on its face unaware that Liz was never coming for it. Mom finally put it in the basement on top of the garbage bag that was tied shut with all Liz's other gifts. When mom threw out Liz's bike, she also rid the basement of the bear. I remember she stuffed it inside a large black bag so the garbage men wouldn't see it. She was afraid they would take it and tie it to the front of their truck.

I also remember Liz and me watching Walt Disney on Sunday nights on the 25-inch color TV that Dad had won from International Harvester. I'm glad I did this with Liz. It's not often an older brother hangs out with their little sister. When she became sick, I talked to her more. I knew she was going to die before anyone else. I'm not sure why I felt this way, but I did. I even asked

Mom one night what she would do if Liz died. Mom said, "Let's cross that bridge when we come to it."

Liz's death, I suspect was hard for everyone, including me. I was angry, but I only understood this to be anger years after it happened. At the time, it was hard to understand what I was feeling. The night Liz died, only Dad came home. He called from his room for Marie and me to come. He told us Liz died—Dad was all choked up and I didn't know how to place the reaction. I had never seen Dad cry before. It's strange, even today, I think about my reaction. It was like my feet were frozen to the floor. Marie's too. The three of us stood, frozen. Dad didn't hug us or try to make it okay or pretend. He just said, "Liz died." Then he cried.

The funeral was held at Toon Funeral Home. I'll never forget the name of it. Two days before the funeral, I went to the funeral home with Mom and Dad. I'm not sure why I was the only kid there with them or why I was there at all. Someday, I'll have to ask Mom why I tagged along.

Anyway, I was at Toon Funeral Home because we were picking out Liz's casket. I remember the funeral director asking me if I was sure I wanted to go inside. I told him I would be fine. I was fourteen back then. Later, I wished Mom and Dad would have left me home or at least outside while I waited for them, but as you know all too well, time moves forward and there is no going back. The moment I stepped into the room, it hit me that Liz was really dead. Caskets were displayed as if we were choosing a new couch. This was my first realization that Liz was never coming back. I wish I could tell you that choosing a casket was the worst of it, but it wasn't.

The funeral was worse.

The absolute worst part about the funeral was carrying the casket down the stairs. Do you remember when St. Joan's church was in the basement of the junior high school? That is where Liz's funeral mass took place. Tim, Jim, Gabe and I were the pallbearers and in charge of carrying Liz's casket. It was so small, but Gabe was worried that Tim might not be able to handle the weight so Jim and Gabe were at opposite corners and Tim and I were at opposite corners. Gabe said to Jim, "If Timmy starts to buckle, I'll pull up and you push down." I remember thinking this is called leverage. I know, weird that I would be thinking about science at this particular time. I tried to focus on calculated movements, but the sounds of our soft footsteps were so intensely eerie it was near impossible. Then there was this terrible noise. I looked over at Gabe, but he continued to stare straight ahead, so I trusted that I hadn't heard the unimaginable.

I remember hundreds and hundreds of people at the church including the students, our friends, and so many people I had never met. It looked like one large mass of people swarming the halls, the aisles and the pews. The quiet was relentless—hundreds of people and the only sounds were sobs and crying. Everyone was crying—everyone except for our family. We were all in shock, I guess. I was sitting by myself after the Mass and the only person who came over to me, that I remember anyway, was Mr. Vager, our neighbor to the left of our house. (Do you remember him?) He came over and said nice things about Liz. He said nice things about me too, being her brother and all.

Well, how'd I do? I hope this letter fulfills a need you have. Someday, I would like to hear how you perceived Liz's death as her younger sibling.

Okay, Anna. I'm going to add a piece to this letter that you didn't ask for. I told myself over and over that I was not going to write this because this letter is about Liz, not me, but after reading my responses, it sounds like I was a great brother to Liz. I don't believe I was. There was one thing I did that is terrible.

Liz loved hiding things. She hid things for no reason at all. She hid cookies. She hid coloring books. She hid shoes. She hid everything. The strangest part of this comical ritual is that she had the same hiding place for everything. The stuff ended up behind the gold couch in the living room. If we couldn't find something, there it was, but Liz denied it was her who took the items or hid them.

When she was seven or eight (which means I was around eleven) I told her if she admitted that she was the one hiding things behind the couch I would give her bubble gum. This is the part that kills me. She was so happy admitting she was the thief, but only because she wanted the bubble gum so badly. She was laughing and jumping around. Well, I didn't have any bubble gum to give her. Liz went from laughing to completely wounded. I completely betrayed her trust. I can still see her disappointment. As an adult, I understand kids do things like this, but I knew better. I can't shake it off. I may never be able to forgive myself. Betrayal is an end-all.

I am now going to put this letter in an envelope and mail it before I change my mind and tear it up. I hope you have a happy new year.

Kyle

READING IT ALOUD to my family painted a more vivid and clearer picture of Kyle's torture, more than when I read it silently to myself or aloud to Dr. Ellison. Especially as I stumbled over his written words, *wounded* and *betrayal.*

I swallowed hard. Quietly, with a slow and deliberate purpose, I let go of air clogging my lungs. "I remember that bike," I said. "It was blue, wasn't it?"

"It was," Gabe said. "Kyle said it right. She rode that thing everywhere. I tried to fix the seat for her once, but it shifted more off center. She didn't even care. She rode it standing."

"Oh really?" Mom lightheartedly laughed. "That's why she never sat down while riding."

"One of the best memories I have of Liz is that silly walk-a-bird walk," Marie said. "Especially when she wore her purple dress. It made her white legs almost glow, wobbling around . . ."

". . . like a drunk skunk," Mom interjected.

We laughed at the memory.

"I did that bird dance with her a few times." Marie smiled. "She was always laughing."

"It's definitely what I remembered most," Meg agreed. "No matter what, she giggled all the time. She was always bouncing off the walls."

"Remember when she broke her arm climbing the kitchen's entrance like an inchworm, one scoot of her left leg, then right, then left hand, then right until she was at the top?" Marie added.

"Oh Anna," my mother said, "You remember, don't

you? The two of you were fooling around and in a blink of an eye Liz was on the floor with a twisted arm. Gosh . . ." My mother shook her head at the memory. "That was a bad break."

"I remember," I said, completely mesmerized by our conversations.

"You and Liz were always together, climbing trees, playing on the swing set, and running around the neighborhood," Meg said.

"What I remember most," Frances spoke up, "is Liz and I sharing a room when we lived in Ohio. She always wanted to stay up late and talk when she should have been asleep, and she was so cute I caved every time. But actually I loved it. She was good company for me."

"You and Liz shared a room?" I asked in surprise.

"We did." Frances smiled.

"How about the pogo stick she had," Gabe laughed. "Man, that kid could bounce up the steps on that thing. She talked me into trying it and I almost killed myself. And that hoppity hoppity ball you had Anna. You followed her everywhere on that thing."

"It was a Hippity Hop, and I bet you remember how it popped." I said.

Gabe laughed. "Yep!

"How?" Tim asked.

Gabe laughed again. "I threw a dart at it."

"For Heaven's sake Gabe, you didn't!" Mom sighed.

"Oh, he did." I said, rolling my eyes.

"Mom, there's a lot you don't know," Marie added.

"Liz used to sit on my handlebars as I pedaled at top speed down our street."

"Oh dear Lord, Marie."

This lighthearted laughter felt good to hear. I didn't want it to ever stop, but I couldn't control myself. Not now.

fifty-seven

"Mom? Was it hard to lose a daughter?" I questioned.

This time around the quiet seemed tolerable, maybe because we were all so ready to know.

"Unbearable, Anna."

"How did you get past it? How could you even go on living?"

"Faith." My mom paused. It almost looked as though she was reciting a quick prayer, begging God that she could find the right words to make things better. "It is the only way—to have faith. I knew Lizzy was in a better place the moment she left this world. My angels get me out of bed every morning. I pray and God listens. He gives us only what we can handle."

"Not always," I said, "Seriously, I can't handle all we've been through, Mom."

"It seems that way now, but you can. You're not alone."

"Why don't you ever cry about what happened to Liz?"

"It's always been difficult for me to cry, even as a child. My mother never shed a tear either. There simply was no time for tears when there was work to be done."

"But Liz . . . Mom, she was your daughter."

"She is my daughter, and I love her as much as I love all of you. A mother never stops loving her children, Anna. No matter how distant they may become, I never stop wanting the best for each one of you. Even Lizzy."

Mom shifted slightly. Her hands pressed hard on the table. "How awful for Kyle to hear . . . that sound." Mom sighed, like she needed a moment to compile her thoughts. "When Lizzy's casket was carried down the school steps to continue into the church I heard a thump . . ." Our mom let out a loud gasp before she was able to recover and compose herself.

"Mom," Gabe whispered. "She's okay."

Mom continued. "Lizzy's head hit the front of the casket. I knew she couldn't feel it, but my Dizzy Lizzy . . ."

"Bette," Dad choked. "Lizzy is at peace."

My mother tried to smile, to comfort us through her most painful memory. "My neck ached and my head was pounding. I knew it was God's way to help me through such a terrible ordeal, but it was so difficult . . ." Mom pulled her unbuttoned sweater tight, like she was chilled. "Give me a moment. I need to catch my breath."

"Mom?" Tears were heavy on my cheeks. "Cry tears for Lizzy."

"I think I will," she tried to joke as she covered her face, tears slipping from underneath her closed hands.

Dad put his arm around my mom. *Dad. A protector?*

"Thanks, Jimmy," she whispered.

"Mom," Tim said. "I heard it too. Kyle told me he realized what we had heard." Tim placed his hands over his cheeks cupping his chin in his hands and let out a labored breath. "When we were carrying the casket down the stairs to get into the church foyer, the casket shifted. There was this thud. I saw Kyle look at Gabe." Tim rounded the table looking at our upset faces. "Liz's body shifted and her head banged the top of the casket. I wanted so badly to scream for someone to fix her so she wouldn't lie crooked for eternity, but I didn't. I regretted that for weeks as I lay in bed, sick to my stomach at the thought of Liz buried with a wrenched neck, unable to straighten herself. Kyle felt the same way, but we promised each other never to tell anyone. We just didn't . . ."

"I heard it too, Tim." Gabe admitted. "I wish I would have known you and Kyle did too. I could barely live with that sound. For years, every time I heard a whack of a hammer, I relived that moment. I had to force myself to forget it."

"Did Jim hear it too?" Meg asked.

"I don't know. I never asked him." Gabe answered, regretfully shaking his head.

Mom looked at Gabe and Tim. "I'm sorry. I should have figured you heard it."

"Mom," I asked carefully, "Is this . . . is that why you decided to forget about her?" I stammered.

"I never forgot about Liz. Never." Our mom said.

"What about her school pictures? You took them all away." I asked, grabbing for a tissue.

"It was the wrong decision. I wanted to make you feel better, and I simply made a mistake. I didn't think it through."

"For me? Why?"

"After Liz died. You were so distraught. I tried to explain that Liz was in Heaven but you refused to listen. You'd cover your ears or hide your face. I tried, Anna. I tried to make you understand that her guardian angel was with her but you wouldn't have anything to do with it."

"Then one day, I noticed Liz's picture lying flat on the piano top face down, like it had fallen. I stood it back up again and didn't think another thing of it, until the following day, when I noticed it again, lying flat and face down. I stood it up it again. The next day, I saw you. You were the tiniest, sweetest thing. You climbed onto the piano bench, leaned carefully over the keys, and you kissed Liz's face. Then you carefully turned the picture over, laying it down flat on top of the piano.

"I went over to you and told you that Liz was in Heaven and that it was okay to have her picture on the piano. You jumped from the bench and ran to your room. I tried to talk to you about it again that night, but you still refused any explanation. That's when I collected all the pictures and put them away. I thought it would help you to get over the pain. I was dead wrong. I'm so sorry. It was plain stupid." A heavy, sorrowful sigh came from Mom.

And then long weary sighs came from Gabe and

Frances. Sobs from others. Maybe I should quit, but I simply could not stop myself from wanting to know every last detail.

"She wasn't scared, right? You said she wasn't scared."

My mother didn't need me to elaborate. She and everyone in the room knew I was talking about when Liz lay dying in her hospital bed.

"She wasn't scared. She didn't suffer either."

"How did you react when you found out?"

"We didn't know how to react at first," Mom said. "I remember Dad and I were questioning things like where do we buy a casket. It was so strange, questions like these popping into our heads. But when we were taken into a room to see Liz, our thoughts cleared. It was like a special gift was granted to us at that very moment.

"Dad and I were alone with Liz. I remember she still had a little breathing apparatus to keep her organs alive. Dad and I talked to her about Heaven and how lucky she was to go to such a beautiful place. We told Lizzy that she was safe and that Jesus and Mary would take good care of her. I reminded her of all the people who loved her and all the people she loved. Oh my gosh—how Lizzy loved people. I reminded her of all the ways she made us smile. I felt blessed to have had that time. I was so good to Dizzy Lizzy," my mom said smiling. "I have no regrets."

"Did you . . . donate —" I squeaked.

"We did," Dad choked.

"What was taken from her?"

"We donated Lizzy's kidneys and liver. But Anna, don't think of it as something taken from Lizzy. Think of it as a gift from Lizzy . . ."

"And her eyes, right?" Tim reminded our mom.

"Oh yes, and Lizzy's eyes. How could I forget?"

"Her eyes?" Bridg said, like she hoped she'd misheard. I hoped the same.

"Yes, Lizzy's eyes. There was a need."

"Anna," Bridg asked quietly, "Didn't you used to call Liz Sissy?"

I tried to smile lightheartedly, but I choked instead. "Um-hm" I nodded.

"We used to tease you for calling her Sissy. I remember telling you to grow up and quit being a baby," Marie said. "We shouldn't have."

"I called her Sissy anyway," I smiled. "Liz let me."

"A cup of coffee, anyone?" Dad asked.

We knew our father was not being rude. We all needed this interruption. Dad took orders from Frances and Marie, who complained she hadn't had coffee in nine months and was in desperate need of caffeine. He opened the door in search of the coffee pot he'd drained many times before today. We got up to fill our plates. The sweet aroma from the crock full of Swedish meatballs filled the air.

"Soooo," I said stretching the word as I scooped three "sweetish meatballs" onto a plate. "Does anyone happen to know Liz's favorite color?"

"Pink. Jinx!" Came from Meg, Mom, and Marie all at

once.

"That was quick." Gabe laughed.

"How about favorite teacher?" I continued.

"Oh, that would have to be Mrs. Kidney—Lizzy's third grade teacher." Mom answered.

"Everyone liked her." Tim agreed.

I kept going, especially since everyone seemed to be enjoying it. "Favorite book?"

Frances raised her hand like she was in a fifth grade classroom, "Oh, this one's mine," she said. "Pippi Longstocking."

"Really Frances?" Mom smiled.

"She made me read a chapter most nights."

"What's all this about?" Dad questioned when he returned balancing three cups of coffee.

"Liz trivia," Bridg answered. "How about her favorite doll?"

"Wasn't it Mrs. Peasley?" Marie asked. "No! Hold on! Don't tell me. Beasley!" Marie shouted excitedly. "It was Mrs. Beasley."

We ate, sharing memories not only of Liz, but also of us. I pushed a meatball into my mouth. I couldn't help but sit forward, chewing quietly, and gazing around at this family, who I was proud to call mine.

Tonight, I thought. *There are two letters I must write, one to Kyle and one to Jim.* They both deserve to know that today Liz's memory was restored.

fifty-eight

Saturday, January 5 was the day I'd be going home. I patiently waited in the TV lounge for my parents to arrive, all my belongings next to me, the doll Marie had given me on my lap, and the coin purse in my coat pocket ready to give to Bridg. I had worked on it the last two days. Stamped with her name, stained, polished, zipper in place and two sides sewn together.

WHEN WE ARRIVED home, Murph was on the doorstep shivering in the frigid Chicago wind.

"You're joking right?"

"I'm here aren't I?" Murph said with his silvery smile, pulling his unzipped winter coat closed. His ears, cheeks, and nose were a stinging beet red.

"Murph? It's not even nine in the morning." I grinned.

"You must be frozen stiff. Why aren't you in the house?" My mom said to Murph, who was now jumping in place and blowing into his hands trying to stay warm.

"I rang the bell." Murph said, shrugging his shoulders.

"Bridgett must be sleeping," My mother replied apologetically.

"Because it's nine o'clock in the morning," I teased light-heartedly.

Oreo greeted me wagging her tail and stayed glued to my legs as I walked up the stairs.

"It looks good, Mom." I said, smiling. There was a family picture on the wall near the kitchen, and on top of the piano was Liz's fifth grade school picture. On the other side of the piano was a picture of Bridgett, I assumed because she wasn't in the family portrait.

"It's a start." Mom said.

"So this is everyone?" Murph asked.

"Almost. Bridg wasn't born yet," I said when Murph began counting the number of kids.

"So this is you?" he asked, pointing to the smallest and youngest kid in the photo.

"Yep."

"Is this Liz?" he asked, pointing to the blonde-haired little girl, three years older than I and sitting next to me in the portrait.

"Mm-hm." My heart sped up.

"How did she die?" Murph said, genuinely.

"A brain tumor."

"How old was she?"

"Ten."

"It was around Christmastime, right?"

"January first."

Murph gave me an unexpected hug. "I'm sorry, Anna," he said—his voice filled with sympathy. "Can I ask why you were in the hospital?" he asked. "Only if you want to tell me."

Murph and I sat in the living room. I did my best to retell the last year. Someday, possibly I'd recap the last ten years, but for now I shared more than I ever thought possible.

"Waffles anyone?" My mom chimed from the kitchen.

"Sure," Murph said excitedly. He pulled a toothbrush from his pocket. "Not a problem."

I laughed when Murph showed off his brightly shining silver smile again.

"Here, I made this for you," I said when Bridg sat down for waffles.

"It's cool. Thanks," Bridgett said, unzipping and zipping the coin purse, looking at the stamped letters, and feeling the soft leather. "Really? You made this?"

"Ah-huh," I said, licking syrup off my lips.

My dad came from his room down the hall.

"Bears tomorrow, Mr. Maedhart?" Murph said after he swallowed a large bite of his waffle.

"Championships. I wouldn't miss it," Dad said.

"It's going to be a tough game against the 49ers."

"Have faith young man." My father said, pushing aside canned goods in the pantry, looking for his sardines. His sweater lifted as he reached for the can on the top cabinet shelf and I caught a glimpse of his belt, neatly looped through his jeans, DAD stamped into the leather.

"HELLO," A MAN'S voice said.

"Is Betsy there?" I asked anxiously.

"Sure, hold on!

The seconds ticked by and I debated if I should hang up.

"Hello," Betsy said, energetic like always.

"Hi Betsy. It's Anna from . . ."

Betsy didn't let me finish before she squealed into the phone.

"Anna! I honestly never thought I'd hear from you again. How are you?"

"Fine." I said.

"Fine? That's it? Not great?" She giggled.

"I'm good. How are you?"

"Great," she said. "Anna. I lost your number and searched everywhere for it. It's not listed anywhere. I called the operator and checked three phone books. I even called the hospital begging them to give me your number or the correct spelling of your last name. Well, I guess you know how that went. I thought for sure you would call me eventually, but when months went by, I gave up."

I smiled. *Chad had known all along*. "Sorry."

"No, it's fine. This is awesome." Betsy squealed again.

"Well, in case we get disconnected, its M-a-e-d,"

"Wait. Let me grab a pen and paper." The phone plunked down on a countertop and I could hear Betsy fumbling through a drawer in the background. "Okay. I'm ready."

I recited the correct spelling of my last name and gave

her my phone number.

"Well that's why! It's not spelled at all like it sounds." Betsy giggled. "And let me tell you, I tried every which way."

Our conversation picked up where we left off like we'd been talking every day since the day we met.

fifty-nine

Popcorn balls hung on the Christmas tree's branches in place of the usual decorated ornaments. Beautifully lit strands of tiny lights reflected off the Karo syrup that sealed the popcorn in a ball-like shape, glistening like hundreds of facets on a diamond. A tiny opening through a couple of wide-spread branches gave a clear view into Mom's kitchen. Beautiful flower bouquets covered the countertops.

Tim whispered as he pushed white candles into the cake placed in the middle of the round table. ". . . Seven, eight, nine, ten."

Frances, Gabe and Marie entered the house through the front door bringing presents wrapped in beautiful Christmas paper and tied with sparkling red ribbon. Again, the front door swung open. Kyle and Meg were there from Texas, and Jim, from somewhere in the world.

"Where's Bridg?" I whispered so as not to be heard. I looked around the kitchen, but she couldn't be found in the mix of my siblings.

"Anna, I'm here, behind you."

I turned. "Let's join the others."

"No. Stay here with me," Bridg said, her voice quivering.

I stared into Bridgett's eyes trying to read her thoughts. "Why?"

"Because Sissy's coming soon," Bridg whispered in my ear.

Bridg pointed to the front door. It opened slowly. Liz entered. She was not a ten-year-old child like I remembered. She was an adult.

"Mom said today is her anniversary," Bridg whispered. "She's been gone for ten years."

We stared as our siblings welcomed her into the kitchen. I stepped from behind the Christmas tree to join the others.

"No, don't go," Bridg begged, pulling at my arm. "Don't leave me."

"Come Bridg. Come with me. You belong with us."

"I'm scared," Bridg cried, pointing toward the kitchen.

Liz danced toward us. I pried Bridg's fingers from my arm and walked toward Liz with open arms, wanting to hug my sister.

Bridg's screams became wounded sobs. "Please Anna, don't leave me."

"Come Anna. Come with me," Liz whispered, motioning me toward her.

"No, Anna! Come back! Please, come back," Bridg screamed.

I glanced at both sisters, torn between the two. "I can't. I can't. Forgive me." I begged for my sister's mercy.

As I turned and ran toward Bridgett, I heard Liz whisper. "I knew you could do it."

I woke without a gasp or a scream. My eyes fixated on my digital clock radio. The time was 1:10 a.m. I clicked on the small bedroom lamp and tiptoed to my desk, unafraid of the dark room, and took out the new journal and pen I received for Christmas. I snuggled back into the warm sheets. Oreo slept soundly, curled into a ball near my feet. I began on page one.

January 10, 1985

Dear Liz,

Do you remember the day you told me to let go? We were at the swimming pool. Just thought I'd let you know, I am letting go, of the bad memories. As for the good memories and your kindred spirit, you will live in my heart forever.

It was easy to close my journal without the entry lingering in my thoughts. And it was just as easy to lay my journal on my nightstand out in the open for anyone to see, if they wanted. I turned to my side thinking of so many things.

I once thought Liz and Ziggy were luckier because they had died. My immaturity and suffering wouldn't allow me to see it any other way until I broke free of the chains I believed controlled my existence. I had believed that the fifth floor was my prison. One day I quietly stopped eating.

If I had not, I would have walked the same path as my siblings. The day I chose to deprive my body of nourishment, hoping to drown my pain, I changed our destiny.

The fifth floor was never my prison. It was my freedom. I was the lucky one.

acknowledgements

I am forever grateful for my siblings' willingness to open their hearts to my interview requests and to share with me their childhood journeys. *Just Like Ziggy* would not have been possible without their stories.

To my husband Mike, my biggest fan and constant reminder to take a much needed break after a long day. Thank you sincerely for your dedication and work ethic that keeps our household running.

Thank you, with gratitude, to my editor Joni Holderman. We have grown into a commendable team. Thank you for your guidance and support through the editing process. Your undivided attention to detail is impeccable.

Again, graphic designer Elizabeth Watters captures our heart and soul through her cover art. Thank you for going beyond what was asked of you. Your creativity is among the best.

From first readers to proofreaders and everyone in-between, these behind the scenes people skillfully combed through lines of text. Many thanks to Elizabeth Meagher, Linda Peaslee, Candy Tumidalsky, Daphne Tantalo, Kevin Moriarity and J. Scott Wilson.

Made in the USA
Lexington, KY
01 October 2016